McFeeley's Rebellion

By the same author

Christ in Khaki
The Honey Gatherers
Let Me Die Yesterday
Coming to the Edge

Non fiction

Murder in Dorset

McFeeley's Rebellion

Theresa Murphy

ROBERT HALE · LONDON

© Theresa Murphy 2012
First published in Great Britain 2012

ISBN: 978-0-7090-9949-9

Robert Hale Limited
Clerkenwell House
Clerkenwell Green
London EC1R 0HT

www.halebooks.com

2 4 6 8 10 9 7 5 3 1

Typeset in 10.5/14pt Palatino
Printed in the UK by the MPG Books Group

Prologue

S LITHERING AND SLIDING in the mud, an expression of distaste twisting his florid face, Colour Sergeant Gray made his way through the darkness along Slap Arse Lane. That spring of 1685 had been a wet one in Ireland that had turned much of the Curragh Camp into a quagmire. There was a heavy drizzle now to add to the misery of the camp followers who lived rough among the furze bushes. The usual number would be found dead from exposure in the morning. Perhaps they were the lucky ones, escaping a more agonizing death from the diseases of their profession. He could hear them making sounds as he passed, a moaning caused by either loving or dying. The colour sergeant was on an unwelcome mission, but he would do his duty. Coming upon the silhouettes of the abodes of the slightly more fortunate whores, he had to steel himself to investigate if the man he sought was here. To do so would be to see sights that repelled him and smell smells that would revolt him.

A sudden movement had the colour sergeant spin round. A soldier had come slinking furtively from one of the tents. Hatless, his tunic flapping open, he was as thin and bent-backed as a whippet. He had taken his first long stride when the colour sergeant's hissing order turned him first into a statue and then a quivering wreck.

'Oh, God…!' the soldier gasped in fear.

'No, just Colour Sergeant Gray, lad,' the colour sergeant managed to find a touch of ironic humour in his despondency. 'Your name and regiment, soldier?'

'I was just …' the soldier began, desperately trying to dream up an excuse.

'I know full well what you were *just* doing, soldier. Your name and regiment?'

'Mottram, sir,' the soldier stammered. 'Kildare militia.'

'Ah!' Gray gave a little grunt of satisfaction. Despite standing knee-deep in unchaste women, his guardian angel had not abandoned him. 'So you know Sergeant McFeeley?'

Mottram looked up at the intensely dark sky. He looked to his left, to his right, in front and behind him. He looked everywhere but at the colour sergeant, who barked impatiently, 'Well? Do you know him?'

'Sir,' Mottram said at last in the affirmative.

Gray was feeling easier about Mottram now, whose narrow face had an innocence suggesting it was curiosity rather than sin that had led him into the Curragh's 'Babylon'.

'Sergeant McFeeley is down here somewhere, lad. Can you tell me where he is?'

The young soldier shook his head emphatically.

'You will be helping Sergeant McFeeley by telling me where he is, soldier.'

Looking at Gray anxiously, suspiciously, Mottram did a check: 'Is that true, sir?'

An exasperated Gray discovered he was envious of the immoral, swashbuckling, two-fisted Colm McFeeley. It took most non-commissioned officers years to achieve a tiny fraction of the loyalty Mottram was showing. McFeeley commanded it instantly, not through fear, although he could be menacing, but with his innate charisma.

'The sergeant is wanted at headquarters and delay could have serious consequences for him,' the colour sergeant said tersely.

Mottram sagged a little at the knees and his jaw fell. Then he stretched a long arm to point at the hovels the more successful and ambitious harlots had built out of gorse and mud. 'The one that has smoke coming from it, sir.'

Nodding, the colour sergeant said sharply, 'Away back to your tent, lad. If I ever hear of you being within pissing distance of Slap Arse Lane again you'll be in big trouble.'

The private soldier took a few tentative steps away from Gray, expecting to be called back at any moment. When this didn't happen he increased his speed and lengthened his stride in thankfulness, leaving behind a colour sergeant who felt alone and isolated.

Gray's nostrils twitched as peat smoke reached him from the hole in a roof. A propped-up sheet of corrugated iron, rusting and as ugly as everything else about the place, served as a door. Gray had made a fist, ready to knock, then dropped his hand when he realized how ludicrous such an action would be. He wasn't calling at the rectory for Sunday tea. He kicked the iron to one side and bent to peer into the rough dwelling.

The ceiling was too low for standing erect, but both the soldiers and the women joked that this was no handicap when taking their horizontal exercise. In the dim light of a makeshift lamp he could see two figures sitting apart on bags of damp, rotting straw that served as beds. One was McFeeley with a cup in his hand, his fair hair tumbling down over one eye and a welcoming smile on his handsome face. Gray silently cursed the man for being as cool and detached here as he was on either a parade ground or battleground. Colm McFeeley always seemed to be under-playing his role in life. It was as if a major part of him had stepped back to be a permanent and cynically amused observer.

The woman, who was on the colour sergeant's right, had long black hair and an unexpected youthful prettiness. There was a wholesomeness to her that was totally out of place in Slap Arse Lane. Yet it hadn't escaped Gray's notice on his sudden entrance that she had to swiftly tuck her bare breasts back inside her opened dress.

'You're wanted, Sergeant, at once,' Gray announced, finding that distaste made him keep his eyes slightly averted from McFeeley.

Colour Sergeant Roland Gray was married to as good a Protestant woman as you'd find on a two-day march. An ideal wife, she lived in the camp with him, taking care of his every need. The physical side of their relationship made no demands on them. Gray lived according to holy rules. It was St Paul who had said that it was better to marry than to burn.

'Where and by whom?' McFeeley asked, his superior education as evident as always in his enunciation and grammar.

'My orders are to escort you to the Four Winds Hotel, Sergeant,' Gray replied.

'Will I see you again?' the girl asked anxiously as McFeeley left the dugout.

'No,' he told her unfeelingly as he stepped out into the night and fell in beside the colour sergeant on a walk that would take them to the suburbs of Dublin.

They were side by side but separated by an invisible barrier. The colour sergeant only wanted to get this sordid duty over. Anger had him inquire, 'Have you no shame, Sergeant?'

Delaying a reply as they came out of the muddy lane onto a hard road, McFeeley dislodged wet clay from his boots before he said, 'It shames me to kill a man, even in battle.'

'You deliberately misunderstand me,' Gray complained. 'I was referring to those awful women. There are many fine soldiers lying diseased and disabled in the hospice because of them. If you lack respect for your body, surely you must fear destroying it.'

'I select my women with as much care as I select men for a dangerous expedition.' McFeeley gave the senior sergeant a grin. 'I only choose newcomers.'

Gray heard this and understood why the girl in the hovel had been so different to the grotesque, foul-mouthed, drunken whores he was used to seeing hanging around the camp. God only knew why she had joined the ranks of the oldest profession. Still able to view a memory of the girl, surrounded by an aura of sweetness, he felt a new anger towards McFeeley.

'You could have saved that young girl, Sergeant,' he said accusingly.

'How?'

Finding that he didn't have an answer, Gray was rescued by them reaching the hotel. He was determined not to go into the building with McFeeley who had made no attempt to do anything with his mud-stained uniform and his too-long, untidy hair.

McFeeley found Captain Critchell waiting for him in the foyer of the hotel. Claude Critchell was a middle-aged man whose face was marked by acne from his youth, and probably too much alcohol since. Having served under him at the large camp at

Loughlinstown, McFeeley recalled that the captain was boring company when in his cups. On those drunken occasions Critchell would claim to be of pure Anglo-Saxon stock descended from Ethelred, brother of Alfred the Great.

'Good of you to come, my dear fellow,' Critchell greeted him. 'You look somewhat dishevelled. Were you not a superb horseman I'd suspect some filly had thrown you.'

'No, I managed to stay on,' McFeeley replied with a smile. 'What's this about, sir?'

'I'm not at liberty to say, my dear fellow,' Critchell said. 'But I can say that you will be going on an immediate transfer to England. Waiting here to see you is none other than Lord John Churchill, the most important man in the British army. I will take you to him without further ado, Sergeant.'

Following the captain along a dark passageway, McFeeley noticed that Critchell was beginning to stoop from age. His glorious fighting days were over. A few more months in an administration job like this and his heroic deeds would be forgotten by everyone but Critchell himself. Fighting for your country was a short-lived occupation that went unappreciated. The financial rewards were pitifully meagre and heroism extremely fleeting. Although aware of this, McFeeley had been in the army since a boy, and had no intention of leaving. If asked why, though, he would be stuck for an answer.

They entered a room in which an elegantly dressed man sat slightly hunched at a desk, studying papers that lay in front of him. Good-looking in a smooth-faced way that was the trademark of his class, he was, McFeeley guessed, around his own age in the mid-thirties. As Critchell and he entered, Lord Churchill neither looked up nor gave any sign that said he knew they were there. A tall elderly man stood behind Churchill. Taking his cue from His Lordship, the tall man looked straight ahead to indicate that he too hadn't noticed them.

A few minutes went by in which Captain Critchell cleared his throat noisily without result. It was so quiet that McFeeley knew that Churchill was using an old aristocratic ploy to remind peasants of their place, and he began to bristle a little.

Then Churchill vigorously tapped the documents in front of him with the army 'walking out' finger of his right hand, and looked up at McFeeley to speak as if they were in the middle of a discussion. 'I must say that this is a far from an admirable history, Sergeant.'

It was only then that McFeeley realized that it was his army record on the desk. The papers must make bad reading but it had never worried him. A soldier should be judged on the battlefield, not from some scrawled words on a piece of parchment in an office. He watched Churchill push himself up from the desk with both hands, speaking as he rose.

'Nevertheless,' the nobleman went on, 'you have not been called here for criticism or reprimand. In fact, and as a soldier I find this difficult to utter, it is your series of insubordinations and your ability, if that be the word, to remain at all times an individual in a disciplined force that recommends you.'

Churchill was then standing upright, stretching his body a joint at a time, starting with the ankles. He was taller than McFeeley, but his narrow-chested physique suggested that his battle campaigns had been fought with a pen rather than a musket.

With all the advantages in life that meant he didn't need to, Churchill spoke in a blustering way, firing out words at a speed that suggested he feared argument. McFeeley felt that this was from a basic shyness in the lord. Definitely not a sly man, he did, however, speak more confidently when not looking directly at the person he was addressing.

'The world is changing, McFeeley. England is changing, and the army has to change accordingly,' he announced as he studied the ceiling 'We have a new monarch. His Majesty King James II is on the throne and each and every one of us shall serve him loyally. But we shall all be put to the test ere long, Sergeant. There is dissent in the kingdom, and His Majesty has enemies abroad, not the least of whom is the bastard James Scott who makes claim to being the legitimate son of Charles II, and therefore the nephew of James, our monarch.'

'James Scott is the Duke of Monmouth,' Critchell elucidated for McFeeley.

'I am aware of that, sir,' McFeeley said, annoyed at being regarded as some doltish and illiterate foot soldier.

'Our enemies are a new breed, McFeeley.' Churchill locked eyes with the sergeant for the first time. 'No longer are the cannon, the sword or the rifle sufficient, Sergeant. Guile must now be met with guile. It is my intention to add a new dimension to the British Army. You, Sergeant McFeeley, are the man on whom my hopes will rest.'

Brushing his unruly hair back with both hands McFeeley considered patting off the now dry mud on his uniform, but stopped himself from making a mess on the floor. He could detect the fragrance of the young woman still with him. He found a perverse amusement in bringing the scent of a whore to be breathed in by someone like Lord John Churchill.

'I don't understand, sir,' he said.

Returning to his seat at the desk, Churchill asked Critchell to outline the plan for McFeeley. Walking up and down as he spoke, the captain explained that McFeeley would be taken from his regiment and brought to England alone. Once there he would work in any capacity that he was ordered to. For instance, Critchell gave an illustration, he might be assigned to any regiment, perhaps as a private soldier, maybe as an officer, depending on what the intelligence work he would be engaged in demanded.

'I will be required to gather information,' McFeeley remarked.

'Exactly,' Critchell nodded.

'In the present climate, with both Catholics and Protestants taking an avid political interest,' Lord Churchill said tiredly, 'one finds it increasingly difficult to decide who to trust. You will be our eyes and our ears, Sergeant.'

'For the present,' Churchill explained. 'Though at times you may be asked to play the role of anything from a foot soldier to a colonel, to the army you will be a sergeant. I have no doubt that you will be successful in this post, so eventual promotion will be a certainty.'

'Special privileges will follow, should you decide to take on this dangerous mission,' Captain Critchell told him, coming round the desk to face McFeeley squarely. His grave expression had chased away the softness that McFeeley had noticed when first seeing the nobleman. He was now an officer whom McFeeley would be prepared to follow.

Having already made up his mind, McFeeley was mentally phrasing his acceptance but cancelled out the idea as Churchill raised a hand in a staying gesture.

'My conscience would not allow me to have you give your answer without one final aspect of this matter being revealed to you,' Churchill said. 'It is that if at any time an enemy of His Majesty King James II should manifest an army, then you may well be required to become part of that army so as to keep us informed of movements, plans and developments. Think on it well, Sergeant McFeeley.'

'I have done my thinking, my lord. I welcome the challenge that you offer me.'

'Good man, I knew we could rely on you, Colm,' Critchell said, delivering a friendly and admiring slap to McFeeley's shoulder.

One

I T WAS A June midnight in which the tiny seaside town of Lyme, held secure by lofty hills on three sides, slept a troubled sleep in an uneasy world. Some kink of nature in the Dorset skies gave the moonlight a bluish tint that enhanced the deep purple of the sea and cast shadows to have the shoreline stand out dramatically. That summer's night was tranquil with the sound of water lapping against the pebbles of the beach as gentle as a lullaby. It defied the imagination to produce a reminder of the fierce south-westerly gales that in winter smashed constantly against the Cobb. No insomniac seagull dared wing its aimless way to ruin the peaceful scene. Out in the bay three large ships had ridden at anchor long enough to blend with the moonlight like grey ghosts.

On the beach two men stripped naked, their careful movements indicating that they were mindful not to ruffle the velvet softness of that special night. One of them was Colm McFeeley, his fair hair burnished by moonlight. The second man was a mixed race soldier known only to his comrades as Private Jack. No one knew whether this was his first name or surname. McFeeley had selected Jack for this mission because of his physical strength and his taciturnity. An incessant talker made a dangerous comrade on a night raid.

Folding their civilian clothing, they both placed it in bags, which they carried to push into gaps in rocks that stood above high water. Coiling a rope around his bare waist and securing it, McFeeley gave Jack a nod that said it was time to go. Both men had a sheathed dagger with a nine-inch blade strapped to their lower legs as they walked the final few yards of the irregular narrow strip of white surf that marked the shoreline. Then they waded through the water, their progress recorded briefly by the rippling sound of the sea their legs disturbed. Keeping to their feet as the water rose first to their hips, then their chests, they lurched forward and began to swim as the mildly chilly hands of the sea touched their shoulders.

Both capable swimmers, they made slow strokes that were deceptively strong and moved them through the water swiftly. Nearer now, they were able to see the three vessels clearly. Nearest to them, with ungraceful lines and pushed low into the sea by a weighty cargo, was a two hundred ton fly-boat that lay at anchor close to a one hundred ton ketch that was also heavily laden. Treading water, McFeeley studied the two vessels, conscious that they contained the arms and ammunition of the Duke of Monmouth's as yet unformed army. Jack had stopped swimming, too, and was looking through the night at McFeeley, awaiting orders. Turning his head a little, McFeeley took in the thirty-two-gun, three-masted fifth-rater, the *Helderenberg*, that he had heard Lord Churchill and others laughingly say had cost the Duke of Monmouth £5,500. The fact that Private Jack and himself were swimming out here in the middle of the night was evidence enough that, despite the laughter, neither this ship nor the Duke of Monmouth could be regarded as a joke.

Taking a mouthful of salt water to prepare him for swimming again, McFeeley spat it out and gestured with his head towards the *Helderenberg*. Swimming parallel to each other, the two men moved through the water with the graceful ease of dolphins until they came up to the giant hull of the ship. Close in against the side of the ship, Jack used his eyes to ask a question: were they to go up the anchor rope? Shaking his head, McFeeley made a sign that they would climb up the hull. It would be a difficult task in the dark, but if the Monmouth soldiers aboard suspected they might have visitors they would be watching the easy route up offered by the anchor.

Although occasionally needing to pause for some time while sending out a hand or foot to search for a new hold, the climb presented them with no real problems. The wood was rough against their naked skin, and each small slip caused abrasions that they didn't really notice. Taking care not to be detected from inside the ship, they went silently and successfully up past the lower deck.

Everything was going more smoothly than McFeeley had expected. This was his first mission under Captain Critchell, and he had spent long in its planning. Critchell had merely told him of the arrival in Lyme Bay of the Duke of Monmouth. The captain had simply conveyed Lord Churchill's command for full details of the strength of Monmouth's army, his arms, ammunition and plans. Both Churchill and Critchell had left it to McFeeley's discretion as to how he carried out the order. The sergeant knew that this either showed they had great faith in him, or, more likely, leaving the opportunity open to shift responsibility for failure straight onto him.

As he thought on this, so did failure loom large. Up above them, blocking their way to the upper deck, was an overhang of some three feet. They were stuck. The sea was a long way below, a reminder for them of how well they had done, but the final short distance to the deck was denied them. There was no time to go back down and risk climbing the anchor rope. Dawn would come before they could complete what they had come to do. Even the half-light of day would mean their capture, and the mounted messenger due to rendezvous with them on the hill west of the town would wait in vain.

Clinging on with his hands, McFeeley first bent his left knee and found a hold for that foot, then did the same with his right knee and foot. First testing the foothold he had, doubled up with his knees against his chest, McFeeley took a deep breath and expelled it sharply as he sprang outwards and upwards, his hands stretched up over his head. He found himself in mid-air without support, the lapping of the sea against the hull of the ship, though far below, was strangely loud to him. The fingers of both his hands clutched only at air. He felt the momentum of his spring slackening, and then he ceased to move through space and was held in mid-air for what seemed an eternity by some invisible support.

Waiting for the fast downward movement to begin, knowing that it would increase in velocity so that he would hit the sea with a splash that would not only damage him, but would alert the soldiers on board the ship, he was astonished as his fingertips made contact with wood. McFeeley grasped eagerly at a thick beading which ran along the lower edge of the overhang. He held on to it, his naked body swinging this way and that. Tilting his head back, McFeeley looked up and despair hit him hard as he saw only smooth wood between him and the edge, so near but never to be within his reach, which would have allowed him to climb over to drop onto the deck. There were neither handholds nor footholds above him, and his only hope was to build up a swing that would hopefully throw him back to where he had clung to the side of the ship before leaping.

But the priority was to stop Jack from making the same mistake as he had. McFeeley looked down at Jack, intending to call softly to tell him to remain where he was. It was too late. Even as McFeeley opened his mouth to shout did Jack throw himself out and up. Both of the soldier's hands smacked against the beading beside McFeeley's, but Jack's body was heavier than McFeeley's, and gravity pulled him down before he could get a grip on the beading.

With no more than a grunt, Jack plummeted. But he twisted himself sideways so that McFeeley felt his hands slide down the back of his thighs and over his calves before clutching at his ankles. As Jack's fingers took a firm grip, McFeeley braced himself to take the shock of the full weight of the soldier.

When it came it was much worse than McFeeley had anticipated. It jolted him right up through every joint, causing pain and strain before reaching his hands, wrenching his left hand from the beading and threatening to tear away the right. Clinging on with one hand, supporting both his weight and that of Jack, McFeeley found that he was under too much physical stress even to breathe. He became aware of a drumming in his ears, and then he was tuned into the blood pumping through his body, a noise similar to the deafening, hissing rush of a waterfall he had stood beside while in Africa.

Calling up every reserve of his strength, he forced his aching right arm and hand to hold on while he struggled to bring the left side of his body and his left arm up. He couldn't do it. The dangling weight of Jack's body was too much. Dropping his head he threw caution to the winds and yelled down at him:

'Let go with your left hand!'

Jack didn't understand, and McFeeley needed to shout again.

This time Jack heard him and took him by surprise, releasing McFeeley's left ankle before he was ready for it.

Recovering, his right arm stretching, creaking and aching intolerably as it took all the strain, McFeeley swung his left arm out and up; it hit the beading and his fingers fought desperately for a hold. At first gaining a tenuous grip, he was able to consolidate it and then he was supporting Jack and himself with both hands.

They both understood what had to be done then, and Jack began swinging towards then away from the ship. Picking up Jack's rhythm, McFeeley went with the swinging. Their pendulum movement increased until the inward swing put Jack within some six feet of the side of the ship.

Timing it perfectly, Jack released McFeeley's ankles and went hurtling towards the wooden hull. Looking down, McFeeley saw him hit hard. He could hear the thudding sound of his body and the crack of his head against the side. For one frantic moment McFeeley could see that Jack had been knocked unconscious. He was falling away from the wall when he came round and clutched at the wooden hull, getting a grip and holding on while waiting for his faculties to return.

McFeeley hung motionless, arms and shoulders aching as he worried over the possibility of Jack's impact with the ship alerting those on board. He waited, expecting to hear a cry of alarm come from above, but all he heard was the rhythmic wash of the sea against the hull below him. It must be, McFeeley reached the conclusion, that the *Helderenberg* was built too solidly for such a sound to be heard.

Satisfied, McFeeley prepared to leave the overhang and return to the hull himself. It was a hazardous exercise, even though he didn't have to drop the same distance as Jack had. Swinging back and forth, back and forth, he felt that he had it judged right, and let go. Spending a brief time of uncertainty in another bottomless world, McFeeley then collided with the rough wooden side of the ship. Bruised and winded, he quickly gained hand and footholds. Some quick thinking was needed. The insuperable overhang demanded a change of plan, and a scheme was already forming in McFeeley's head.

Jack was looking up at him. He was fully conscious but blood ran from his wide-nostriled nose and there was an ugly swelling on his left temple. Either the movement of the sea had increased or slamming against the hull had caused McFeeley giddiness, for he felt sick as he looked down. Blinking his eyes hard a couple of times, he found that the three-master was rocking slightly and slowly as before. As his spinning brain slowed down, McFeeley realized why Jack's muscles bulged and knotted in his arms and shoulders as he clung to the curved waist of the side of the ship. Jack had to be suffering badly from concussion and was having difficulty in holding on.

Taking one hand from the hull, McFeeley pointed astern. That was the way they had to go. The stern of the ship was perpendicular, but it had no overhang. Waiting until a nod from Jack confirmed that he had the message, McFeeley then began edging along the side of the ship. A little below, Jack, every bit as tough as he looked, was following him. Sometimes a little shaky when placing a foot, or fumbling as he tried for a grip, Jack was keeping pace with him.

They came to the sharp angle at the stern. The unknown that was around the corner made McFeeley apprehensive. Should the precipitous stern of the ship offer no grip for either hand or foot, then he would have to abandon the mission. Not ever having known defeat, McFeeley wasn't certain that he could handle being a loser. With his right hand and foot he held precariously onto the hull as he leaned out to take a look at the stern. For a fraction of a second he was rocked by a blast of air of surprising force on such a windless night. For that short space of time he was in danger of losing his hold. As his body jerked violently in alarm he experienced an intense sensation of falling, but even though it took him a while to realize that he had done so, he was able to hold on. But it was at the expense of skin torn from his fingertips as he gripped hard until his slipping right foot came up against a projection capable of supporting it.

Taking deep breaths to regain his equilibrium, McFeeley looked up at the stern and released a rushing sigh of relief. Some careless god who had been looking the other way until then had arranged for a net to be left drooping over the rail. It dangled within easy reach of Jack and himself.

McFeeley and Jack exchanged pleased grins and began their ascent.

At the time the two intrepid soldiers were climbing to the stern rail of the *Helderenberg* an anxious Lord John Churchill took his seat at an extraordinary meeting of the Privy Council in the Palace of Whitehall. Presiding was His Majesty King James II, whose eyes were red-rimmed and face haggard from worry and fatigue. Ready to share his monarch's problems, Churchill had personal worries that threatened to take precedence. The unease of the assembly was such that he found it to be almost tangible. Each and every member of the board still grieved for the attractive, smooth charm of the late Charles II. They found it difficult to come to terms with the conscientious industry of the abrasive James. That very day the new king had stripped the Duke of Monmouth of his title, leaving him as plain James Scott with a reward of £5,000 on his head. It was now a treasonable offence to say that the illegitimate Scott was the legitimate son of the late Charles II.

In Churchill's judgement the only comfortable member present was Henry Jermyn, Catholic adviser to the king. Jermyn had no need to straddle the fence between religions that dug painfully into the crotches of every other member of the Council. At the age of fifty-one King James had time to reconcile a country divided by Catholicism and Protestantism, especially if he soft-pedalled the former as had his brother. Monmouth was the immediate threat to a long and peaceful rule for James. No one could be sure if the duke was the legitimate son of Charles, but the fact that he represented the Protestant religion had the majority of the people behind him.

At that moment the Duke of Monmouth was causing Lord Churchill great concern. Churchill's wife, Lady Sarah, and Rachel her companion, were staying at Forde Abbey near Axminster in Devon as the guests of Sir Edmund Prideaux, who had served as Oliver Cromwell's Attorney General. Mellowed and politically castrated by age, Sir Edmund was no danger, but his wealthy son, also Edmund, had strong Whig sympathies and had been plotting with Monmouth over many years. If Edmund should capture the women, Sarah in particular, then they could be used as hostages to negate Churchill's effectiveness as a soldier against Monmouth.

As he sat there watching James get to his feet, Lord Churchill wasn't sure where his loyalties would lie if it came to a case of king and country or wife and sister. It was a possibility too distressing to contemplate.

'I was awakened at four o'clock this morning,' King James began, addressing an assembly that was droopy-eyed and befuddled by wine and lack of sleep, 'by customs officers who had ridden from Lyme to inform me that the ships of James Scott had anchored in that Dorset bay. Since that time I have taken certain necessary measures. Important though those measures be, the essential is a military solution, which is the purpose of this extraordinary meeting of the Council.'

'If it please Your Majesty,' Lord Chief Justice George Jeffreys began, getting to his feet, disturbing the air with a foul gas comprising alcohol, stale sweat, and medicinal tinctures, 'I understand that the mobilization of the West Country militia is already in hand under the second Duke of Albermale. I would respectfully remind His Majesty that Colonel Percy Kirke has recently returned with his troops from Tangier. May I humbly offer the advice that five companies of Colonel Kirke's foot regiment should be moved to a position west of Salisbury, together with four troops of the Blues and two companies of the Royal Dragoons. I am confident this would refute beyond doubt any military action likely to be instigated by the Duke of Mon— James Scott.'

'Reactionary poppycock,' snorted Baron Guildford, the Lord Keeper, a squat, obese man who had become increasingly irritable in his two-year period of tenure on the Woolsack.

'You hold a different view, my Lord Keeper?' the King asked sharply.

Standing, his heavy, red cheeks wobbling from both the movement and indignation, the Lord Keeper replied, 'More of an observation than a view, your Majesty. When words are to be manipulated or the law to be interpreted so as to benefit one side to the detriment of the other, then indeed I would not hesitate to turn to the Lord Chief Justice. But this could quickly become a matter of war, your Majesty, which surely must dictate that we turn to a soldier.'

Face red with anger, lips moving to spew out silent angry words in advance of an irate tirade, Jeffreys was getting to his feet once more, but James gestured for him to be seated, and turned to Baron Guildford.

'And who say you this soldier should be, My Lord Keeper?'

'Perhaps I may be permitted to deal with this, Your Majesty,' Henry Jermyn said in a low, controlled voice. He was aged around forty, and although not handsome had a powerful personality and a high intelligence that disguised the irregularity of his features. A too-large nose was bent at a sharp angle by a high bridge, and his lower jaw had an overbite that was so unpleasant that Jermyn went to great lengths to avoid being viewed in profile.

Knuckling both of his eyes, turning the red rims a deep crimson, the King raised a questioning eyebrow at Baron Guildford. 'Have you any objection, Lord Keeper?'

'None, Your Majesty,' Guildford stood with a jowl-jiggling bow. 'I admit that Jermyn is far better qualified than I to deal with this.'

'Nay, Your Majesty, I would go no further on matters military than to introduce a brilliant soldier whose father, Sir Winston, is fittingly the Member of Parliament for Lyme,' Henry Jermyn said, certain that his proposal would be accepted by a king strongly influenced by popery. 'We should place the matter in the capable hands of Lord John Churchill.'

However, the king looked somewhat miffed, and Churchill knew why. James would want his friend, the Earl of Feversham, a Frenchman who had been trepanned after a falling beam had crushed his skull during the Great Fire of London, at least nominally in charge of the army that would oppose Monmouth. Churchill himself had received his military training under Feversham's uncle, the famous Marshal Turenne.

'I have a military commander in mind,' James said, proving Churchill's supposition to be right, 'but I would welcome hearing from you on this, Lord Churchill.'

'Your Majesty,' Churchill bowed, hoping that concentrating on the matter in hand would quell his worries over his wife. It was a forlorn hope. Only half his mind handled his address to the Privy Council, while the rest gnawed at all the daunting possibilities of what could be taking place down in Devon. But he made a good job of it, warning against alienating West Country folk by using Colonel Percy Kirke and his 'lambs' as the men of his regiment were known, a regiment whose brutality had it notorious.

'Thank you, Lord Churchill,' James nodded, so worn-looking now that he appeared ill. 'I recognize the sagacity of your words on what we should not do. Can you suggest some constructive action?'

'I have already commenced constructive action, Your Majesty. By dawn I confidently expect a messenger carrying details of James Scott's military strength and his projected campaign.'

This impressed the king and some two thirds of the Privy Council, with the sceptical remaining third openly scoffing the notion that military intelligence could be gathered so swiftly, especially so when, as far as was known, neither Monmouth nor any of his soldiers had yet set foot on land.

As the meeting broke up, so did the enormity of what he had taken on hit Churchill for the first time. He had effectively gambled his reputation, his career, perhaps even his very peerage, on an undisciplined army sergeant whose record read something like that of a transportee on a convict ship.

There were still a few hours left before dawn, but Churchill knew that anxiety over his wife would prohibit sleep, while frantic worry about the trust he had vested in Colm McFeeley would make the sleepless hours drag past intolerably slowly.

They came over the ship's rail together, landing lightly on bare feet; McFeeley pulled his body into the shadows at one side of a wooden stanchion while Jack concealed himself at the other side as an armed sentry slowly walked the deck towards them. Wearing old-fashioned back-and-breast armour and dressed in a campaign coat of red laced with purple, a uniform that belonged to an age long gone, the soldier was a strange sight.

The two men stayed in hiding, regulating their breathing so as to make no sound. Not looking in their direction, the sentry walked up to the rail, looked over it down at the sea, muttered to himself what could have been a curse and then ambled back the way he had come.

As he signalled Jack to move out with him, McFeeley had no clear idea where to find what he sought. It had to be on the lower deck, so he moved along the now deserted upper deck swiftly. Finding a hatchway, he lifted it and went in, sliding down to the lower deck, with Jack closing the hatch up above before joining him.

Moving along the dimly lit gangway, McFeeley studied the closed doors, pausing for some indication of what the cabins might contain. Every door was bare, and he was wondering which were the quarters of Monmouth's military officers, when a cabin door opened a few feet up ahead of them. A man clad in a long, red-and-white-striped-nightgown stepped out into the gangway, standing with his back to the open door, head drooping sleepily as an annoyed voice called from inside the cabin.

'Where you going, William?'

'To the heads,' William replied with a grunt.

The voices told McFeeley that these were private soldiers. This meant that the officers occupied cabins further along the gangway. It was useful information, but the big question was in which direction did the toilet the man was going to lie. If he turned left, then McFeeley and Jack could stay with their backs flat against the wall until he returned to his cabin, Should he come their way, then there was no way they could remain hidden. The man turned right.

As the fellow came towards them with a slow, rolling gait, McFeeley bent and slipped his dagger from its scabbard. Straightening up with the knife at the ready in his hand, he knew that the next few steps the Monmouth soldier took would be his last walk on earth.

The soldier stopped, and McFeeley felt Jack tense beside him in the belief that they had been spotted. McFeeley was ready to leap and was actually springing forward as the Monmouth soldier moved his hands. Checking himself, McFeeley choked back a laugh as the soldier lifted the front of his nightgown, farted loud and long, then urinated where he stood.

Bare feet splashed by the gushing cascade, McFeeley, like Jack, moved not a muscle until the Monmouth soldier gave a grunt of satisfaction, dropped his gown, then turned and went back into the cabin, closing the door behind him.

Made anxious by the delay, McFeeley moved off along the gangway with Jack close behind him. He estimated that they had reached the officers' quarters, but couldn't come up with a plan to find a high ranker without revealing their presence.

He pulled in against the wall then, reaching a hand out behind him to signal for Jack do the same, as another cabin door was opened. Prepared for this to be an officer, McFeeley was staggered to see that the man who stepped out into the gangway wore a suit of royal purple. There was something about him, indefinable but very special, that cast a strange spell to hold the hardened, cynical Colm McFeeley in awe. For the first time in his life the sergeant found himself affected by the presence of another person. It wasn't like the power a woman holds over a man, a power that flees at the end of the sensational sex act. This man exuded some kind of energy that McFeeley had to fight against to avoid being overwhelmed. He was young and graceful, and even the dim light in the gangway caused the silver cross of the Knight of the Garter to sparkle brilliantly on his breast. McFeeley knew that this was the enemy. This was the Duke of Monmouth.

Speaking in through the open doorway, the duke said, 'A very good night to you, Clarence.'

With that, the duke walked away from where McFeeley and Jack stood, the former unable to believe the lucky break he had just stumbled upon. Whoever was in the cabin was a high ranker. It is doubtful that the duke would have visited anyone but his second-in-command. Drawing his knife as the door was quietly closed, McFeeley gestured for Jack to do the same.

They stood one each side of the door as McFeeley turned the handle slowly. Feeling it give, he gave a quick nod of his head to Jack and they both jumped into the room.

Standing sideways to them, partway through unbuttoning the tunic of a colonel, his elderly face frozen in a network of lined surprise, was a man of short stature whose white hair contained just a few flecks of black as a reminder of the colour it had once been. A sword was propped in its scabbard close to him, resting against the

bunk. An alert McFeeley stepped closer, his knife held in a threatening way before he saw the idea of grabbing the sword cancelled
out in the colonel's eyes.

A quick glance around the cabin told McFeeley that he was really
in luck. The green and gold flag of rebellion was propped in one
corner waiting to be taken ashore and erected. Charts were pinned
to the walls and papers that included graphs were littering a small
table. The ideal prisoner had fallen into McFeeley's hands.

Still not recovered from having two naked men come crashing
into his cabin, the colonel flinched as McFeeley brought the point of
his dagger up to press lightly against a prominent Adam's apple
that protruded through the open collar of the tunic.

'Up on deck!' McFeeley ordered.

'Who are you?' the colonel demanded, regaining some of his
composure and courage.

'No questions, just move,' McFeeley said.

'I am a colonel, sir, Colonel Clarence Calvert,' the colonel said
haughtily. 'I soldiered under Cromwell.'

'You may have raped and pillaged, but nobody *soldiered* under
Cromwell,' McFeeley replied bitterly, pricking Calvert's skin with
the dagger just enough to cause blood to trickle.

They got him out through the cabin doorway then. McFeeley and
Jack were on either side just to his rear, their daggers held against
the colonel's back, demanding silent obedience. In this manner they
reached the upper deck without encountering anyone. But as they
closed the hatch they saw the silhouette of the sentry from earlier
approaching.

Pulling the colonel down with them, McFeeley and Jack
crouched behind a capstan that was waist high. There was plenty
of shadow to conceal them, and the sentry was passing, totally
ignorant of their presence. But the sudden doubling up of his body
had compressed the innards of Calvert's extended belly, and his
stomach complained with a grumbling that sounded like thunder
in that still night.

'Post number three …' the sentry was yelling, bringing his
musket round to them as Jack leapt over the capstan to land on the
deck in the soft, sure-footed way of a cat.

Knocking the barrel of the sentry's musket upwards with his left forearm, Jack plunged his knife into the soldier's heart, but was not fast enough to prevent a reflex action that had the sentry discharge a shot. The Enfield 1853 sent a bullet harmlessly into the air, but the blast of the powder was an echoing crack that would have been heard by everyone on board. Pulling Calvert to his feet, aware that they had only seconds in which to escape from the ship, McFeeley dragged him to the rail. The colonel, tripping over the body of the sentry, lost them time. A dual effort by McFeeley and Jack had him back on his feet, with Jack holding Calvert as McFeeley hurriedly uncoiled the rope from around his waist.

'Get your clothes off, quick!' McFeeley snapped at the colonel.

'Look here …' Calvert began an indignant protest, then gave a short scream as Jack sliced his clothing upwards, accidentally catching the skin as he did so.

They pulled off the colonel's ruined clothes then, ripping them away until he stood as naked as they were, his drooping stomach giving the impression that he had swallowed a cannonball. Tying one end of the rope around his own waist, McFeeley allowed a length of about six feet between him and the colonel before looping the rope round Calvert's chest and pulling it up under his armpits. McFeeley then tossed the remainder of the rope to Jack, who allowed the same distance between himself and the colonel as McFeeley had, then tied the rope around his own waist.

'Over the side,' McFeeley shouted, expecting the colonel to move as fast as Jack and himself. But Calvert had dug his feet in, and they were forced to pick him up bodily and throw him, shrieking, over the side of the ship.

It wasn't what McFeeley had planned. Even though he and Jack wasted no time in leaping over the rail, the plummeting colonel pulled them awkwardly so that they hit the side of the ship twice before reaching the water.

Smacking against the cold water knocked the breath out of them, and the struggle Calvert was putting up underwater dragged them down deep. His lungs bursting by the time he was able to reach the surface, the weight of the colonel on the rope dragging him back under again, McFeeley was able only to partially fill his lungs.

Under the water it was pitch black. He went hand over hand and along the rope until he felt the soft body of Calvert. Then the hard muscles of Jacks's arm and shoulder brushed against him. Relieved, McFeeley worked in unison with Jack. Holding the colonel, pushing themselves up to the surface with their feet, they were able to keep their heads and that of the colonel above water while they took in air as Calvert gagged and choked.

Three muskets were fired from the ship, but the bullets went too wide to be heard hitting the water. Confident that the soldiers on board were firing blindly, McFeeley and Jack caught hold of the rope tight against the colonel with one hand and swam with the other as they towed him backwards, his mouth at all times above the water.

Reaching the beach seemed to take an eternity, but then they were out on the pebbles, pulling Calvert ashore. The colonel had stopped coughing and, to McFeeley's consternation when he checked, had ceased breathing as well. Rolling the tubby colonel, who had breasts like a woman, onto his side, McFeeley held his narrow shoulders as he thrust his knees into the soft flesh of Calvert's back. Continuing to apply on and off pressure with his knees, although at first there was no result, McFeeley was then rewarded by the sound of a gurgling that began deep inside of the colonel to end with a gushing splattering of seawater out of his mouth.

Still coughing and retching on the water remaining inside of him, the colonel was at least alive. They got him to his feet. The elderly man was a pathetic sight, his hair plastered to his face; body stooped, and stomach drooping. His genitalia had shrivelled. Colonel Clarence Calvert had been neutered by the cold.

Retrieving their clothing from among the rocks, McFeeley and Jack dressed quickly. Then they took one end of the rope each to lead the colonel like a prize bull off the beach and up over a grassy bank. As dawn neared, the moon had retreated in anticipation and it was the darkest time of the night.

From memory, McFeeley located the half hut, half dugout that he had found while on reconnaissance for the mission. Once used but since abandoned by either fishermen or smugglers, the small place had a sturdy door. When the colonel had been brought in, shivering and complaining that he was an old man, McFeeley tossed him a couple of fraying millers' sacks to wrap himself in.

Huddled in the sacks, body still shaking violently, Calvert sat on the earth floor as instructed by McFeeley, who took sheets of paper, a quill, and ink from where he had previously stashed them. Jack looked on, his face impassive, nothing to do because the colonel was in no condition to make a bolt for it.

Making a pad from the paper, ink quill poised, McFeeley sat on his heels and said, 'I want you to tell me, Colonel Calvert, what arms and powder Monmouth has with him, and then I want to have details of his strategy planned for after the landing.'

Breath rasping now, a rattle of salt water in every breath that he took, the old man sat with his heavy-lidded eyes closed, shaking and shivering, trying to wrap the old sacks even more tightly around him. Jack, making one of his rare ventures into conversation, put McFeeley's fear into words.

'This old chap will die before we get a word out of him, Sergeant.'

Not able to deny this, but not wanting so dire an outcome to be spoken of in his own voice, McFeeley stayed quiet. The dangerous mission, hopeless on the face of it, had been accomplished so successfully that he couldn't bear to think of it all coming to nought. Still hunkering, he moved his feet to waddle closer to Calvert.

'I want all the details, Calvert, and make sure that what you say is correct. We'll be shutting you in here while we go to check on the information you give, and should you prove not to have told the truth, then we won't return to let you out. Now, start talking.'

To the surprise of McFeeley and Jack, the colonel spoke slowly, slurring his words, without opening his eyes. 'We did it, General. God was with us that day. Tuesday, aye, yes, it was Tuesday. The third of September, that was when we showed them, General. For the small price of twenty English dead and fifty-eight wounded we killed three thousand Scots and took ten thousand prisoners.'

'He's rambling,' Jack cursed.

'Sssshh,' McFeeley cautioned, an idea forming in his mind as Calvert continued to verbally fight Cromwell's battles of the past.

'Their stronghold was Edinburgh Castle, but, by gad, we captured that on Christmas Eve—'

'Mr Calvert,' McFeeley interrupted the lighted-headed muttering in a stern voice. 'I am Commander-in-Chief, Oliver Cromwell.'

'Sir,' the old colonel, still shivering so much that his head bobbed from side-to-side, shouted his response respectfully, his eyes remaining closed.

'I want you to give me a full report on this Monmouth fellow,' McFeeley said in the same overbearing manner as before.

Calvert obeyed the command, and by careful questioning, it took McFeeley just some fifteen minutes to learn and write down all that he needed to know. McFeeley made his notes: four cannon, a high but unrecorded number of carbines and pistols, five hundred pikes, five hundred swords and two hundred and fifty barrels of powder. There were eight hundred men aboard the three ships, but the loyal yeoman farmers, peasants and artisans of Dorset and Somerset who would flock to his colours, once ashore, would massively increase Monmouth's army. Monmouth intended to head west through Taunton and make his headquarters at Bridgwater, from where he would march on Bristol with an army that, though rustic, would be some six thousand strong.

McFeeley folded and sealed this report. Through the door of the dugout he could see the heavy red sun of a new day ease itself sluggishly above the eastern horizon. It was close to the time to meet with the messenger who would take this report to Captain Critchell, who would in turn take it to Lord Churchill.

What Calvert, all the time gasping for breath, had also told McFeeley was that Monmouth's first engagement on landing would be east of Lyme, at the town of Bridport, where the local constables were preventing eager young men from leaving to join Monmouth. There was no time for Lord Churchill to take army action to warn the militia at Bridport, so Jack and he would have to alert the garrison there.

While McFeeley and Jack retrieved and unwrapped the muskets they had secreted in the dugout, and were cleaning them, Calvert, dribbling salt water, breathing noisily, had his head on one side and was mumbling incoherently.

A seagull's cry belatedly greeted the dawn as McFeeley went to the door and looked out. In the bay, boats were being lowered from the Monmouth ships. McFeeley discovered, and it unnerved him, that his eagerness to get into action was dulled by the image of the Duke of Monmouth that had remained in his mind since having seen the man who would be king on board the *Helderenberg*. Though conscious of where his duty lay, McFeeley couldn't help but admire the young and energetic fighting man with the courage to go it alone. While pleased with the report he had compiled, and keen to get it to Churchill, McFeeley recognized that there was a significant part of him that would have preferred to stand shoulder-to-shoulder with the inspiring Duke of Monmouth.

Yet dreams were not for soldiers. Colm McFeeley had lived the fairy-tale life once. It had ended on a night of dense fog a dozen years ago. A lieutenant then, under the command of Prince Rupert, he had led his men groping their way over sandbanks to the Nore, where they had driven off the Dutch who had sailed up the Thames estuary with the intention of sealing off the English fleet. It had been a crazily spasmodic battle with the fog hampering both sides equally. For the first time ever McFeeley's soldier's mind had not been working to maximum capacity that night. Plagued by worry over Rosin, his wife who was due to deliver their first-born at any moment, he had missed the infiltration of his ranks by a squad of Dutch soldiers. McFeeley had learned he had been outflanked when his sergeant major had died with a Dutch bayonet through his throat.

That tragedy had been an omen of worse to come. Now as he tried to concentrate on Monmouth's three ships he couldn't avoid the image of Mother Shannon's face that had been haunting him for years. The crone of a midwife had come running to meet him as he went back into camp on that terrible, foggy night. Tears streaming down her lined face, slack lips working over toothless gums, the old woman had broken the sad news to him. Rosin had died in childbirth and the baby had been stillborn.

While still shattered by the loss of his wife and the tragic birth, McFeeley had been the subject of a military inquiry that had reduced him to the ranks. Over many long years he had gradually fought his way up again in his military career, but he had never succeeded in filling the void left by the death of Rosin.

By an immense effort of will he shut off the past and came fully into the present. It was time to rendezvous with Critchell's messenger. Going back into the dugout where Jack sat tinkering with his musket, McFeeley wanted to be on the move.

'We'll be on our way, Jack.'

Getting to his feet, Jack gestured with his head towards the now quiet Calvert. 'We won't need to come back for him.'

'I was only bluffing,' McFeeley answered. 'We've no way of checking if what he said was true, but I thought that I could frighten him into giving an accurate report.'

'I knew that,' Jack said as he tore open a paper cartridge, poured the powder into the barrel of his musket, and then rammed the bullet in. 'What I was telling you, Sergeant, is that the old man is dead.'

Possibly due to McFeeley's train of thought while outside a few minutes before, this hit him astonishingly hard. Walking over to where the old soldier sat in death, he looked down at him. Calvert's pride at being an ex-Cromwellian officer mattered not now. The colonel had gained the dubious distinction of being the first victim of the Duke of Monmouth's rebellion. Yet this would not gain Calvert a place in history, for only Jack and McFeeley would ever know how he had died.

Dropping down onto one knee, McFeeley pulled the sacks from around the colonel. There was no time for a burial, so he laid him flat then covered him completely with the sacking. It was an occasion that asked for a prayer to be said, even silently. McFeeley turned quickly away because he hadn't prayed in twelve years.

Two

LADY SARAH CHURCHILL was feeling tired. It was breakfast time but she had to stifle a yawn as she shared a table with Sir Edmund Prideaux, the aged but lovely-in-a-motherly-way Lady Prideaux, and the golden-haired Rachel, Lady Sarah's companion. Lady Sarah had been unable to sleep since a quarter past two that morning when she had been awakened by the sound of horses' hoofs. They had been distant from the bedroom that she shared with Rachel, and she estimated that they had been at the front of Forde Abbey.

Her worries were increased now to find that Edmund wasn't joining them for breakfast. Although Rachel was enamoured of the young lawyer, Sarah was always ill at ease in Edmund's company. He had none of his father's quiet and reassuring charm. Sarah felt that she could ask Sir Edmund a question about the night without overstepping the mark of a guest's politeness.

Thanking the butler with a smile as he placed toast in front of her, Sarah welcomed the act of buttering it so that she could make her enquiry without having to look at either her host or hostess.

'Did you hear horses in the night?' she asked, adding. 'Well, early in the morning to be exact. Around two o'clock.'

From under her eyes Sarah caught the anxious glances that Sir Edmund and his lady exchanged with each other. He started to reply with. 'Well, I think that perhaps ...'

'Your conscience prevents you from sleeping, Sarah,' Rachel jokingly accused her.

For some reason Sarah had been nervous since arriving here this time. Normally she enjoyed Forde Abbey, and had readily agreed when Rachel, who had decided to pursue Edmund Prideaux, had asked her to share a short break in Devon.

'Edmund was away on business, and arrived home fairly late. I haven't seen him yet this morning, Sarah, my dear, but I will ask him if it was two o'clock,' Lady Prideaux explained.

'I thought that your main interest this morning would be in riding, Sarah,' Sir Edmund said. 'I hear you are determined to master Goodyear, a formidable stallion. I admire your pluck.'

'Foolhardiness,' Rachel commented without a trace of malice. 'I never mount up unless I'm sure that I'm on a docile hack.'

It's a pity you don't apply the same principle to your men, Sarah thought, doing an inner blushing at her risqué simile. Rachel's sense of fun and blatant use of suggestively orientated language made her a liability at times, particularly when at prestigious gatherings at which John Churchill was present. Yet Sarah was very fond of her. Whatever Rachel lacked in social skills and morals, she more than made up for in honesty and loyalty.

Even so, she was beginning to regret having agreed to visit Forde Abbey. As much as she liked Sir Edmund, opposition to James II was coming to a head and Prideaux was one of the leading squire rebels. If some move against the King should be made while she was in this house, then Sarah would seriously compromise her husband. She was well aware that King James II hated, and possible even feared, his rebellious nephew.

'I believe, in all modesty, Sir Edmund, that I can this morning get the better of Goodyear.'

Unnoticed by any of them at the table, Edmund, the son of the house, had entered the room, standing just inside of the doorway as he spoke to Sarah.

'Not this morning I am afraid, Lady Sarah.'

'Good morning, Edmund,' his mother said, anxious eyes seeking the butler who was not in the room. Standing, the old lady went past her son, patting him fondly on the arm while informing him. 'I'll have Clive bring your breakfast.'

'No, mother, I can't spare the time,' Edmund called after her, then turned to Sarah and Rachel. 'You are lucky ladies. When I mentioned to George Speke that you were here at Forde Abbey, he insisted that you spend a few days at his manor in White Lackington. All arrangements have been made. A coach awaits you; my ladies, simply pack a short-stay bag each, and bring your maids along with you.'

'Do you consider this to be wise at this point in time, Edmund?' Sir Edmund asked.

'Absolutely, Father,' Edmund smiled a practised smile that he knew made the very best of his good looks.

Lady Prideaux came back into the dining room, a frown exaggerating the age lines in her face as she asked her son, 'Who are all those men outside, Edmund?'

A jolt of fear went through Sarah. The sound of many horses in the night came back to her, and she waited anxiously for Edmund's reply.

'Just friends, Mother, simply friends who will be riding on within the hour,' Edmund answered with his easy smile. Then he turned to Sarah and Rachel. 'The coachman will be waiting for us, Rachel, Lady Sarah.'

'I am rather excited about spending a little time at White Lackington,' Rachel smiled. 'Will you be there with us, Edmund?'

'Of course, my dear.'

'Edmund,' Sir Edmund addressed his son in a serious tone. 'I must ask you to spare me a minute or two. It is a matter of extreme importance. Might I suggest that we go into the drawing-room?'

'No time, sir; I regret to say,' the son said. 'No doubt whatever it is you wish to speak about will last until I return from White Lackington.'

Sir Edmund was not satisfied with this, Sarah could tell, and his deep concern worried her further. It was on her mind as she reluctantly packed a trunk, helped by Ruby, her maid. Rachel was smiling happily as she sang a popular song while packing her trunk. In ordinary circumstances Sarah would have been as pleased at the change for a few days as Rachel was. But circumstances were far from ordinary. Her suspicions were further aroused when they were ready to leave and Edmund kept them inside of the house until the sound of his 'friends' riding away had faded. Sarah guessed that the men had been armed.

In the courtyard where the coach and coachman awaited, she was hoping for a glimpse of Sir Edmund. Disguising her movements by fiddling with her vanity bag, Sarah wrote a brief note to him, explaining that she believed herself to be in danger and requesting that he have the coach followed and Rachel and herself taken from it. On the pretence of soothing Goodyear, she pressed both the note she had written and a coin into the hand of Simon the Prideaux's young groom.

'Please see that Sir Edmund gets this note, Simon,' she whispered. 'Do not let me down.'

'I won't, my Lady,' the boy promised.

Edmund was calling to her, urging her to hurry, and she joined Rachel in the coach. Edmund mounted up on a chestnut bay and went on ahead to arrange lunch at an inn.

Constantly looking behind her, to the chagrin of her companion, Sarah was vastly relieved when, some minutes after Edmund had ridden off, she could see a modest dust cloud gaining ground on the coach. It was a rider who was sure to bring an end to the growing nightmare that this journey was becoming for her.

'Who is it?' Rachel enquired without real interest.

'I'm not sure …' Sarah began truthfully while wondering who Sir Edmund would send after them. The old gentleman would have perfected a plan of action, of that she was certain. Then her hopes were shattered as she recognized the approaching rider as Simon.

Riding up to the side of the coach, breathing hard, his face puffed and red from exhaustion, the boy leaned close to Sarah, attempting a conspiratorial whisper, but his breathlessness spewed out his words as a harsh semi-shout.

'I couldn't give your letter to the Master, my Lady.'

'Why ever not? '

'The King's men did come to the Abbey and they tooked the Master way.'

None of this made sense to Sarah, and she said snappily and haughtily, 'What are you talking about, boy? Why should something like that happen?'

'Haven't you heard, my Lady?' Simon asked in disbelief.

'Everybody do be talking about it, The Duke of Monmouth has landed at Lyme!'

Most of the groom's words were distant and echoing to Sarah, but the content of what he had said got through to her. His hand reached into the coach, the coin she had given him held in his fingers.

'You will want your money back, my Lady, as I didn't do what you asked.'

Sarah couldn't answer, she felt terribly faint. A darkness was closing in all round her and her head was spinning, She was aware of the boy releasing the coin. She heard it rattle against the floor of the coach as the groom rode away.

'Oh good, here's Edmund coming back. I'm really looking forward to lunch,' Rachel said enthusiastically.

The sound of Rachel's voice pulled Sarah back from the abyss of unconsciousness. But she didn't welcome the escape because nothingness would be preferable to contemplating an immediate future that she was certain would be horrible. Wishing that she had obeyed her instincts and remained at Forde Abbey, she shivered as Edmund Prideaux rode up to the coach.

As McFeeley and Jack galloped into Bridport on horses stolen from a farm near to Lyme, a mist had settled to have things normal appear to be unpleasantly eerie. They were riding through the silence of a graveyard, with the hoofs of their mounts muffled. There was neither sight nor sound of the 3,000 men of the Somersetshires said to be guarding the town. They were aware that an advance party of 100 tough Monmouth musketeers was close behind them. Backing them would be a composite strike force of 1000 soldiers. From what the two of them could see of it, Bridport was going to be the rebel Duke's first victory, a total rout due to the defenders being unprepared.

They rode up the broad main street and were close to the road that intersected it about halfway along its length, when a soldier on guard, startled by their sudden looming out of the mist, tremblingly pointed a musket at them.

Releasing the rope he had used as improvised reins, but staying in the saddle, McFeeley kicked the musket out of the sentry's hands and reached to catch hold of his tunic with both hands, effortlessly lifting him from the ground so that they were face to face.

'Where are your officers billeted?' McFeeley snarled his question.

'Yonder,' the sentry stammered, pointing to the Bull Inn that stood on one corner of the intersection.

Throwing the soldier to the ground rather than just dropping him, McFeeley rode to the inn. He and Jack dismounted together, and he ran into the inn first.

Two soldiers, a corporal and a private, leapt up from where they had sat dozing in a corner. The corporal reached for a rifle but McFeeley got him by the throat, slamming him back against a wall, asking demandingly. 'Where are your officers?'

'What's going on here?'

Still holding the corporal immobile, McFeeley turned his head to the militia officer who had come out of a side room. 'Who are you, sir?'

'Edward Coker, I asked what is going on here.'

'The town is about to come under attack from Monmouth's soldiers,' McFeeley told him tersely.

Coker laughed disdainfully. 'And who might you be?'

'Sergeant McFeeley, Kild ...' McFeeley stopped himself from identifying the militia that he no longer belonged to.

'You look more like a muck-spreader off some Dorset farm,' Coker said as another officer came out of the room to stand by him. With a grin, Coker said to McFeeley. 'This is Major Wadham Strangway, tell him what you've just told me.'

'Monmouth is about to attack Bridport, sir,' McFeeley made the statement urgent.

Strangway laughed, then turned to his fellow officer and they had a good chuckle together. Coker turned to McFeeley. 'Whoever you are, get yourself out of here.'

'But, sir,' McFeeley protested.

With a threat in his stance, Wadham Strangway stepped towards McFeeley. 'For a start, Monmouth is in France. Secondly, if he has an army then it won't amount to ten men, and thirdly, no military commander would launch an attack in mist such as we have here this night.'

As the officer finished speaking a volley of shots rang out. This was followed by some startled shouts that wiped the grins from the faces of the militia officers.

'We need rifles and ammunition,' McFeeley told them as Jack stepped forward.

'Fix them up,' Coker nodded at the corporal, then asked McFeeley. 'Did you two arrive on horses?'

'Yes, sir.'

'Then we are commandeering them,' Coker said. 'Come on, Wadham!'

As he and Jack took a musket apiece and bullets from the corporal, McFeeley turned to shout at the officers who were going out of the door into the street. 'Wait, sir.'

They ignored him, and McFeeley ran to the door, standing with his back against the jamb, using the building for protection as he looked out into the misty night. Riding out of the fog was a Monmouth colonel, bearing down on Coker and Strangway, both of whom were preparing to mount the horses that McFeeley and Jack had rode into the town on. Edward Coker fired a pistol just as McFeeley aimed his rifle at the rebel colonel. McFeeley had no time to pull the trigger; Coker's bullet hit the colonel somewhere at waist level. The Monmouth officer doubled over, clutching at his side, barely able to stay in the saddle as he wheeled his horse about and was swallowed up by the mist.

Swinging up on to a horse, Coker shouted excitedly to Strangway. 'I got him, I think!'

A musket cracked in the fog and Coker stood upright on the horse, supported by his knees, before keeling over sideways. A shot had ripped his skull open and his brains splashed bloodily onto the doorjamb beside where McFeeley stood.

Glancing at the mess, McFeeley remarked to Jack, 'That's the last thinking he'll do!' Then he yelled at Strangway, who was looking down at the dead Coker, wheeling his mount wildly this way and that. 'Get down off the horse, sir!'

It appeared that Strangway had instantly obeyed the shout. But he came off the horse too quickly, landing thuddingly on the ground, coughing blood as he died noisily and convulsively.

In the mist outside it was complete chaos. There was indiscriminate shooting going on and riderless horses were charging around in panic as McFeeley and Jack, both running at a crouch, left the Bull Inn. An idea came suddenly to McFeeley, having him run back into the inn and snatch up the Somersetshire standard before coming out again to rejoin Jack.

'Head that way!' he shouted at Jack over the general clamour, using an arm to indicate the east.

Monmouth's men, with unlimited success, were coming from the west, which meant that any stand made against them needed to be made some distance to the east. Jack went off down the continuation of Bridport's broad main street at a lope, while McFeeley spun on his heel to study the panicking horses that were wheeling round him. Spotting one that was saddled, he ran to leap on it from behind, clutching the Somersetshire flag in one hand, gaining the saddle with an ease that would shame a skilled acrobat. Reaching down for the reins, he controlled and pacified the horse before riding to the west, bullets whistling and singing round him as he went, holding the standard aloft and yelling over and over again. 'To me! Somerset men, Dorset men, to me!'

Continuing west until the rebel fire became too thick to risk going further, he swung the horse about, still calling out his rallying cry as he rode back eastward. The leaderless local militia had been milling around in confusion, and they welcomed McFeeley's directive. By the time he caught up with the running Jack, McFeeley had a considerable number of musketeers in tow, some mounted, others on foot. Reaching a bridge at the eastern extreme of the town, he crossed it and then dismounted on reaching a stretch of flat grassland

'Form up in three ranks!' McFeeley shouted, and his followers, counted off and put into place by Jack, immediately obeyed.

Striding along the front of his improvised company of musketeers, McFeeley gave the order to load. The mist was thinning now, allowing daylight to take over fully.

'Pay attention,' he ordered, and not one soldier questioned his authority. 'They will come at us over that bridge, which will bunch them together. You will wait for my order to fire. On my first command only the front rank will fire. Once you have discharged your weapon, kneel and reload. The same applies to the centre rank when the order is given to fire. When the rear rank has fired, and if it is necessary, the same routine will be repeated.'

It was just a matter of waiting then. McFeeley walked to the bridge and took a look along the wide road. Keeping out of sight he saw the rebel foot soldiers advancing with a carelessness born of easy victories so far in Bridport. To a veteran like himself the Monmouth troops heading his way seemed to lack discipline. Some were so confident that they carried their muskets at the trail.

Going back to his newly formed, modestly sized army, he alerted his soldiers superfluously, for the drumming of rebel feet could clearly be heard – and was growing louder by the second.

When the Monmouth men came over the bridge it was some eight abreast and without any attempt at formation. So relaxed were they that they didn't see the three ranks of waiting musketeers until McFeeley shouted his first order, and then it was too late.

'Front rank! Front rank fire!' McFeeley shouted.

At the concerted cracking of muskets the entire first row of rebels went down as if scythed, and several of those further back fell dead or wounded.

The surprise was so complete that the impetus of the Monmouth soldiers coming up behind pushed those in front of them on to stumble over their fallen comrades.

'Centre rank! Centre rank fire!'

More Monmouth men were mown down, a youngster, a dark stain of blood spreading fast across the breast of his tunic, came staggering on, holding his musket by the barrel and dragging its stock along the ground. He was heading for McFeeley, who raised a hand to stop Jack who was moving forward to protect him. The boy, who had taken up arms for the rebel duke, had the round, bland red face of an agricultural worker. Just feet from an immobile McFeeley, he tried to lift his musket but was too feeble. He smiled a silly smile at McFeeley, as if being mortally wounded and unable to lift a musket was amusing. Then he crumpled. His knees gave way first and the rest of him followed. The lad was dead before he hit the ground.

Behind the fallen rebel the Monmouth musketeers were colliding with each other in a mad dash to retreat. McFeeley's voice was hoarse as he yelled the order. 'Rear rank! Rear rank fire!'

Hit in their backs as they went, the rebels tumbled into the dust as McFeeley saw that his front and centre ranks had reloaded, and then ordered his rear rank to do the same.

'Take up pursuit!' he ordered, leading the way by crossing the bridge at a trot.

The rebels were on the run and the local militia, inspired by McFeeley and euphoric as they leapt over the bodies of those they had slain, was in full pursuit. But then McFeeley held his musket on high as he yelled out a one-word command.

'Halt!'

Stopping as a disorganized group, the Somersetshires looked up ahead to where rebel cavalrymen were skirting past their retreating infantry and heading for them at a gallop. Fortunes had changed swiftly. The local soldiers were standing exposed and vulnerable as the Monmouth horsemen bore down on them, and they turned their heads to McFeeley in desperation.

'Form up into three ranks,' McFeeley ordered. 'As before, wait for my word of command.'

Recognizing that he and his squad faced annihilation, McFeeley resigned himself to his fate while making a personal pledge to take as many rebels as possible with him. The horsemen were so close now that every steaming breath of the mounts was clearly visible, and he saw the face of the officer commanding as he held his sword high.

'Front rank! Front rank fire!' McFeeley yelled.

His musketeers fired. Two cavalrymen were shot straight out of the saddle, while the horse of a third shrieked out its agony and did a nose-dive into the ground, throwing its rider whose neck snapped with a crack that was as loud a shot from a musket.

With the horsemen close enough to preclude an order for his centre rank to fire, McFeeley was astonished to see the officer in charge of the cavalry, abject fear on his weak-featured face, rein up his mount, scream out an order, then do an about face to gallop off, closely followed by his horsemen.

McFeeley couldn't credit what had taken place. The cavalry officer was in such a funk that it was obvious he wouldn't stop until he had returned to whence he had come – Lyme.

Realization of their miraculous reprieve slowly dawned on the men of the local militia. One of them did a nervous giggle. This triggered off laughter that turned into cheering as they came forward to pound McFeeley on the back in congratulation.

Some forty dead rebels lay around them. Monmouth's first battle had ended in defeat. Bridport had successfully been defended. McFeeley, though pleased with the result, remembered the competent and impressive Duke of Monmouth he had seen on board the *Helderenberg* and concluded that the battle for Bridport had been a fluke. Once Monmouth was established there would be many hard fights ahead.

Perplexed by the intrigue that beset her, and exasperated by the inanity of Rachel's pursuit of Edmund Prideaux, Lady Sarah Churchill ate dinner at White Lackington automatically. Excellent though the food was, she didn't really taste it. She was aware, however, of John Trenchard's covert but sensual study of her from across the table. Trenchard, the son-in-law of old George Speke, and Member of Parliament for Taunton, while sitting at his side was Sir John Hooker Vowell, a prominent Devonshire Member of Parliament and an ardent Whig. These two eminent guests were just two in a long line of visitors to the Speke manor since she had been there. They were callers who conversed in whispers, or walked away from the building before engaging in any conversation. She had witnessed many clandestine meetings in addition to hearing Prideaux's late night visits to her companion's bedroom. Being accustomed to Rachel's sexual proclivities, Sarah was unperturbed by them, but was disturbed by the golden-haired beauty's infatuation with Prideaux, having her scoff at Sarah's contention that they were both prisoners at the manor. Prideaux, distanced at the table from Sarah by Rachel, was showing the effects of drink. Edmund had in fact been drunk on each of the three evenings they had spent at White Lackington, but on the two previous occasions alcohol had made him merry to the point of being boisterous. In contrast melancholia had settled on him this third evening, and it had John Trenchard make a comment.

'Why so glum, Edmund? Rest assured that the arrest of your father is nought but a precautionary measure.'

'Perhaps so,' Edmund was prepared to concede, 'but to me it is a dire warning that such measures by the King may preclude any real chance of an insurrection.'

'Absolute nonsense!' snorted Trenchard, an ugly, bombastic man who would forsake caution for self-promotion. 'You have seen the patronage of my rebels' club in the Red Lion Inn at Taunton, Edmund.'

George Speke, old and frail and suffering from an illness that made him shake, particularly when reaching out a hand for something, looked troubled and appeared to be about to say something, but his son-in-law was continuing, trying to reassure the still doubting Edmund Prideaux.

'Nothing can stop the rebellion, Edmund,' Trenchard said, his enthusiasm having him stand from his chair, turn a circle and sit once more. 'I have personally committed 1,000 foot and 200 to 300 horse soldiers.'

Clearing his throat noisily to make a gap in the conversation for the words he wanted to say, George Speke advised. 'I say, John, show some prudence with your assertions while we have lady guests present.'

By that time entirely convinced that she and Rachel were prisoners here, Sarah realized that the old man was not in on the plot. Though he was too old and feeble to offer any help, she felt better knowing that he wouldn't stand for his home to be used for a kidnapping. Speke was a Whig and a member of the Green Ribbon Club squires of the West, but he was a straight-dealing, honest old man.

'We are free to talk, sir,' Edmund Prideaux told Speke, suddenly nowhere near as drunk as he had earlier appeared to be. 'Both ladies will remain as your guests for some little time. Lady Sarah will shortly be writing a letter to Lord John Churchill, and what she has to tell him will ensure that the King's enemies will not come rampaging through the West Country.'

'I will not be a party to so despicable a plot, young Prideaux,' Speke said, shaking his old head in emphasis and unable to stop the movement.

'It is already in hand, sir, and your conscience is absolutely clear,' Prideaux said.

'It is my understanding that King James has placed the Earl of Feversham in command,' the old man said, looking pleased at having found a flaw in Prideaux's plan for Lady Sarah.

'That appointment was made out of sentiment – a favour to an old friend, not military strategy,' Trenchard said with a little laugh. 'Feversham is a French fool with a plate in his head, whose only activities are eating and sleeping. He is in nominal command, Father. Doesn't the fact that the King has raised Churchill to the rank of brigadier illustrate who is really running James' armies?'

This was the first Sarah had heard of her husband's promotion. She was initially thrilled but then confused, for it all meant nothing while she was here at White Lackington and John was wherever he was. It was daunting to think of the inner battle that would rage inside of loyal soldier John Churchill when he was faced by a choice between King and country or his wife. What would he choose? Her's was but one life and should her husband decide to save it, then it was likely to be at the expense of thousands of other lives.

Sarah's anguished pondering was broken in upon by the clatter of many horses' hoofs outside.

'That's John back with the first batch,' Edmund said, a pleased smile on his face as he stood.

This answered another question for Sarah, who had noticed that John Speke, the son of old George, had been absent from the manor since Rachel and herself had been there. Apparently he had been out buying mounts for the rustic cavalry that the rebel duke would be forming.

'I hope that our first gift to his Grace Monmouth will not be too motley a bunch of nags,' Trenchard said in what sounded like semi-prayer as he stood and left the room with Prideaux.

'Don't judge us too hastily, Lady Sarah,' the old man pleaded when he was left alone with Sarah and Rachel.

'I am aware that you have no role in it, sir,' Sarah replied, trying to sound benevolent where the old man was concerned, but unable to remove haughtiness from her tone, 'but I cannot be expected to take kindly being kidnapped and held for ransom.'

'Quite so,' George Speke nodded sadly as indistinct voices and the movement of horses came from outside. The white head still bobbed up and down long after the nod had served its purpose. 'I will do all that I can to assist you within the limitations imposed by my age and frailties.'

'I appreciate that, sir,' Sarah managed a smile despite the desperation of her situation.

'Though I will not condone you being used in such a way, Lady Sarah, I will never deny James Duke of Monmouth,' Speke said, then his eyes misted over as he visited that far place of reminiscence that is only accessible to the aged. 'He stayed here five years ago, you know. A truly marvellous man, and that was a really wonderful time. Never has White Lackington known anything like it, Lady Sarah, Miss Rachel, before or since.

'2,000 persons on horseback brought him to the Manor, and there was another 20,000 here to receive him. It was necessary to tear down the railings all around the Manor to accommodate the multitude. He ran races and wrestled with the local gladiators, ladies. It was August then, and I can still see that fine, handsome young man winning every time to have applause and cheering echo over the lush meadows. He picnicked with us on the cornflower-bordered heaths.

'He laughed and joked with us, drank our cider and our elderberry wine under the park trees. I am in no way a religious fanatic, Lady Sarah; it is that man that I worship. Bear in mind when the fighting starts that it is erroneous to regard it as a war of religion. King James is Catholic, but the man who will lead his armies, your good husband, is a Protestant. Religion is often the excuse but rarely the issue, Lady Sarah.'

Sarah was sure that it wasn't tiredness that caused tears to leak from George Speke's eye's he finished speaking. Prior to hearing his descriptive recall, Monmouth had been for her no more than a distant memory, and since just a name spoken in speculation, in anger, or in fear. Now he had become a man. A man who loved life and knew how to live it to the full. Hatred and the wars it spawned were impersonal. Would a soldier be able to slay an enemy he knew well?

'I must get away from here, sir. Can you take me to Ilminster tonight?' Sarah asked hurriedly, aware that Trenchard and Prideaux would return at any minute.

'To do that would be to endanger you even more, Lady Sarah.'

'I don't agree,' she protested. 'I have friends there who will help me.'

Tilting his skull-like head to listen for the return of the men who had gone outside, George Speke told her in a low voice. 'This is a most difficult and dangerous time, Lady Sarah. It is impossible to tell where loyalties lie. You would be wise, and certainly safer, to remain here at White Lackington.'

There was much truth in what the old man said. With the Monmouth rising so close it was possible that she would ask someone she believed to be a Royalist for assistance, only to have her throat slit by a supposed friend who was really a rebel. It disheartened her to do so, but Lady Sarah Churchill had to agree with George Speke.

There were troop movements throughout the south of England. The militia of Gloucestershire, Herefordshire and Monmouthshire had moved in to defend Bristol from an anticipated attack by Portsmouth. 12 companies of the Foot Guards, and seven companies of the Coldstream, some 1150 men in all, were heading for a rendezvous with the Wiltshire militia. Not far behind them were 16 large cannon with carriages, powder, ball, shovels, pickaxes, etc., the trundling main artillery train from the Tower of London. While at the same time a smaller train of eight lighter guns – four iron 3-pounders and four brass falcons – had set out from Portsmouth with Sherborne in Dorset as its destination. Lieutenant Colonel Charles Churchill, the brother of John, was commanding five companies of infantry, most of them veterans from Tangier. A total of 1,800 foot soldiers, 150 cavalry, together with 26 cannon, heading for the West Country. John Churchill himself was riding ahead of his infantry and reached Bridport with an advance guard of 300 horsemen. The commander-in-chief, Lord Feversham, was moving down from London with a troop of Life Guards and sixty Horse Grenadiers. The net was closing on the Duke of Monmouth.

Colm McFeeley, having been promoted to lieutenant in the field for the action that had saved Bridport, was serving as a temporary attachment to the five companies of foot that were under the command of Colonel Percy Kirke. They were camped on a low hill above Axminster, and on the afternoon of a blisteringly hot day, McFeeley, restless and bored, was doing some rifle practice assisted by Jack who had, as insisted upon by McFeeley, been promoted to sergeant. There was tension in the camp and much talk of the coming battles with Monmouth. In the way McFeeley had noticed before, most veterans were made anxious by anticipation, whereas the unblooded were blissfully ignorant.

A young private soldier came up to him and saluted smartly. 'Compliments of Captain Allenby, sir. He would like to see you right away.'

Tossing the carbine he had been using to Jack, who deftly caught it, McFeeley said laconically. 'Keep practising, Jack. I have a feeling I'll need you to cover my back.'

Following the soldier to the adjutant's tent, he found Allenby to be a small man with quick movements and intelligent eyes. As McFeeley entered the tent, the adjutant had two glasses in one hand and a bottle filled with dark alcohol in the other. Raising the bottle by way of invitation, Allenby asked McFeeley in a broad North of England accent, 'Which do you prefer, Lieutenant, abstention or horse piss?'

'If those are my only options, Captain, I'll go for the piss.'

Pouring them a glass each, Allenby wryly gave some advice. 'Never let the army manipulate you into becoming adjutant, McFeeley. I've ceased to be a soldier to become a general manager. I could be running a mill back home, taking my pick of the comely maidens looking for work.'

'Why do I feel like a maiden under threat right now, Captain?' McFeeley enquired with a grin as he accepted a glass and took a sip.

'I was told that you are a perceptive man, Lieutenant,' Allenby smiled. 'Among other things.'

'It could be best to leave the "other things" for now,' McFeeley suggested.

Allenby chuckled. He was McFeeley's kind of man. 'I'd like to discuss them with you, but duty dictates that I must brief you for a mission.'

'I have been selected because I am not one of the "lambs",' McFeeley stated rather than questioned.

'Indeed, indeed. This is a delicate matter, McFeeley, involving as it does, Lieutenant Lawrence Peters, the nephew of Colonel Kirke.'

The place part way down McFeeley's spine that was infallible in sending him warnings was acting up now. If what he was here for was straightforward, then one of "Kirke's lambs" would have been entrusted with the task, not a temporary newcomer like himself. The fact that a close relative of the commanding officer was involved was sure to be an added, serious complication.

About to speak, Allenby paused while orders were bellowed outside at a squad doing drill. When the foghorn voice of a sergeant lost some of its volume and the sound of many feet beat a retreat, the adjutant began to speak without looking at McFeeley. 'Lieutenant Peters, who is the son of Colonel Kirke's sister, is a man that I judge to be more suited to life as a poet than a soldier, and I imagine that he shares my view. But, what with family tradition and all that sort of thing, he found himself serving under his uncle and ...'

'... and he's run off,' McFeeley filled in for the adjutant, who spun to look at him sharply.

'They didn't warn me just how perceptive you are, McFeeley!'

'Forgive them,' Captain,' McFeeley grinned. 'They didn't know.'

'I'm amazed that you are only a lieutenant.'

McFeeley laughed. 'You'd have been more amazed yesterday – I was only a sergeant then.'

Uncertain as to whether the lieutenant was joking, Allenby became serious as he got down to the business he had called McFeeley there for. 'Lieutenant Peters left on foot, taking a musket and no rations with him, McFeeley. As you will be mounted, and he will need to stop to find food, catching up with him shouldn't prove to be difficult. The problems begin after you have found him.

Colonel Kirke will deal personally with his nephew when you bring him back to camp. The thing is, Lieutenant, only the commanding officer and myself, you, too, now, of course, know of Lieutenant Peters' absence. Colonel Kirke wants him brought back in with the utmost secrecy.'

'I'll do what I can,' McFeeley promised.

'It would be in your own interest to do better than that by ensuring that you do exactly what the commanding officer wants,' Allenby cautioned. 'Colonel Kirke is a difficult man, McFeeley.'

'I've heard all about Colonel Kirke, Captain,' McFeeley said grimly, then lightened up as he stretched out a hand with his emptied glass in it. 'That must have been a fine horse. I'll have another and then be on my way.'

Filling both glasses, Allenby enquired. 'Where will you start?'

'Peters would have headed for Axminster straight off,' McFeeley replied, draining his glass. 'It should be easy to pick up his trail there.'

Three

I N SPITE OF the district being largely pro-Monmouth, McFeeley found a publican who had sold Peters a brandy and had seen the lieutenant take a road south-west out of town.

McFeeley rode steadily for half an hour without seeing a dwelling of any kind. The first sign of human habitation came when he topped a grassy rise to see a farm cottage standing alone and desolate as a desert island. Riding closer, McFeeley could see that it was little more than a hovel that relied on an attached barn for mutual support. A woman and a boy stood together, aggressively defensive as they watched his approach. She was of chunky build, heavy breasts resting upon folded arms that were brown-skinned and bare. A sprinkling of grey painted highlights into her black hair, but the passing years had etched character into her face without affecting its attractiveness. Aged about thirteen years, the boy was sullen and he sneered at McFeeley's uniform as he reined his horse to a halt and dismounted.

'My father's gone off to join Monmouth,' the boy told McFeeley with childish glee.

'Go on back down to the bottom field and get on with your digging, Lennie,' the mother ordered. Then she turned her pale greyish eyes onto McFeeley, in a penetrating gaze and inquired, 'I suppose you're looking for one of your kind?'

Still holding the reins of his horse, he nodded. 'You've seen an officer pass this way?'

'Rest awhile, tie your horse to that post,' she told him. 'I can offer you bread and cheese.'

'Thank you, but I haven't come far,' he told her as he secured his horse. 'When did you see this soldier go by, Mistress…?'

'Yates. My man is Thomas Yates who, like the boy said, has gone off to fight a war, Lieutenant. You are a lieutenant?' she studied his insignia with a frown.

'Yes. The name's Colm McFeeley.'

'I'm Lucy,' she said, her study of him more intense than ever.

The meeting had become stilted, almost as awkward as two young people interested in each other but both embarrassed by that interest. McFeeley asked, 'When did he go past, Mistress Yates?'

'Lucy,' she corrected him archly. 'He didn't go by; he's here. Can you see that pond down there? That's where he is but I don't want him here. He's so strange and very quiet, isn't he?'

'I've never met him,' McFeeley replied. 'You say this pond is down there?'

'Yes. He's hiding in those rushes. I gave him some food, but he frightens me.'

In her eagerness to show him the pond her chubby forearm had come against McFeeley's hand. Her skin was warm and silky smooth. Though he couldn't be sure then, or after, how her breast came to rest on his arm. He hadn't moved, so she had made the contact, accidentally or on purpose.

Letting her arm slide down, keeping it in contact with him at the same time, she clasped his hand in hers. Looking him straight in the eye, all self consciousness and shame driven away by a sudden urging inside of herself, she huskily announced, 'I need a man.'

Time and circumstance didn't permit polite preliminaries or encourage small talk. Her statement had been as uninhibited and artless as the raw nature of the countryside that surrounded them. McFeeley's response was equally as basic, but his warning mechanism was active. He looked to where the woman's son bent to his work, and then at the tall rushes concealing Lawrence Peters.

'I have to take that man back to camp,' he said.

'He'll still be there … afterwards,' she replied in a matter of fact way that didn't fit with what was happening and the way her fingers entwined with his as she took him towards the barn.

She was undoing her dress before he had closed the door of the barn behind them. McFeeley himself was now beyond the point of return. The straw spread on the floor of the barn was as enticing as the four-poster bed of a lady in a palace. She came to him then, fumbling at his uniform, her eyes heavy-lidded and breathing through her parted lips in a deep, erratic manner.

Five minutes later he was brought briefly back down to earth by what he took to be the sound of the barn door being opened. Lifting his upper body he turned to look over his shoulder. He believed that he saw the boy standing in the doorway, but the woman fiercely pulled him back down to her and he wondered if he had imagined seeing Lennie.

When it was over and he stood hurriedly dressing, she commented in a drawling voice, 'I know men lose interest after-wards, but your haste, Colm McFeeley, is an insult to me.'

'I think your son looked in at us,' he explained, although aware that she had spoken jocularly. 'I'm worried that he has warned Lieutenant Peters that I'm here.'

She had dressed by the time he had pulled on his boots, going out of the barn with him as he looked and saw that the boy was working in the field. Untying his horse he put one foot in the stirrup, pausing as she placed a hand on his arm and asked a tentative question.

'You will come back to me?'

'Of course,' he lied as he swung up into the saddle and rode down to the tall rushes.

Dismounting before he reached the clump of reeds he went forward carefully on foot, expecting to discover that Lawrence Peters had fled after being warned by Lennie Yates. Gently parting the reeds, he first saw the dark green-brown water of the pond. Then an alarmed McFeeley knew that he had been wrong about Peters fleeing, but right in believing that the boy had told him that McFeeley was there. Nothing had prepared McFeeley for this scene. Lieutenant Lawrence Peters was sitting up, sideways on to McFeeley, whose arrival Peters seemed not to have noticed. He sat with his knees raised and the stock of his musket held between his feet. The firearm came up at an angle so that the muzzle was pressed against Peters' forehead. As McFeeley reached the clearing, Peters, whose arm wouldn't stretch as far as the trigger of his musket, was holding a stick with which he probed for the trigger.

'Nooo!' McFeeley shouted, but even as his cry filled the air, the musket exploded. There was a puff of smoke, an acrid stench, but Lawrence Peters sat upright, as immobile as a statue.

The shot seemed not to have affected Peters in any way. But then the head turned in McFeeley's direction. The top part of the front of his head had been blown away, but the eyes were intact and had a terribly glassy stare that fixed on McFeeley as he fell backwards. The lieutenant had been dead from the time of the shot had been fired. He had just taken a long time to lie down.

Every room at White Lackington had been taken. Neither Rachel nor Sarah went to the dining room for their meals now because the talk around the huge table buzzed with expectation of a visit by the Duke of Monmouth. Taking their meals in a small side room, they had been seeing less of Edmund Prideaux. Rachel's midnight trysts with him had become infrequent.

Having had no option but to write the letter required by both Edmund Prideaux and John Trenchard, Sarah had been relieved at how innocuous the wording had been. All that they had required of Sarah was proof that she was in the hands of Monmouth supporters. Putting an address on her letter was forbidden.

Together with Rachel she was walking in the manor grounds on a morning as bright and sunny as those that had preceded it of late, but which had a few clouds searching for each other in the sky. It was a sign; the old gardener sagely told them that the hot weather would break before long.

Walking towards them were Edmund Prideaux and John Trenchard. When the four of them met, Prideaux, plainly carrying out something pre-arranged with Trenchard, split Rachel away to leave Trenchard walking with Sarah. While their conversation remained general and unspecified, Sarah found that she was enjoying herself. John Trenchard, for all his dry, serious looks was good company. But then he switched the conversation and she found herself on guard.

'I welcome this opportunity to have a word with you in private, Lady Sarah,' Trenchard began. 'I make no apology for being a Whig and pledging my support, my very life even, to the cause of James

Duke of Monmouth, but I find that the way young Prideaux is using you to be deplorable.'

'But, sir,' she protested as they strolled beside a lake in which darting fish flashed their silver backs in the sunlight. 'You were with Edmund when he had me write that letter to John.'

'Please understand, my dear Lady Sarah,' Trenchard pleaded, 'that it would have been unwise of me to show dissent. Though I intend to help you from being held here indefinitely as is young Prideaux's intention, I will do so within the limits of not endangering the Monmouth campaign.'

'But you will help me?' Sarah inquired, wanting reassurance.

'I give you my word, Lady Sarah.'

They walked over a pretty little bridge. Sarah reached with the intention of plucking a beautiful red rose from a cluster growing on a bush that grew by the yellowstone wall of the bridge. She made a little 'Ooh' exclamation as a thorn pricked her finger. His hand touching hers, John Trenchard picked the flower and gave it to her with a smile.

'Will you be able to return me to my husband, do you think?' she asked.

'That is what I aim to do, and I'm sure that I will succeed,' Trenchard said, stopping by a highly scented flower bed, turning to face her and taking the rose from her hand, holding it level with her face, comparing her beauty with that of the flower. 'I will be back here the evening after next, and, with your permission, I will come to your room and we will finalize everything.'

In her relief of at last seeing a chance to get away from White Lackington, Sarah agreed readily to this but later had second thoughts. Until that afternoon Trenchard's interest in her had manifested as nothing other than a lecherous leering. She felt that she may have made a terrible mistake in agreeing to him coming to her room, and dreaded the coming of the night when she would be alone with John Trenchard.

Lieutenant Colm McFeeley sat in the saddle with the body of Lawrence Peters draped over the horse in front of him. Standing facing him, trembling with rage, mouthing irate words that as yet had not linked up with any sound from his vocal chords, was Colonel Percy Kirke. The colonel, a balding, bumptious fellow, stood in front of officers both commissioned and non-commissioned, who had gathered together as McFeeley had ridden into camp. Captain Allenby was there, at the side of his commanding officer but looking detached from the proceedings until he walked to the horse to lift the linen that McFeeley had tied round Peters' head. Letting the material drop after a brief examination of the wound, the adjutant went back to stand by Kirke, who had found his voice at last.

'I command soldiers, not murderers, McFeeley. Don't dare try any kind of mitigation with me. There is no justification for you causing the death of Lieutenant Peters.'

About to voice a denial, McFeeley began, but broke off as he saw Allenby surreptitiously shake his head.

'You have something to say, Lieutenant?' Kirke roared.

'Nothing, sir,' McFeeley replied, just loud enough to be heard.

'I should think not,' the colonel said, then began rapping out orders. 'Provost Marshal – have the medical officer take care of Lieutenant Peters' body, and place Lieutenant McFeeley under arrest.'

'I will see that Lieutenant McFeeley is confined to his quarters, sir,' Captain Allenby said.

'That will not be necessary, Captain,' Kirke said.

'It is customary in the case of officers, sir,' the adjutant reminded his commanding officer.

'Goddammit, Allenby!' Kirke shouted in rage. 'We are not dealing with some minor offence here. This is murder, Captain! Murder! McFeeley will be placed under close arrest at once.'

Allenby was wise enough to make no further protest as McFeeley was pulled from his horse and manhandled over to a gun carriage where his back was slammed against a wheel. Kirke was strutting around, his knees stiffened by anger, issuing orders that had the company blacksmith arrive to chain McFeeley to the wheel of the carriage.

In the hot afternoon sun, having to stand because he was so restricted by the chains, McFeeley's ankles began to swell so that the manacles bit in, splitting the skin and the flesh, causing him excruciating agony. His temperature rose so that his mind began to play tricks on him. Rosin walked up, calmly passing the sentries to come to him, smiling in the way she used to greet him so many years ago. They spoke of their deep and undying love for each other.

Then he decided that Rosin had a right to know about Lucy Yates, and he started to make a garbled confession. But she lovingly chided him. 'Quiet, my darling,' she said, placing a finger on his lips, then she disappeared, not walking away but suddenly evaporating in front of his eyes.

Blood began to trickle from both of his ankles and for one lucid moment he recognized that pain and the heat had combined to have him hallucinate, but the next instant he lost everything once more. The sergeant major, whose death on the Thames' flats had been attributed to McFeeley's negligence, came marching smartly up. 'I forgive you, sir,' the soldier said before executing a militarily perfect about-turn and striding off.

Blacking out then, McFeeley didn't regain consciousness until daylight was fading. His mind created its last illusion then by bringing a vision of Lieutenant Lawrence Peters who thanked him for something without specifying what, before disintegrating in a shower of sparks.

When night came, the cold lowered his temperature and put an end to the fantasies, while increasing the pain of his manacled ankles and the stiffness of his chained body. Sleep was impossible that night. By the time dawn streaked the sky with first red and then gold, McFeeley had retreated inside himself to a depth that left him barely aware of his suffering and his surroundings. But he snapped back into clarity as he saw Captain Allenby and the blacksmith coming towards him.

Compassion in his eyes as he saw the condition that McFeeley was in, the adjutant said, 'A Captain Critchell has ridden into camp, Lieutenant, with orders for you to be immediately released.'

The blacksmith first cut through the manacles, causing McFeeley pain so intense that he lost consciousness, kept upright only by the chains that held him. Allenby looked at the damaged ankles and straightened up to shout an order for one of the sentries to fetch a doctor or a nurse.

As McFeeley's arms were freed, although pain and stiffness prevented him from using them, Colonel Percy Kirke came up, an expression of bitter anger on his face as he gestured for his adjutant and the blacksmith to step back. He came close to McFeeley, his breath reeking foully. The colonel's tone was adjusted so that his words reached McFeeley's ears only.

'I gather that you have friends in high places, McFeeley. Don't let that fool you. To have all the legions of angels on your side would not save you. I will get you, McFeeley.'

'It is safe to assume that Lady Sarah Churchill is being held either here, here, or here,' Captain Critchell told McFeeley as he fingered the map in front of them three times. Barrington Court at Shepton Mallet, was owned by Edward Strode, who, like George Speke at White Lackington, and Captain John Hucker at Taunton was a Whig and known as a supporter of Monmouth. 'Wherever she is the house cannot be stormed without putting Lady Sarah in danger.'

'So it is a case of one woman against the massed armies of the king?' McFeeley surmised.

Doing a circular walk inside of the tent he had been allocated at the Axminster camp, hands behind his back, head drooping in thought, Critchell said. 'Not exactly, Lieutenant. To be exact, the rebels are holding two women, Lord John Churchill's wife and Rachel, her companion. Lord Churchill is, above all, a loyal soldier who has sworn to serve the monarch. He would now be prepared to put all personal considerations aside and confront Monmouth, but King James, in his kindness, has stipulated that three days be allowed for an attempt to be made at rescuing the two women.'

'Which is where I come in,' McFeeley stated rather than asked.

'Yes,' Critchell said, seemingly not inclined to enlarge on the subject at that stage.

Still feeling some weakness McFeeley was pleased by the way his bandaged ankles were supporting him. Waiting for the captain to go on, he reviewed the recent past. Had he not dallied with the voluptuous Lucy Yates, then he might have been in time to prevent the suicide of Lawrence Peters. That way he would not have incurred the wrath of Colonel Kirke, a formidable and implacable enemy.

Possibly Kirke's enmity was nothing when compared to what he had shared with the farmer's wife. McFeeley was ready to risk his life to gain nothing more than a small hill from the enemy, but at those times only a part of him was involved. He only came fully alive when in the arms of a woman.

Yet even that hadn't been the same since the death of Rosin. When his wife had left she had taken something vital of him with her. In recall he was shaken by how dynamic the vision of her had been during his strange time when fastened to the wheel. Then he heard Critchell speaking.

'It involves you becoming a member of Monmouth's army, Colm,' the captain was saying.

'To find out where the women are being held and report back?' McFeeley questioned.

With a negative shake of his head, Captain Critchell looked uncomfortable. He looked around the tent and commented. 'It's still only early morning, but I could really use a drink.'

'If you need a drink to tell me what to do, what will I need to do it, Captain?'

'More courage than I have, Lieutenant, of that I am certain,' the captain admitted gravely. 'We are asking you not just to locate the two ladies, but to free them from the clutches of the rebels.'

McFeeley had not anticipated anything like this. Critchell had said that the king was allowing just three days for whatever had to be done. He could join Monmouth's army, but to do what Critchell was asking would mean reaching the duke's hierarchy on the first day. He pointed this out to the captain, who had an answer that proved to McFeeley how far and fast the newly formed intelligence agency of Lord John Churchill had progressed.

'We know that a man named Fraser intends to collect the £5,000 on the duke's head by killing him,' Critchell explained, 'and we are aware of the time and the place, which is Chard, where Fraser is going to shoot Monmouth. What you must do, Colm, is not only prevent Fraser from killing the duke, but to make sure that you are seen doing so.'

McFeeley grasped the plan. Monmouth would be so grateful at his life being saved that he would immediately take McFeeley onto his staff. He said dubiously, 'Whoever Fraser is, he won't be going under his own name. How will I find him and follow him?'

'His looks are most distinctive,' Critchell replied. 'He is said to have a scar from a sword that runs from his left temple, across and down the corner of his right eye, all the way down to his jaw.'

'It shouldn't be difficult to notice him,' McFeeley remarked wryly.

It was noon when McFeeley sat at a table in a roadside tavern on the edge of Chard. Though his injured ankles pained him, the long walk of that morning had exercised his muscles, cleared his head and made him feel good generally. The place was crowded with men, rustics in the main, all unarmed and enthusiastic about joining Monmouth. A middle-aged bawd with long and greasy fair hair circled the noisy, smelly tavern, hoping to distract one or two from their military aim so as to earn her living. She tried a smile on McFeeley, but he looked straight through her. To carry a musket would have been to draw auspicious attention to himself so he was armed only with a dagger concealed beneath his artisan's smock. To his left, sitting in a corner, ugly and morose, was the badly scarred man who had to be Fraser.

A huge man suddenly loomed up in the open doorway, roaring out in a deep voice befitting his barrel chest. 'We go to serve the Protestant duke! King Charles's son, the lovely hero! A-Monmouth! A-Monmouth!'

Cheering and shouting welcomed him and his cry. The man sitting on the bench next to McFeeley, a weasel-faced fellow with sly, shifty eyes, banged both clenched fists on the table as he yelled. 'A-Monmouth! A-Monmouth!'

Striding in, the huge man sat at McFeeley's table, his bulk having a seesaw effect on the bench that came close to unseating both McFeeley and the weasel-faced man beside him. He called for a drink at the top of his voice, while at the same time the bawd was smiling in expectation as one of the older men was taking round an empty tankard into which the men dropped coins. Not sure what was happening, McFeeley flipped a coin into the pot. All the time he kept a wary eye on Fraser.

Beside him an argument had sprung up between the man passing around the tankard and McFeeley's sly-looking neighbour. The weasel-faced man was refusing to contribute to the kitty.

'With the woman I've got back home I've no need to see what this ugly wench has,' McFeeley heard the sly man object.

'You always was a mean bugger, Thomas Yates,' one man shouted complainingly.

The name spun around inside of McFeeley's head until it attached itself to a memory of the vivacious Lucy. Astounded by the coincidence, McFeeley exclaimed, 'Small world!' aloud.

'You got something to say?' Thomas Yates asked him belligerently.

'Not a thing,' McFeeley assured the man, not wanting to mix in anything.

'You'se the only bugger who ain't paid nothing, Yates,' a gawky creature complained.

'Chip in, you mean bastard,' someone else shouted.

Facing too much opposition, a cursing Yates grumblingly and grudgingly tossed a coin into the tankard that was then placed on a table in front of where the bawd stood.

'Come on then, m'dear, let's see your rabbit-hole,' a farmer-type called, generating laughter.

'I'll wager it looks more like a horse's collar,' someone shouted. Unabashed, the bawd gathered up her skirts with both hands. Pulling them above her waist, she held them with one hand while pulling down her baggy-legged bloomers with the other. To the crude shouts of men and the delighted sounds made by callow youths she did a slow pirouette to put herself on show to everyone around her. Doing a half-turn, she woman bent over, flipping up her skirts to display huge white buttocks.

The bawd was doing a second turn, this time bending over, when McFeeley saw Fraser had got to his feet and was easing his way through a crowd of men too enthralled to notice his passing. Preparing to leave, finishing his drink, McFeeley heard disgruntled muttering from beside him.

'I want my money back,' Thomas Yates grumbled.

The bawd's smile became a snarl as she was about to pick up the tankard and Yates's hand snaked across the table to grab a fistful of coins. Her clawing fingers missed Yates's eyes and face by a tiny margin as he ducked under several pairs of hands that were reaching for him. He would have escaped if the huge man, who had shouted his praise for Monmouth, hadn't gripped his shoulder.

McFeeley was keen to get out of the tavern and on the trail of the scar-faced man. He was on his feet, skirting Yates who was struggling in the grip of the big man, when a scuffle near him, one of many that were breaking out, tipped over a bench, the sharp edge of which caught his ankle as it fell.

As the bench slammed into the bloody groove carved by the manacles, pain shot through the whole of McFeeley's body. Partly knocked off balance, he collided against the big man. Taking advantage when the impact loosened the fingers holding him, Yates made for the door. Blaming McFeeley for him having lost his man, the big fellow aimed a punch at him. McFeeley could see the massive fist coming at his face but he was paralysed by agony and couldn't take any evasive action. A huge fist slammed into his jaw. A light of great brilliance filled his head. Then everything went black.

McFeeley came round to find himself half-lying over the corner of a table. There was a general melee going on all round him, with the big man felling everyone he could reach, while others fought among themselves. The scene was being played out to a background of curses and crazy laughter from the bawd, who was standing on a chair enjoying the mayhem going on around her.

Hearing her laughter turn into a yelping scream, McFeeley saw a group of struggling men stagger to accidentally knock her from her rostrum. The bawd disappeared in a welter of flying fists and kicking boots as McFeeley went dodging through the combatants and out of the door.

He stopped outside; the bright sunlight was a welcome contrast to the dimness inside of the tavern, and he eagerly drew in deep breaths of fresh air to push out the gas of sweat, alcohol and the stink of breath that had polluted his lungs inside of the hostelry.

With no way of knowing how long he had been unconscious after receiving the blow, McFeeley looked for Fraser. But the long straight road ahead to Chard was deserted. Yet so was the equally long and straight road behind him. Guessing that Fraser headed for Chard, McFeeley decided to hurry to the town in the hope of locating Fraser and preventing Monmouth's assassination.

He hadn't realized the magnitude of the task that faced him until he reached the start of the wide, dog-legged main road of Chard. It was packed with people, most being the yeomen, peasants and artisans who had flocked to Monmouth's colours. In the main armed only with pitchforks and flails, or home-made pikes, they sported sprigs of the rebel duke's 'Leveller Green'.

Making his way, with difficulty, through the throng, McFeeley kept a sharp lookout for a scarred face, but he accepted that there was little chance of finding one man among so many. The high number of people there was a tribute to the Duke of Monmouth. No other Englishman could inspire so many thousands to follow him.

Much further up the road now, McFeeley found that the people he was squeezing past stood in respectful silence. He could hear a voice raised in a rousing speech. Unable to find Fraser, McFeeley knew that he had found Monmouth as he heard the shouted words. 'I have come to defend the truths contained in the Good Book, and to seal them, if it must be so, with my blood.'

Hearing these words from Monmouth, even though he could not see the duke from this far back in the crowd, a man standing close to McFeeley shouted, 'By God, for this man I would die.' In the way of the majority of Monmouth's 'troops', this man carried a primitive weapon fashioned from a scythe blade riveted to a staff of about eight feet in length. Despite the ludicrous appearance of the weapon, McFeeley's soldier mind told him that it would be more useful in hand-to-hand fighting than the standard musket with plug-bayonet.

Pushing on through, he reached a clearing formed by the crowd being held back by rebel soldiers armed with muskets. It was a peaceful control aimed at preventing the Duke of Monmouth from being mobbed by admirers. To McFeeley's left Monmouth's transport was stationary and in line at the side of the road. It was a sight that astounded McFeeley by evidencing how light the rebel duke was travelling. There were no more than thirty-five supply wagons, drawn by oxen and carthorses, and the four cannon he had brought from Holland with him were strapped onto ploughs. Thinking of the massive forces that James II was gathering to go against Monmouth, he found himself not only pitying the duke, but feeling a great fear for him and the men he had gathered to serve him.

Forcing his way to the front rank of the crowd, McFeeley's ears were filled with joyous cries of, 'A-Monmouth and the Protestant religion', before silence descended as they waited for their hero to continue his speech to them.

He found himself standing beside a man in his mid-twenties who, with a friendly smile, extended his right hand to McFeeley and introduced himself. 'Daniel Defoe'.

The stranger seemed to be of a mind that the name would mean something to McFeeley, who shook the proffered hand while he said, 'I don't know the name.'

'Methinks that one day my name will be known,' Defoe replied in absolute modesty. 'But first I will pledge my all to the Monmouth cause. What did you say your name is, friend?'

McFeeley told him, able to see Monmouth now. This was his second sighting of the man, and it was every bit as exhilarating as the first. Looking every inch a prince, in his royal purple suit and with the sun twinkling on the silver Garter star above his heart, his dark brown periwig was neatly combed, while the sword at his thigh confirmed his image as a leader ready for war.

Beside Monmouth was a man with a brace of pistols in his belt and a musket on his shoulder. Obviously the duke's right-hand man, he gave the impression of being the complete soldier, but there was something familiar about his face that niggled at McFeeley's mind.

'Who is that man with the duke?' he asked Defoe.

'Lord Grey of Werke,' came the answer, and before Defoe could add, 'he's in command of Monmouth's cavalry,' McFeeley had identified Lord Grey's weak, dissolute face as that of the man who had turned in fear and galloped away when leading the horsemen at Bridport.

Having been seduced away from his mission by studying the Monmouth set-up, McFeeley brought his mind back to Fraser. The Duke of Monmouth presented an easy target as he stood addressing the crowd. But Fraser was after the £5,000 reward for killing the rebel duke, so he was not likely to fire from among people who would tear him limb from limb.

Scanning all the high vantage points from which a musketeer could put a bullet into Monmouth, McFeeley glumly realized that it could be any one of some twenty places. He considered taking Defoe into his confidence, having him search ten of the buildings while he took the remaining half. But that would take considerable time, and Monmouth was definitely coming to the end of his speech, so the shot had to come at any moment.

A rapt silence had settled on the Monmouth multitude. Everyone was waiting to give him an adoring ovation when he had concluded speaking. Over the top of the duke's voice, the keen ears of McFeeley picked up one single and insignificant sound. At first it meant nothing to him. Then he found himself trying to place it without knowing why. Intuition had played an important role in his life to date, and now it was urging him to concentrate. It had been a dull, metallic sound. He waited for it to occur again, but it didn't.

McFeeley looked around him, desperate now to identify the sound. In a split second everything came together in his head. The sound had definitely come from the long, low, fifteenth-century church on his right. The bell-tower was not high, but it was tall enough to permit a direct bead on the Duke of Monmouth. McFeeley knew beyond all doubt that the sound he had heard was that of a nervous or careless Fraser catching his musket against the bell.

'Defoe,' he said tersely, catching his new friend by the arm, 'run to His Grace and have him seek shelter – now!'

'I don't understand …' Defoe, intelligent though he was, was bemused by McFeeley's behaviour.

Trusting his instincts while accepting that he could be wrong and the consequences serious if he was, McFeeley grabbed a musket from the Monmouth soldier nearest him. Taken by surprise the man relinquished his firearm easily.

Running off towards the church, his feet kicking up dust, McFeeley saw Defoe struggling with two of the soldiers positioned to hold back the crowd. McFeeley was relived to see Defoe break free and run towards the rebel duke. Muskets were levelled at him, but the soldiers couldn't risk firing at Defoe for fear of hitting Monmouth. No such restriction applied to McFeeley, though and as he skidded to a halt at the church door, a bullet chipped stone splinters from the wall beside his head.

Four

CRASHING IN THROUGH the church door, McFeeley blinked away a half-blindness brought on by the shadowy interior. A darkly clothed man at the altar turned to rebuke him in the practised voice of a preacher. 'Bring not the weapons of death into the house of the Lord, sinner. I am Reverend Mr Rich. Leave, young sir! Go now before you incur the wrath of the Lord.'

Running past him, McFeeley headed for the small but sturdy door into the tower. Raising his right leg, he kicked the door open. It thudded against the inner wall as a cry of outrage came from the direction of the altar. Standing at the foot of a rickety spiral staircase, McFeeley discovered that the tower was much less lofty than he had imagined. He could see the single bell with what had to be the scar-faced man with his back resting against it, musket aimed down into the road below. Realizing that his noisy entrance into the tower would have pushed Fraser into a panic action, McFeeley yelled Fraser's name, his voice booming like that of something disembodied in a tomb.

Even as he shouted, a shot was fired above. Knowing that Monmouth had been the target, McFeeley fired his musket. In reply he got something like the yelp of a kicked dog; Fraser's musket fell first, followed by Fraser tumbling down the twisting staircase. Rolling the last few steps, he landed on his back at McFeeley's feet. From the blood staining Fraser's homespun shirt, McFeeley could tell that his bullet had caught the man in the left side a little below the heart.

His deep, long and jagged scar having turned purple, Fraser lifted his eyelids to look at McFeeley. Drawing his knife, McFeeley

66

went down on one knee to slice open the wounded man's shirt. What he saw told him that Fraser had only a short time left.

'You're a king's man, aren't you,' the scar-faced man said weakly.

Giving a nod of confirmation, McFeeley folded the injured man's shirt back over the deep wound, and told him, 'You're not going to be around to collect the reward on Monmouth's head.'

'Reward!' Fraser gave a chuckle that set blood gurgling in his lungs, and a red froth bubbled from the corners of his mouth. 'I was not seeking the reward, but carrying out my orders. You are looking at what is left of Captain Hamish Fraser of the King's Own Royal Regiment of Dragoons.'

McFeeley was shocked at having shot and fatally wounded a fellow soldier. This caused him grief but he felt a great rage as he saw that Fraser had been set up as an assassin, and himself sent out to kill him, all for the sake of McFeeley gaining Monmouth's confidence so as to secure the release of Lady Sarah Churchill. He understood that sacrifices on the battlefield were unavoidable. But that was a very different thing to the cold and inhuman way in which Fraser and he had been used.

He was attempting to make the injured man more comfortable when he saw a pair of gaitered legs beside him. The Reverend Rich stood there, looking down forlornly at the stricken Fraser.

'Has the Duke of Monmouth been injured, Your Reverence?'

'No. The bullet fired caused a minor wound to the hand of a man standing nearby.'

Overhearing this, Fraser showed a courageous, wry humour by remarking, 'I will die knowing that I failed in my last act on earth.'

A voice that still had the sound of Monmouth despite being weakened by the thick walls of the church, reached McFeeley, and was followed by a roar of concerted cheering from the crowd as a fit of violent coughing overtook Fraser. Blood gushing from his mouth, he died.

Wanting to do something for Fraser but stymied by the finality of death, McFeeley turned his head to ask Rich, 'Can you do something for him, sir?'

'The angels will hold him in their arms,' Rich said, adding, 'it is you who is desperately in need of help, my son.'

'Then when, and if, my time comes to need help, I hope that you will be there, sir.'

In the doorway of the church, steeling himself to step out into a world he suddenly lost any enthusiasm for, McFeeley turned when the clergyman called softly to him. 'Your kind is always alone when their time comes, my son.'

This sent an ice-cold sensation through McFeeley as he walked outside, stepping back a pace as the crowd yelled his praises, calling him 'the saviour' as they came running his way. They were held back by Monmouth musketeers who protectively escorted McFeeley to the Duke of Monmouth. He was standing with Lord Grey, an embarrassed and uncomfortable Daniel Defoe and a woman whose beauty would have been remarkable even had the raw essence of sensuality not been stirred into it. The result was a sexual force that emanated from her with such power that it temporarily drove everything from McFeeley's mind, except his sorrow at having killed Fraser.

Reaching Monmouth, he dropped to one knee, ready to kiss the hand of the duke. 'Your Grace ...' McFeeley began, but the hand holding his brought him to his feet.

'It is I who should be kneeling before you, my dear friend,' Monmouth said, his special appearance having an even greater affect on McFeeley than the sight of him aboard the *Helderenberg* had had. 'You have saved my life, I shall be eternally beholden to you and this young fellow here, I have asked him to join my army as a ranking officer.'

A blushing Daniel Defoe said, 'I am most grateful to you, Your Grace. But as yet I have no experience as a soldier. All I ask is that Your Grace allows me to trail a musket for you.'

'Indeed you shall,' Monmouth clapped Defoe on the shoulder. With a smile at McFeeley then, the duke said, 'And you, sir, I sense that you have seen service on the battlefields of the world?'

'I have, Your Grace.'

'Just as I thought from the set of you. And your name, my friend?'

'I am Colm McFeeley, Your Grace.'

Placing his outstretched right hand on McFeeley's shoulder, the duke asked, 'You are truly a man's man. Will you join me?'

McFeeley's mind was in turmoil. What was happening now was what Lord Churchill and Captain Critchell had planned, and it was McFeeley's duty to accept. But having learned what the king's army had done to Fraser, and out of admiration for the Duke of Monmouth, McFeeley was uncertain of his reason for accepting Monmouth's offer. Feeling that no half decision would suffice, McFeeley was pushed into it by the impatiently waiting duke who stood drawing his sword in front of his unfurled banner of Leveller Green inscribed in letters of gold, 'Fear nothing but God'.

'I will be both honoured and proud to serve you, sir,' McFeeley dropped to one knee, the tip of Monmouth's sword touching him lightly on each shoulder.

The conviction that he was a traitor gripped McFeeley with a sickening intensity. It was a malady made acute by having no focus. He felt that he was letting down the duke he now knelt in front of; and King James II, Lord Churchill, Captain Critchell and even his treasured memory of Rosin.

'You will ride at my side, Colm McFeeley,' Monmouth told him as he regained his feet. 'Now, allow me to introduce my commander of horse Lord Grey of Werke.'

Taking the hand of the man who had run from him at Bridport, a relieved McFeeley saw no recognition in the pale eyes, only an inherent weakness. Then the cool hand of the stirring woman was in his as Monmouth introduced her.

'May I present Lady Henrietta, Lord Grey's wife.'

There was no fear but a lot of fire in her dark eyes. As if by the use of some kind of witchcraft, she was looking inside of McFeeley, seeing much of his past life, seemingly reading the details of every carnal relationship he'd ever had. It was a peculiar experience for him.

'You would seem to be the man of the moment, Colm McFeeley,' she smiled brilliantly.

Noticing that Lord Grey had given his attention to a young man who was bringing up a string of some thirty horses, while very aware that the duke was watching him and Henrietta, McFeeley retained her hand as he said, 'To my regret, Lady Henrietta, I have let many important moments slip past me.'

'Then I will make it my mission to see that you don't miss any in the future,' she said softly.

'This is John Speke, McFeeley.' Monmouth gestured towards the man who had come up with the horses. 'John is one of my most active supporters, as you will see from this fine collection of mounts he has brought me. Tonight we will wine and dine at the home of George Speke, John's father, at White Lackington. There will be a ball, the lull before the storm, as it were. A man fights all the better for having the scent of a woman in his nostrils. We'll have to provide you with a uniform, my friend. Your yokel dress will deter the ladies at the dance. Have you come far to join me?'

'A long way,' McFeeley replied, deliberately keeping it vague.

'I thank God that you arrived in time,' Monmouth said with a fervency that had McFeeley covertly study him, but McFeeley was certain he had just detected an abject shrinking away from thoughts of his own death. As a veteran, McFeeley knew that a soldier over-concerned with his own safety was a liability. What he had glimpsed in the duke could signify that in a crisis he might well be a disaster as a leader.

'An attempt was made on my life while we were at Lyme, McFeeley,' he explained now, possibly suspecting what McFeeley had witnessed in him, and trying to excuse it.

A horse was brought up for him to ride at Monmouth's side, and they moved off at the head of a long convoy of horsemen, carriages, and foot soldiers. McFeeley thought it likely that Lord Churchill's wife and companion would be at White Lackington. He was uncertain as to whether or not he wanted to carry out his mission. Apart from Lord Grey of Werke, who McFeeley could not even be civil to, he liked the rebel duke and his officers. It occurred to McFeeley that he was more influenced than he realized by the double-dealing of his superiors that had led him to kill Captain Fraser.

Recognizing that he was soon to be forced into making the most dramatic and traumatic decision of his life, he had no idea what that decision would be. A man of honour, McFeeley hadn't lost sight of the allegiance he had sworn to the king, but he felt that the deception played on him regarding Fraser cancelled out his oath to King James II and his predecessors.

Lady Henrietta rode with her maid in a coach close behind Monmouth, Grey and McFeeley. The lovely woman's aura was such that it easily crossed the distance between them to tantalize McFeeley. What should have been an enjoyable sensation for him was torture. Each time McFeeley conjured up an image of Henrietta, the dark, meaningful eyes and the mouth that was provocative whether smiling or pouting, it was immediately replaced by the face of Captain Fraser in death.

'The men behind us, McFeeley,' the duke remarked, his movements the easy rhythm of an accomplished horseman, 'they have risen up to support me. I thank the Lord for them, but it is the tenant farmers and their workers at our rear who gladden my heart, for they would not dare follow me without the consent of their landlords. The greater part of the country is behind me, my friend.'

'It is rumoured,' Lord Grey addressed McFeeley directly for the first time, 'that there are many serving with the militia who are ready to change sides.'

This alerted McFeeley, who took a sideways glance at Grey. He wondered if this was just a chance remark or whether Grey suspected that he was a king's man. It might even be that Grey, whose cunning was compensation for low intelligence, recognized him from Bridport.

'All who want to join me will be welcomed,' Monmouth said.

'We must determine not to welcome turncoats, Your Grace,' Grey warned.

A distraught Lady Sarah Churchill was in no doubt that John Trenchard had misconstrued her inaction for acquiescence. She regretted earlier allowing him to take a liberty during a dance. Yet although she blamed herself she could not find much in mitigation. The manor at White Lackington had been in a state of high excitement since early evening when Monmouth's army, a column more than three miles long, had been seen approaching. With the soldiers camping nearby, the rebel duke and his officers had been rapturously welcomed. In all the commotion Sarah had become disoriented. She was all alone, while Rachel, still besotted with Edmund Prideaux, clung to him for support.

James, Duke of Monmouth had made a short speech before dinner, which gained him much acclaim. John Trenchard had sat at Sarah's side at the table. His wife, who showed no feelings for and little interest in her husband, was spending her time fussing round her elderly father. At the table Sarah had forced herself to broach the subject that was all important to her.

'Will I be gone from here before this night is over?' she had inquired of John Trenchard.

He had replied quietly and a little tetchily. 'All in good time, Lady Sarah, all in good time.'

This wasn't either a promising or an encouraging reply, and Sarah was glad of the diversion provided by Monmouth's presence. Sitting alone in the camp of the enemy, she remembered the duke was a dynamic man with looks and a style that were captivating.

She reminded herself that she was on enemy territory. There was no protector to make her feel secure. All she had was a tenuous possibility of being saved by Trenchard, together with a growing unease brought on by the way the officer sitting at Monmouth's side was studying her.

Fair-haired and ruggedly handsome, the man had a toughness about him that suggested he would be more at home roaming the woods than sitting stiffly at a banquet table. It was the officer's uniform he wore which linked up with some inner quality to impart a poise and dignity that many of the more sophisticated and more educated men at the table lacked.

Made embarrassed by his interest in her, she almost welcomed Trenchard's invitation to dance. Yet the stranger's eyes had found her again on the floor. He was dancing with a gorgeous woman who, elegantly dressed and with her hair piled stylishly high, had ridden in as part of the rebel duke's entourage. As this couple had passed Sarah and Trenchard in the dance, the man looked so deeply at her that she had given an involuntary shiver startled her partner.

'Are you cold, Lady Sarah?' Trenchard had asked.

'No, it's just ...' Sarah had begun but couldn't finish. Even she didn't know what it was about the Monmouth officer that had caused this extreme reaction in her.

Sarah knew that it wasn't fear. She regarded it more like meeting someone you were close to in the past and hadn't seen for ages. It was that kind of a jolt, and Sarah Churchill found herself entertaining the absurd thought that she remembered the officer from the future.

It was during this unusual and abstract deliberation that Trenchard had steered her right to the edge of the floor where the heavy shadows were deepened by the dark purple drapes hanging at a huge window. Pausing in the dance, Trenchard had placed the tip of a forefinger mid-way between her chin and lower lip. By applying gentle pressure he opened her mouth, kissing the inside of it in a profoundly sexual way.

Taken by surprise, Sarah had made the mistake of not resisting. Making no response, her body had remained rigid. An absence of protest on her part had convinced John Trenchard that she welcomed his attentions. A short while later, as they had stood side by side at the rear of the assembly of guests listening to various Whig dignitaries paying tribute to Monmouth, Trenchard had furtively dropped his right hand behind them to fondle her buttocks. So tightly were they packed among the other guests that Sarah could not have made an avoiding move without causing a disturbance.

This second incident had further encouraged and excited Trenchard, while making it clear to her that she was in a dire situation. He later leaned close to Sarah, his voice hoarse, to say, 'I will not keep you waiting long before coming to your room tonight, Lady Sarah.'

Soon afterwards Sarah's heart leapt as she saw the fair-haired Monmouth soldier heading her way across the floor. Confident that he was about to ask her to dance, she had to fight back an agonized cry of disappointment as she saw the woman who had come with Monmouth take a course across the ballroom floor that would have her intercept the officer before he could reach Sarah. To Sarah's chagrin that was exactly what happened. In the path of the fair-haired officer, the woman said something to him. Though he listened intently, his eyes remained on Sarah and she found herself willing him to continue in her direction. The woman placed her hands on the officer's shoulders and the two of them moved away in a dance.

'I had been waiting for that since the moment I first saw you at Chard,' Lady Henrietta said as they came back into the manor.

The change from the night air to the heavy atmosphere inside the manor brought an alteration to McFeeley. Henrietta had an air of danger about her. Aware of it from the start, McFeeley had pushed it to one side after they had danced. Now the warning had returned with a vengeance, and he rued having surrendered to his ever-demanding base urges. A remark made by John Speke had confirmed McFeeley's suspicion that Lady Henrietta was Grey's wife but Monmouth's mistress.

'And you, McFeeley,' she asked, brushing down her clothes, her hand movements jerky at his lack of response to her statement. 'Had you been waiting as long as me?'

'Longer,' he assured her, 'All of my life, Henrietta.'

This pleased her and she smiled but he could detect an under-lying misgiving in her that he was insincere, simply flattering her.

But that evening of divided loyalties had become further compli-cated by an inexplicable, invisible connection between him and a beautiful woman who, nevertheless, was a total stranger. It took a discreet inquiry of host George Speke to learn that she was none other than the woman he had been sent out to save – Lady Sarah Churchill.

Back in the hall, McFeeley was struck by the forced gaiety of the assembly. It was plain to him that fear of the morrow had everyone desperate to enjoy today. Without a word, Henrietta, who had moments ago been in the throes of a passion that could well have hovered on the borders of insanity, left him as if they had been casual acquaintances, exchanging no more than a few polite words. Plainly fearing that her short absence from the rebel duke's side may have weakened her position, she eased back into the group surrounding him, getting close, her eyes adoring and her mouth inviting.

Scanning the huge room, McFeeley saw Lady Sarah Churchill, her lovely face serious as she carried on a conversation with an attractive woman he took to be her companion. The man who had been her constant escort that evening was not on the scene right then.

McFeeley moved through the crowd heading for Lady Sarah Churchill. Although she had her back to him and there was no way that she could have seen McFeeley coming toward her, she spun round, startled when he was within a few yards of where she stood. Their eyes met, and he could tell that she was willing herself to turn away. Failing, she lowered her gaze, her lovely face reddening as he reached her.

Lieutenant Francis Tonge strode through the camp. As immaculately turned out as ever, he was a credit to Lord Oxford's Horse in particular and the army in general. Young and handsome, although a constantly stern expression had carved too many lines, too soon into his face, he had every reason to be confident, and yet his stride shortened as his pace was slowed by an attack of nerves as he neared the tent of Lord John Churchill. Lieutenant Tonge had been summoned and had obeyed at once, leaving himself no time to even hazard a guess as to why the brigadier wanted to see him. Saluting as he entered, he stepped into a tent in which Churchill occupied the only chair, which was positioned behind a table, a captain standing beside him. With his new rank of sergeant, Jack stood to one side with the bearing of a soldier but with much of his straight-back pride diminished by his awe of being in such high-ranked company.

'Good of you to come so swiftly, Lieutenant,' Churchill said. 'This is Captain Critchell, who will issue you with your orders. Your regimental commander speaks most highly of you.'

'Thank you, sir,' Tonge replied. Never having previously seen Lord Churchill, hearsay had led him to expect to find a man walking easily through life along the path of privilege and wealth. But the brigadier, though only a few years Tonge's senior, looked very tired and haggard. Tonge had seen officers in a better state than him after being engaged in protracted battles, whereas Churchill yet had to sniff the acrid smoke from a Monmouth musket.

'I understand that you have seen action against the Turks, Lieutenant,' Churchill said, looking directly at the officer in front of him. This was the first time he had raised his head.

'I was with the Polish army, sir.'

'That should stand you in good stead here, Lieutenant, as you will be taking out a party of men on a very important, but dangerous, exercise,' Churchill told the young officer, then looked up at Critchell. 'Be so good as to detail the situation to Lieutenant Tonge, Captain.'

'First things first, Lieutenant,' Captain Critchell began with a touch of levity, 'I should remind you that you are now back in the British army.'

'I have learned that the bullets of any army do not respect uniforms, sir.'

'Quite, quite, Lieutenant. Now, let me introduce you to Sergeant Jack,' Critchell said. 'He will be going with you.'

'With respect, sir, I have a sergeant of my own who has served with me for several months. This is in no way a comment on the sergeant here present, sir,' Tonge explained.

'Of course not, Lieutenant. I appreciate that you are looking at what you see best from a standpoint of military expediency. When I explain the situation you will understand why it is our sergeant who will serve as your second-in-command,' Critchell replied. 'What I tell you now is strictly secret. We have a lieutenant out there somewhere whose brief is to rescue two ladies that are believed to be held captive by Monmouth activists. That lieutenant and Sergeant Jack have successfully completed several hazardous missions together, Lieutenant. Jack knows how our man thinks, and that is most important in this kind of work.'

'The lieutenant is overdue, sir?' Tonge inquired.

Critchell replied. 'That question is impossible to answer, Lieutenant Tonge.'

There was anxiety inside this tent that was so intense Tonge could imagine a silent scream bouncing off the canvas walls. The mixed race sergeant looked capable enough, but he also had the sort of untamed look that Tonge was used to seeing in the British army's punishment blocks. This was taking on the appearance of a suicide mission. In previous times this wouldn't have worried Tonge. But he had been married just three weeks, and his bride, Nancy, was in camp with him. Tonge wondered if Churchill and

Critchell knew of his recent marital situation when they had chosen him. Then he dismissed his curiosity as being ludicrous. Neither the brigadier nor his pet captain would give a damn about a subordinate's personal life.

'We don't know where the ladies in question are being held,' Critchell resumed. 'We have no idea where our lieutenant might be at this time, and neither do we know exactly where Monmouth and his main force are. All that you will have to go on when you take your party out are assumptions, Lieutenant.'

'Can you explain what I am to assume, sir?' Tonge asked, liking less this exercise the more he learned about it.'

'If I may be forgiven, sir,' Critchell said as he had Churchill move his arms so that he could roll a map flat onto the table. 'Come here, Lieutenant. Good. Now, we do know that Monmouth is making for Taunton, and it is reasonable to assume that the ladies are being held somewhere along the way. In fact, we would say that they are here, at White Lackington, or further up here, in Taunton.'

Lord Churchill then further unnerved Tonge. 'Wherever those ladies are, Lieutenant, we cannot hit Monmouth in any force until we are satisfied that they are not in an area of danger.'

'Your mission is a threefold one, Lieutenant,' Critchell went on. 'Without engaging the enemy unless it is unavoidable, you are to bring us a report of Monmouth's position, his strength at that time, plus his direction and speed of travel.

'Secondly, with Sergeant Jack as your guide, you are to seek out our lieutenant. If he has not yet achieved his objective of securing the release of the two women, then your third task will be to assist him in doing so.'

'Very good, sir,' Tonge said, asking, 'what is the name of the lieutenant, sir?'

'It is not necessary for you to know that, Lieutenant, as Sergeant Jack will identify him for you. Now, have you ten good men in mind that you can take with you?'

'Yes, sir, I know who to take,' Tonge assured the captain.

'And you can leave within thirty minutes?'

It wasn't really a question but an order. Tonge's mind turned to Nancy, wondering how she would take to them being parted for the first time since their marriage. In a way he was glad that it was such short notice. If he hadn't been leaving until dawn, then he was certain to be weakened by his new bride's tearful build-up to a farewell.

'Thirty minutes, sir,' he confirmed for Critchell, who had followed him from the tent.

With a sly look backwards to measure the distance so as to ensure that they were out of earshot where Lord Churchill and Sergeant Jack were concerned, Captain Critchell moved close to Tonge and spoke in a low voice.

'You fully understand the situation involving the two ladies, Lieutenant Tonge?' he asked.

'I do, sir,' Tonge replied, at a loss as to why he had been chosen if he was considered too stupid to grasp a simple situation.

'The rebel army is gaining strength by the hour, Lieutenant,' Critchell said with emphasis. 'Monmouth has to be hit soon, but an attack can't be launched when it might imperil the two ladies.'

'I fully understand,' a restrained Tonge said, annoyed by the constant repetition.

'I believe that you do understand me, Lieutenant Tonge,' Critchell seemed convinced. But he went on. 'As long as the two ladies are beyond danger, Lieutenant, in one way or another.'

'Sir!' Tonge saluted, did a parade-ground about turn, and marched off.

It wasn't until he was back at his quarters and was taking his wife in his arms to prepare her for notice of his imminent departure that the truth hit him. Captain Critchell had given him permission, had ordered him, to kill the two captive ladies if that was the only way to ensure that an immediate campaign could be launched against Monmouth. Holding his wife he felt waves of horror passing through him at the prospect of killing two women in cold blood. Shrinking away from carrying out such an act, he also knew that he would have no choice if it became necessary.

Ensuring that his face betrayed none of his feelings, being close to Sarah Churchill stirred McFeeley's animal instincts, while in complete contrast he wanted to adore her as if she were an angel sitting on a heavenly throne. He had orders to rescue them, yet he was certain that neither she nor Rachel were in danger. It was plain that those supporting Monmouth simply wanted to use the captives to reduce the effectiveness of the king's army. To even the odds, so to speak.

Now Sarah and he stood facing each other; two strangers with something stronger than the pulling between lovers tugging at them. With her attempt to appear coy defeated by her interest in him, she asked a trifle fearfully, 'Who might you be, sir?'

McFeeley put off his answer for a few moments. Whatever he said would dictate whether he was to follow the rural songs of Monmouth or fall back in behind the sombre drum of the king's army.

'I am a lieutenant with—' McFeeley began, breaking off when he noticed a minor commotion happening near to Monmouth. A newcomer had caused a stir. A tallish man, he was stooping his shoulders a little to speak to the duke, who was listening with avid interest. There was something wrong, and McFeeley said, 'Excuse me, Lady Sarah,' before making his way to the rebel duke and the agitated people around him.

'Please!' Lady Sarah did a plaintive pleading as he left her.

Seeing her companion of earlier in the evening coming back towards Sarah, McFeeley could tell that the man disturbed her. That was her reason for almost begging him to stay with her. McFeeley made her a promise in thought that he would soon return.

On his way across the room McFeeley speculated that a message had been brought to Monmouth that the much-needed uprising in London had begun. It was overdue, and the duke had sent his personal chaplain, Nathaniel Hook, to the City with orders to get things moving. The plan was to split James's troops and have them fight on two fronts. Monmouth needed either that or a miracle.

An ashen-faced Monmouth introduced the new arrival, a tall, lean man with a mop of brown hair that had thickly defied middle age, a skeletal jaw and a great Roman nose. 'This is Reverend Robert Ferguson who has, I regret to say, brought news of a most alarming variety.'

'Most alarming, most alarming,' an animated Ferguson squeaked in a Scottish accent. He had piercing eyes that he fixed on McFeeley. 'They are close, man, and moving in fast.'

'The Duke of Albemarle is almost beside us with the Devonshires,' Monmouth expanded on what the clergyman had said for McFeeley.

'Aye!' The excited Ferguson took over, 'and Sir Edward Phelips is flanking us with the Somersetshires and the Dorsetshires.'

A pensive Lord Grey said, 'And we will soon have Feversham and John Churchill to contend with. Will you direct that we move out this very minute, Your Grace?'

The duke was thoughtful. All in the little group, including Henrietta, stood waiting respectfully to hear whatever he decided. To McFeeley a night move, though Ferguson's news made it seem prudent, would be a mistake because Monmouth's troops were untrained. Those of his countrified army who did have muskets first had to be given hours of drill by his ex-Cromwellian officers.

McFeeley noticed now as he had before in his short acquaintance with Monmouth, that it took only a whiff of a crisis for the duke to lose his buoyancy. He anxiously asked, 'If we tarry here a while, McFeeley, how long will it take to make a man proficient with a musket?'

'He can be taught how to fire it in hours of intensive drill,' McFeeley replied, 'but it takes many weeks of practice before handling a musket becomes automatic.'

'You are saying that we have nothing to gain, and much to lose by remaining here at White Lackington?' Monmouth asked.

'I would not presume to say anything other than that you are in command, Your Grace,' McFeeley said, wisely and humbly.

'Shall I send orders to alert the camp, Your Grace?' Grey inquired, making his suggestion sound like a foregone conclusion in his anxiety to get away.

'Give me a little time,' Monmouth said, walking away with his head bowed. 'I must be alone.'

They all watched him go, each wondering what his decision would be, and some, McFeeley noticed, were, so early in the Monmouth campaign, wondering if the duke was capable of making the right choice. There was a niggle of doubt in McFeeley, but he reserved his judgement on the rebel leader until he had something definite to evaluate Monmouth by – such as his first encounter with the enemy.

Five

SEARCHING THE CROWDED room for Lady Sarah, McFeeley failed to find her. Guessing that she had retired to her room for the night, he cursed himself for not having found out where it was. A sudden feeling of isolation had come over him. The clique to which Lord Grey and Henrietta belonged were still together, faces strained, talking little as they waited for the return of Monmouth.

He went out through the door which Henrietta and he had used to re-enter the manor. But when he stepped out onto a stone-paved terraced to lean against a pillar at the top of a set of steps, the fragrance of night flowers brought back vividly the recent memory of Lady Henrietta and what they had shared. The demure, composed Lady Henrietta Grey, who now mingled with the other guests inside, was not the ripe, ribald woman who had lain with him in the darkness.

Descending the few steps, he walked along a path where the silhouette of Monmouth stood with his back to him, one hand resting on a statue of Oliver Cromwell. Without turning, the duke spoke, making a name into a question. 'McFeeley?'

'Yes,' McFeeley answered, walking up to join the duke beside a small pool, which the statue stood guard over. Water hurried down a cataract of little height. The rippling played a tinkling little melody against stones, close to tuneless but somehow made haunting by the night.

'They await me. They do,' the duke said dully. Looking up at the statue, he asked McFeeley in a conversational manner, 'What do you know of Cromwell?'

'That is not a question to put to an Irishman, sir,' McFeeley replied, his voice tight.

'Reactionary trivia,' the duke dismissed Oliver Cromwell's most ruthless campaign with a gesture of one of his hand. 'He was a benevolent dictator, McFeeley. He lived by the sword and died of a fever. Could the likes of you and me be fortunate enough to die in our beds, McFeeley?'

'It's not something I've given mind to,' McFeeley shrugged. On that warm night he went cold inside as he found himself breathing in Monmouth's self-doubt and fear.

'What makes men so different?' the duke pondered dispiritedly. 'Even Richard, the son of this great man, was too weak to inherit the world of strength created by his father. They wait in there for me, McFeeley, and I cannot fault them. They are ready to give their lives and ask nothing in return but for me to rid them of a hated Catholic king whose cruel taxes punish them while his "Clarendon code" does persecute them. They are the faithful, McFeeley, but every one of them is of the lower level. When I landed at Lyme the upper class did not welcome me. They hid their valuables and fled. I brought with me in my purse just ninety guilders, which is nine pounds. In Lyme I borrowed four hundred pounds, and that has now been spent, too. I have no money to make payments or to pay bribes, McFeeley. To go on is to meet my death and bring the majority of those following me to their deaths.'

When McFeeley made no reply, the duke walked away to the house. In his wake McFeeley saw Monmouth stop just inside the door at the same time as he heard Dr Ferguson's bellowing tones. Moving in behind the duke, McFeeley saw the cleric pacing up and down in front of the crowd.

'It is the same throughout all our West Country,' the clergyman was telling the assembly. 'We Englishmen know the Duke of Monmouth is the one man of quality in the kingdom who believes passionately in the rights of the Common Man.'

On seeing the duke standing inside of the door, Ferguson stopped speaking. But he had already worked himself and his audience up into a frenzy of loyalty to Monmouth. There followed a long silence in which it seemed even the breathing of everyone in the vast ballroom had been held in abeyance. Standing behind the duke, McFeeley saw him jerk his shoulders back, straightening himself up but he couldn't find his voice. Trying again, making his back rigid, he spoke in a firm, confident voice.

'I want all commanders to go to the camp and assemble their men. We leave within the hour.'

'God bless the Protestant duke!' Ferguson cried, his eyes alight with an extremist's fervour.

Observing Monmouth, McFeeley wondered how much of his renewed determination was down to recovered courage and how much was owed to bravado. Whatever, he had witnessed a thin wedge of weakness in the duke that was fast eroding the admiration he had so recently felt for him.

'Your decision to press ahead is most welcome, Your Grace,' said a slender young man accompanied by the man McFeeley had seen with Lady Sarah for most of the evening.

'Thank you, Edmund,' the duke replied. 'I must stress that we will be facing stiff opposition.'

'Negated considerably, Your Grace, by the plan that John and myself are ready to implement.'

Mouth pursed dubiously, Monmouth spoke in some discomfort. 'I find it difficult to have myself begin a rebellion from behind the skirts of a woman, Edmund.'

'That won't be the case, Your Grace,' John Trenchard put in. He was older than McFeeley had estimated from a distance, possibly twice the age of Lady Sarah. 'We seek only to dissuade Lord Churchill from unleashing all of his might until we are fully prepared.'

'I am not certain that will happen. Lord Churchill is a soldier first and a man last.'

Ignoring this, Prideaux looked to where the host, George Speke, was engrossed in conversation with Dr Ferguson. 'While Speke's attention is held elsewhere, Your Grace, I will secure a carriage for the two ladies, and leave it to John to bring them out quietly from the manor.'

Trenchard looked pleased with this arrangement. It was a sight that had McFeeley make up his mind. Monmouth interrupted his scheming.

'Please see me when the men have been assembled, McFeeley. If you agree I would like you to take a scouting party out ahead of us,' the rebel duke said as McFeeley walked away.

Retiring to blend with velvet drapes that concealed an alcove, he watched and waited. At the far side of the room Henrietta and Monmouth stood close together in a deep discussion. John Trenchard was talking to John Speke. Commanders were animatedly agreeing on tactics and Dr Robert Ferguson was kneeling in prayer. Then his attention was drawn to Trenchard ascending the wide and majestic stairs at the north end of the ballroom. Following at a distance McFeeley watched Trenchard reach the top of the flight stairs and turn to his left to go along the landing and up a second flight of stairs. When McFeeley reached the second landing there was no sign of Trenchard. Obviously he had gone into one of the rooms leading off the landing.

There were four doors on McFeeley's left and three on the right. He knew that he would have to employ a system of elimination. It involved risk and it had to be done swiftly. Opening the first door ajar he waited, listening. There was no sound, not even a solitary snore. He moved to the next door to achieve the same result. With the third door ajar he found himself listening to a breathlessly whispered conversation between lovers. Eavesdropping made him feel guilty but he had to do it. If Lady Sarah Churchill had welcomed John Trenchard to her bedroom, then Lord John Churchill would have lost a wife and James Duke of Monmouth gained an officer.

Hearing a female voice husking out phrases in abandoned passion, McFeeley was astounded. He had heard them himself, word for word and very recently. It was a short mental step to identify the voice as that of Lady Henrietta. Then the man spoke. Though gasping from exertion the voice was easily recognizable as the Duke of Monmouth. Quietly closing the door, McFeeley did a mental, cynical smile. The man who flinched from starting a battle from behind a skirt had no objection to preparing for combat from under one.

Still having a silent chuckle over this, McFeeley stiffened as he heard a muffled female scream. It had come so unexpectedly that he could place its location as the room on the opposite side of the landing. Bursting the door open with his shoulder, McFeeley jumped into the room. With eyes trained to take in detail fast, McFeeley saw the room's illumination came from two smoking candles standing on a dresser. On a bed placed against a wall a man and woman were engaged in a struggle violent enough to have tangled and twisted the bedclothes so that some had tumbled onto the floor.

McFeeley found himself looking at the back of John Trenchard's grey head. Then a face appeared over Trenchard's shoulder and eyes opened wide by horror were staring at him. It was Lady Sarah Churchill. With a memory of her groomed, superbly dressed elegance in his mind, McFeeley had to adjust so that this frightened creature, her hair awry and lips pulled back from her top teeth in preparation for another scream, could become Lady Sarah for him.

Trenchard turned his head as McFeeley took two long strides to the bed. Clapping his left hand onto the back of Trenchard's head and his right under the man's chin and jaws, McFeeley lifted him right up off the bed, keeping hold of his head and swinging Trenchard round and round before releasing him so that he rocketed over to slam against the wall.

Without any plan on the part of McFeeley or himself, Trenchard was upright when he hit the wall, his feet being some three feet from the ground. Leaping over, McFeeley drove his right fist so deeply into Trenchard's midriff that he was actually able to feel the man's spine against his knuckles. Opening his fingers, McFeeley used the heel of his hand as Trenchard began to slide down the wall. The hand raked up viciously over the older man's face mashing the lips and tearing the lower part of the nose from its root. As Trenchard fell heavily to the floor either unconscious or dead, McFeeley turned to the bed from which Lady Sarah had got up shakily.

She was desperately trying to cover her bare breasts and abdomen with the jagged flaps of her tattered and badly torn night-dress.

Turning his back, McFeeley ordered. 'Forget that. Get your clothes on and collect your things. I'm taking you out of here.'

'Why?' she asked in a voice suffering badly from a tremor. 'Why would you do that?'

'Get dressed,' he insisted, still turned from her, moving his right foot as blood from Trenchard flowed to threaten it. 'I am a lieutenant with the Kildare militia who has been sent by Lord John Churchill to rescue you.'

'But ... but ... you came with the duke, wearing his uniform!'

'It was the only way to reach you. Now, get dressed at once; there is no time to spare.' If they were to get away from White Lackington it had to be done during the melee and confusion of Monmouth's army moving out.

She called to him. 'I am dressed now.'

He turned as she was brushing her hair, chin held high as she did so. Trenchard was alive, making snuffling, gurgling noises on the floor now. Lady Sarah avoided looking at him.

'Your companion?' McFeeley asked, needing to collect the other woman as quickly as possible.

'Rachel is in the room across from here,' she said.

'You will come with me to fetch her and then we must leave the manor without further delay,' he said as he went towards the door, hoping that Monmouth had left.

Following him, she suddenly stopped, saying. 'Our maids! They are in rooms below stairs.'

Reaching out, his fingers going round her slim wrist, McFeeley applied a gentle tug to move her along. 'We cannot take your servants. They will come to no harm here.'

Opening the door slowly and quietly, McFeeley looked out and released a sigh of relief at the sight of Monmouth making his way hastily down the far end of the landing. He pulled on Lady Sarah's wrist once again but found she was anchored inside the room. He turned to find her standing at right angles to him, distaste on her face as she looked down upon the battered John Trenchard.

'What if he should die?' she asked, aghast.

'Then the world will be a better place,' McFeeley replied as he pulled her out of the room.

Although still summer there had been an autumn dampness in that dawn. Having finally managed to get a fire going in the hollow where the three of them had spent the night, McFeeley was cooking breakfast in a pot. He had stolen both the utensils and the food from White Lackington. They had escaped without any real problem, although he had discovered that every horse and carriage had been put to use by Monmouth's men before he could get to them. It had meant setting out on foot, which was hard on Sarah and Rachel. Rachel was undoubtedly the tougher and more resilient of the two. Sarah still slept now under one of the heavy coats McFeeley had appropriated, together with a musket, powder and bullets, from the manor. Waking at first light, Rachel and had gone to wash at the stream that was over the southern bank that formed one side of a hollow ringed by trees.

With the food about cooked McFeeley became concerned at the length of time Rachel was taking; in these unsettled times there were ruffians of all kinds roaming the countryside. Turning away from the sleeping Sarah, McFeeley picked up his musket and walked swiftly up the bank. Standing still on the crest, he looked to the stream that was not fifteen yards away. Rachel was standing with her back to him, her long hair wet. She was unmoving as McFeeley silently advanced not wanting to startle her, but was surprised when she twisted her head over her shoulder to smile at him.

'What took you so long?' she teasingly inquired.

As she spoke she turned her body to face him. Rachel's breasts were so small that her chest had a boyish look, and McFeeley noticed that the water in her long tresses made them as dark as her body hair. He stood immobile as she walked slowly towards him. Raising both hands she placed them on his shoulders, head tilted back provocatively and her mouth invitingly close to his.

'What of Edmund Prideaux?' McFeeley asked.

'Edmund is somewhere out there,' she replied, 'but you are here.'

She kissed him then. For a moment McFeeley remained rigid, but then he responded.

It was close to half an hour later that McFeeley came back into contact with the world. He was lying relaxed with Rachel in his arms, smoothing her golden hair back from her face by using his parted fingers as an oversized comb. McFeeley was relaxed until he heard woman's cry of fright.

A bird probing for worms at the water's edge took flight, either at the sound or McFeeley's reaction to it. Rachel's eyes remained closed and she slept on. Gently disengaging himself he jumped to his feet. Ignoring the blurred inquiry of a half-awake Rachel, McFeeley partly dressed himself, snatched up his rifle and continued dressing as he ran to the hollow.

Dropping flat before he reached the low crest he peered cautiously down into the hollow. He was thankful to see Sarah unharmed and sitting where she had slept. She was staring in fright at two soldiers, one of whom was pointing a musket at her while the other squatted by the fire eating the food that McFeeley had cooked, occasionally passing a morsel up to his companion. The man beside the fire had a musket lying on the ground close to him. The uniforms they wore told McFeeley that they were with the Queen Dowager's Regiment of Foot.

McFeeley waved a hand backwards to halt Rachel as he heard her coming up the bank behind him. Fat and no longer young, the squatting man would be too cumbersome to quickly re-unite himself with a musket, so McFeeley cancelled him out as any threat. It was different with the other man. He was young, with long hair drooping like string from under his hat. An upbringing in some city's slums had given his narrow face the unmistakable cunning that comes from such an environment, and his thin body was alert with the tension of a hunting animal.

Edging back down the bank to where Rachel knelt, McFeeley explained the situation to her in a whisper. She had dressed, but sloppily so. The fact that it was a perfectly still morning without a breath of air helped McFeeley. He looked to the far side of the hollow at a tall tree with a slender trunk topped by a mass of inert greenery. Putting his mouth close to Rachel's ear, he was astonished that she had the power to arouse him again despite the desperate situation they were in.

'You see that tree directly opposite?' he asked in a whisper and she nodded her head. 'I'm going to skirt round the hollow to get to it. You keep watching the tree, and when you see me shake a branch I want you to shout. Stay exactly where you are, and shout.'

'What shall I shout?' she asked, woman-like and not grasping what he had in mind.

'Anything you like,' he hissed at her through clenched teeth as he moved away.

Crawling along round the bank, McFeeley was puzzled by the presence of the two soldiers. He had expected Critchell to send out a small party in the hope that they would intercept him, but he would need to cover a lot more miles before meeting up with any such patrol. It was his guess that the two soldiers in the hollow were deserters. Once the fight with Monmouth began, the countryside would be teeming with deserters like this pair, all of them dangerous.

Passing the tree as he crept up the bank, McFeeley stretched his musket up to gently shake a branch.

'Sarah!'

Hearing Rachel's shout, confident that it would draw the attention of the two soldiers, he straightened up and jumped into the hollow. Colliding with the standing man he sent him and his musket flying, reversing his own musket with the intention of delivering a blow with the stock to the back of the neck of the young soldier who had been knocked onto his hands and knees. But McFeeley had to change tack swiftly as he saw the squatting man's hand reaching out and grasping his musket. Lady Sarah Churchill screamed and so did the fat soldier as McFeeley stamped on his wrist, snapping it. Kicking away the injured man's musket, McFeeley swung back to the young soldier to find that he had fully recovered and was once again holding his musket on Sarah.

'Put down your firearm, sir,' the soldier said coolly but with a surprisingly well educated modulated accent. 'I have never shot a lady yet, but I'd do so right now; I swear to God.'

Believing that he meant what he said, McFeeley did as the soldier had ordered. Straightening back up from laying his musket on the ground, he saw Rachel run to Sarah, and they clung together.

Swinging his musket now to cover the unarmed McFeeley, the soldier said, 'This isn't what it seems sir; we were leaving King James and heading to join up with the Duke of Monmouth.'

Mystified as to why the young fellow would make such a confession to him, McFeeley suddenly recalled that he was wearing the uniform of a Monmouth officer. He said casually, 'Neither am I what I seem to be, soldier. I'm a lieutenant serving under Brigadier Churchill.'

This, when put into words, sounded like a tall story, but McFeeley was both amazed and relieved to see that the young soldier immediately accepted it.

The problem came with the fat soldier also believing what McFeeley said. He was up on both knees, nursing his broken wrist with his other hand. But then he let go and leaned sideways to pick up the musket. Holding it awkwardly in his left hand, supporting it somehow in his armpit, the soldier, pain and rage distorting his fat face, brought the firearm to bear on McFeeley.

'You can go on your way,' McFeeley told the pair of them. 'If you want to be with Monmouth, then that is your choice, I won't stop you, and I'm in no position to follow you.'

'You're in no position to do anything but die,' the fat soldier said, getting up awkwardly off his knees. He kept the muzzle of the musket pointing unwaveringly at McFeeley's chest.

A helpless McFeeley saw that the soldier was ready to fire. He took a quick look at Sarah and Rachel, guilty about letting them down, worrying over what would happen to them now.

'No, Matthew, put down your musket. Like he said, he isn't going to stop us leaving, and he can't come after us,' the younger man said. Narrow and not unhandsome the face was serious but made to look strange by his unusually long hair. He lowered his own musket.

But the older man, trying to rest his aching wrist this way and that, but finding no way to relieve the agony, was too irate to be denied. Aware that the soldier was about to fire the musket, McFeeley stared him straight in his small, deep-set eyes.

A musket exploded, discharging its shot noisily, but McFeeley felt no effect. Having been wounded several times and aware how excruciating the pain could be, he told himself the difference here must be that he was mortally wounded.

Then things began to come together in his head. He was still standing but the fat soldier was crumpling to the ground. Both Sarah and Rachel had sprung to their feet, hands clapped over their mouths in horror, while the young soldier stood, stony-faced, his musket leaking whiffs of smoke.

'I didn't want to kill him,' he said, as if someone had asked why he had fired the shot.

'I'm glad you did, soldier,' McFeeley said. 'Go on your way now, with my thanks.'

The soldier shook a miserable head. 'There's no point in going now. It was Matthew's idea. I have this feeling that I'm going to be dead soon, so I might as well die for a king as a duke.'

'What's your name, boy?'

'Private Jonathan Piper, sir. Queen Dowager's Regiment of Foot,' the soldier replied. 'Permission to go with you, sir?'

McFeeley looked at the young man keenly. For all his sharpness of features and wild appearance he had impressively large and intelligent eyes.

'You would seem to be somewhat uncertain regarding loyalties, Piper,' McFeeley said doubtfully. 'What is there to show that I can trust you?'

'He's dead, sir,' Piper said laconically, pointing a finger at the body of the fat soldier, then using the same finger to indicate McFeeley, 'and you are alive, sir.'

Defeated by this, McFeeley nodded assent.

It had all the pathos of a tragi-comedy, Brigadier-General John Churchill found himself thinking as his mind resisted the droning, soporific voice of the Reverend Rich spouting a monotone sermon. King Monmouth! It was too ridiculous even to entertain the thought for a split second. Yet Churchill, the High Church Tory, could not come down firmly on the side of King James II. Monmouth had been an enchanting fellow, pleasant company, athletic and as coura- geous as they come. In those days Churchill had been a mere captain of grenadiers and an ardent admirer of the debonair Monmouth who had been a stimulating commander, a superb officer needing only the stabilization provided by an experienced staff. The army had gone way past appreciating Monmouth; it had loved him for the magnificent soldier he was.

'... They who resist shall receive to themselves damnation,' the Reverend Rich said for what Churchill was ready to believe was the thousandth time.

He pitied Monmouth, too, as a man who had a king for a father but was denied the right to be his heir. Once captain-general of the Land Forces, Monmouth was the highly respected leader of a formidable army. Now, due to being wrong-headed, he was a figure of ridicule leading a band of poorly armed vagabonds.

Knowing Monmouth well, remembering when they had supped wine together while laughingly pursuing the tastiest ladies in court, Churchill doubted that he had either the ruthlessness or the dedication to make his rebellion into anything but a disaster.

Churchill, moving his eyes rather than his head, looked around him. If there were any local people at matins, then they were swamped by uniforms. In the pews behind him was a detachment of the Royal Regiment of Dragoons, an impressive line-up of scarlet-coated horsemen. Also making up the congregation was the Queen Dowager's Regiment of Foot, while the dark-blue tunics of Lord Oxford's Royal Regiment of Horse were prominent. It was Churchill's guess that the people of Chard, who mostly favoured Monmouth, had stayed away from the service.

There was a great sadness in Churchill as he watched the black smoke from a candle dance in search of a direction before spiralling upwards. The candle itself was coming to an end, as was the service and, unhappily, James Scott, late Duke of Monmouth. The military net was tightening. His one-time friend might defy the king's mighty army for a week or so, but when it ended so would his life. That would upset Sarah, Churchill knew. Although his wife had had little to do with Monmouth in the past, this had been due to circumstances as well as geography keeping them apart. Yet for all that, she had, in the way of all her contemporaries at court, admired the marvellous courtier that Monmouth had been.

Thinking this brought back the worry over Lady Sarah to John Churchill. As a man of action he was always frustrated by delegation. Yet he'd had no choice but to rely on Captain Critchell to handle the arrangements for the return of his wife from the Whigs who hoped to use her to the advantage of Monmouth. This in itself was indicative of Monmouth's present plight. Such a proud man would once never have permitted any of his subordinates to stoop so low as to abduct a lady.

With the service over, Churchill walked slowly from the church into what always seems to be special sunshine on a Sunday morning. The clergyman was standing by the door, right hand extended and an uncertain smile on his corpse-like face.

Taking the hand, finding it to be unpleasantly dry and scaly, Churchill said, 'My thanks and congratulations on such an apt sermon, Your Reverence. I bid you a very good morning.'

'Good morning to you, my lord, and Godspeed,' Rich replied.

Turning away, Churchill hurried to where he saw Critchell standing waiting for him. 'Any news of Lady Sarah, Captain?'

'Not yet, sir, but it is yet early.'

'You have confidence in this Irish fellow?' Churchill asked, realizing that he was as guilty of reiteration with this question as Rich had been with his sermon.

'McFeeley?' Critchell checked unnecessarily, held in that sweet pleasure experienced by those who have sensational information to impart. 'I have reason to believe that he has achieved some result, my lord. There is talk here in Chard of Monmouth's life being saved when a man was shot, in the church.'

Critchell had nodded toward the building that Churchill had just left, and he turned to look at it, shock on his face. 'In the church! My word, Claude, even that soldier of yours would surely shrink from taking a life inside of a church?'

'I suspect that McFeeley would not see it as a church, sir,' Critchell offered.

'I suppose that he wouldn't, and neither would His Majesty,' Churchill muttered, made despondent by having to face one of the many absurdities that beset him. 'And what of Monmouth?'

'We are told that, as expected, James Scott was given a rapturous welcome in Taunton, sir. But he dallied there ere long, my lord. When he should have been preparing for war he was accepting banners made from the underclothing of schoolgirls and, I daresay, removing the underclothing of some of the girls' female teachers.'

It could be that Critchell was using calumny effectively, but, having known Monmouth, Churchill doubted it. With a smile he was saying, 'James was ever a man who could fight and a man who could—' He swallowed the last word as the Reverend Rich passed by close enough to be within earshot. Critchell chuckled.

'On the assumption that McFeeley is still with Monmouth seeking Lady Sarah, my lord, Lieutenant Tonge will be following the column ready to assist or make contact with McFeeley,' Captain Critchell said.

'Monmouth is heading for Bridgwater, Claude?'

'That would seem to be correct, sir.'

Bowing his head, Churchill said sorrowfully, 'It is coming to a head, Claude. There will be blood on the moon before this is settled. Nothing will prevent me from losing a friend, Claude, and I am relying on you to determine that I do not lose a wife as well!'

Lieutenant Francis Tonge moved up to the ridge to drop down beside Jack who had beckoned to him. He was glad of something to take his interest at last. In the day in which he had been out with his small party, Tonge had been seduced into some kind of half daydream by the glorious Somerset summer. The grass was at its greenest, the trees in full vigour, the hedges they passed shone white with hawthorn, and cranesbills and foxgloves were in flower everywhere. While the soldier part of him fought to keep his mission in mind, the romantic Tonge used imagination to conjure up his bride so that she walked beside him, hand in hand, on the way to a peaceful picnic.

'What is it, Sergeant?' he asked, sad because the image of Nancy faded fast as Jack brought things military to the fore.

Sergeant Jack's reply was to point down to the road far below. Eyes following his finger, Tonge first blinked then knuckled both eyes to be sure that he was seeing aright. The Protestant duke's column was on the march. Supply wagons and four sturdy guns strapped onto ploughs were pulled along by shire horses and oxen. Then came what Tonge estimated were seven thousand men who kicked up the red dust of three miles of road as they marched. At fairly regular intervals the column was interspersed by regimental banners. Monmouth, dressed in purple and with the Garter Star prominent, a black-plumed beaver on his head, was in the vanguard, escorted by his forty hand-picked Life Guards of Horse.

Apart from this the only real military show came with the long row of scarlet tunics worn by the Tauntonites of Basset's regiment. Here and there Tonge could see a red or a yellow tunic denoting either a deserter from the king's militia or a stolen coat. The majority of soldiers in this raggedy army were dressed in workmen's jerkins and breeches while they marched in labourers' shoes. It should have been a dejected army, but it marched with a lively step and Lieutenant Tonge at first couldn't believe his ears when the singing reached him.

'We have to get closer, Sergeant, to determine whether or not the lieutenant and the two ladies are in the column,' Tonge said to Jack. He wondered what response he would get. Though regarded highly by Captain Critchell, Sergeant Jack had been surly and taciturn since joining the party.

'They are not down there,' Jack said in a way that said he didn't doubt his own conviction and wouldn't welcome Tonge questioning it.

Tonge wasn't prepared to let it go. Exasperated, he said, 'Sergeant, there are thousands of men down there. I think it not possible that you can take a glance and say that the three we seek are not among them.'

The procession went on below as Jack gave his officer's words considerable thought. Having changed to a bawdy Taunton song, the voices had lifted in volume, the joy in them reaching up to the king's men as a reminder of what a happy army it was that followed the Monmouth colours.

'Women sit a horse very different to a man, sir, even when astride,' Sergeant Jack then said as he continued to look down at the long column. 'No women are riding down there.'

'But what of the lieutenant?'

'He would not be there if the ladies were not present, sir,' Jack replied.

Lieutenant Tonge found that the restlessness that had been irritating him had now increased. If the lieutenant and the two ladies were not with Monmouth now, they were either making their way back to Lord Churchill's camp, or they had perished. If it was a case of the latter, then though it would be a matter for regret, he wanted to establish it quickly so that he could return to Nancy. Never one to welcome special assignments, this one in particular, Tonge was a soldier who came into his own on the battlefield. He had gained distinction during the assault on the Fortress of Maastrich when, with his left leg shattered by the explosion of a Dutch mine that had killed fifty of his comrades, he had fought on beside d'Artagnan and his musketeers, who up to that time had been held in reserve.

That was soldiering, not wandering the British countryside in summer, looking for two women foolish enough to be captured by the enemy and an officer stupid enough to go after them alone.

Six

TONGE'S PERIOD OF mental discontent was interrupted by a shouted command from one of his squad of ten soldiers. They had been standing behind the sergeant and himself, waiting for orders.

'What say you? Who do you ride with?'

Hearing his man shout, Tonge turned, Sergeant Jack coming up to his side, to see that the soldier had stopped a horseman by thrusting the spike of a halberd against his chest. Showing no fear the rider looked calmly down at the soldier. Expensively dressed, the horseman had an air of sophistication that came only with breeding. When he spoke it was in carefully modulated tones.

'I ride with the Lord, my good fellow,' the rider told the soldier. 'I am a Quaker.'

'Whither are you riding?' the soldier demanded, giving the point of the spike a prod.

'I ride westward,' the horseman replied as Tonge and Sergeant Jack approached.

'Your name?' Tonge asked, standing close, resting a hand on the withers of the horse.

'My name, sir, is John Whiting.'

'And what business is it that takes you westward, John Whiting?' the lieutenant inquired.

'Business that concerns only the heart, sir,' Whiting replied, his smile pleasant. 'I ride to my fiancée, Miss Sarah Hurd, who is at Taunton.'

'Have you seen anyone, a man going cross-country with two women?' Jack asked.

'Might I have this weapon removed from my...?' the Quaker began, continuing after Jack had rapped out an order and the soldier had lowered the halberd. 'Indeed, I did espy a small party consisting of *two* men and two ladies.'

Puzzled by this Tonge thanked the man, adding, 'When was it you saw this party, and where?'

'This very morning, a trifle east of South Petherton.'

'We are grateful to you,' the lieutenant gave a little bow of his head. 'Now, ride on, John Whiting. Do not permit us to keep you from your love one minute longer.'

Giving a half-salute, Whiting moved his horse away.

They ate well that noon. The heat of the blazing sun had made walking inadvisable, and they sat in the cooling shade of trees enjoying a rabbit that Jonathan Piper had shot. Though detached and remote, the youngster had an easy self-assurance about him that lightened the load of McFeeley's responsibility because he was able to entrust several duties, including keeping watch, to Piper. They were heading north-east, but there was no way of telling if Churchill's camp was in that direction, and Lady Sarah expressed her worry about it as she finished her meal.

'Are we relying on chance alone, Lieutenant?' she candidly asked.

Lady Sarah's genteel upbringing made their present situation an ordeal for her. McFeeley was conscious of how tough their long march had been on her. Although of the same class, Rachel had a tomboy facet to her that came with an in-built toughness.

'In a way we are relying on luck, Lady Sarah,' he answered, as always unsettled by her study of him. 'But a party is sure to have been sent out to meet us.'

'What if the rebel forces should find us first?' Lady Sarah asked, not out of fear but interest.

'Then Private Piper can join Monmouth as he wanted to do,' McFeeley evasively replied.

When it was cool enough to be on the move he had Lady Sarah walk up front at his side, with Rachel pacing behind beside Piper. McFeeley encouraged talk to keep the minds of the women away from their own pains and fatigue. Jonathan Piper, speaking in a low voice to a surprised and fascinated Rachel, as well as an astonished, eavesdropping McFeeley, was giving an informative account of Sir Charles Sedley's play, *The Mulberry Garden*, which Piper claimed to have seen in London. This was a suggestive play laced with innuendo and *double entendre*, but Piper handled his description of it with the modesty expected in the company of ladies, although McFeeley suspected that Rachel was willing the soldier to give a more frank account.

'May I ask why you chose life as a soldier?' Sarah asked, breathless from the fast pace.

'I feel that my reason for following the drum will strike you as tedious: the heaviest weight in the world is an empty pocket, Lady Sarah,' McFeeley said.

A little way in front of them a skylark shot up from its ground nest to do a vertical climb, singing a beautiful song.

'A serenade to nature,' Sarah said with a hand up to shield her eyes. She remarked to McFeeley, 'Even as a lieutenant your pocket surely hasn't been filled by the army.'

'No, but the army filled my belly, begging your pardon, my lady,' McFeeley said grimly.

She was angling for the story of his life. No one had ever heard it and, drawn to her though he was, Lady Sarah was unlikely to be the first.

His mother had been Maura Doyle, a serving girl in the house of the governor of Wexford. Made pregnant by his son, Maura had been close to her time on that Thursday morning in 1649 when Oliver Cromwell's troops hit Wexford. Rampaging Protestant soldiers, driven close to madness by dysentery contracted in wild, wet camps during a long, miserable autumn, and incensed by tales of anti-Protestant persecutions, had ripped the town apart. Charging down the Spawell Road the soldiers had herded men, women and children into the marketplace. There, two thousand innocents were slain. The survivors had found Maura Doyle later that day, lying dead across the carcass of a horse, her baby swinging alive, suspended in the world on an umbilical cord.

Philomena O'Driscoll, widowed in the Cromwellian massacre at

Wexford, had eased her grief by caring for the baby, naming him Colm McFeeley after the doctor that had saved his hour-old life on that grim and bitterly cold day. Emigrating to England while McFeeley was still an infant and taking him with her, Philomena, a gentle, loving, staunchly Catholic woman had earned a living in the only way available to her. Home had been a brothel in Whetstone Park, off Lincoln's Inn. There, in spite of the degradations of her enforced profession, Philomena had raised McFeeley well. He had gone short of neither love nor education, and on reaching puberty his chances in a harsh and deprived world were, due to the efforts of his devoted foster mother, far superior to those of his peers.

It was when McFeeley was poised to take a well-paid job and start to repay Philomena for her years of care and kindness that disaster struck. The apprentices of the City rioted on a Shrove Tuesday, the traditional day for their frolics, and for a reason never discovered demolished all the brothels in Whetstone Park. Philomena took McFeeley by the arm and fled among a throng of screaming, wailing, running whores. The military were called up, drum and trumpet sounded alarms, but it was all too late to save the home of Philomena and McFeeley, which was also her business premises.

The area soon became a blood bath as the military fought the apprentices in a bid to regain order. A swung club, accidentally or on purpose, split open the head of a prostitute running beside them. Always kindness itself, Philomena stopped to tend the injured whore, while McFeeley was swept off with the crowd to find himself down by the river. Naive as he was, he didn't realize that the men of the riverside had gone underground, bolting themselves into their cellars. Soon McFeeley learned, the hard way, when a pressgang rounded the corner in front of him. There was no way of escape. McFeeley had been captured and brutalized on the way to being locked up with others they had captured.

At midnight they were brought out under escort to be shipped away. The street was filled with crying women running this way and that along the column as they sought husbands, fathers and sons. At the end of the street he saw her; she was running forwards with arms outstretched. He was calling her name as one of the pressgang swung a cudgel that caught Philomena full in the face. McFeeley cried out as she stood absolutely still, blood running from her nose and mouth. Then she dropped like a stone. That was the last time he ever saw her.

Early the next morning, due to a momentary lapse in vigilance by a guard, McFeeley and a boy of his age named Horlick were able to escape. Neither of them would be pressed into service with the navy. A shot from a musket ripped away the back of Horlick's head while they ran. Another bullet skimmed across McFeeley's right thigh, drawing blood but not interfering with his run.

Close to Lincoln's Inn, determined to find Philomena, he collapsed from exhaustion. As he lay in a shadowy alcove formed in the wall of a church, fast regaining his strength, four men came upon him. Claiming that they, too, had eluded the pressgang, they befriended McFeeley. On the pretence of taking him for a meal, promising to bring him back to Whetstone Park and helping to search for his 'mother', the four betrayed McFeeley for a reward by delivering him up – to the army.

His reminiscence was ended by Lady Sarah Churchill's regretful inquiry. 'I'm sorry, Lieutenant, have I evoked painful memories for you with my queries?'

'Those are the only kind of memories I have, my lady, but you are neither responsible for them nor for my foolishness in visiting the past,' McFeeley assured her.

He slowed his pace. To continue meant entering a long valley and putting them at risk should there be any Monmouth soldiers on their flanks. Rachel and Piper had caught up and were now standing beside them. McFeeley guessed that Piper knew what the problem was: that to protect the two ladies they had to get up onto the crest either to their left or the right, but to do this would tire the women so much that they would be unable to go on. Filled with an inward reluctance, he led them into the valley.

Half a mile on, the valley opened out into a wide, flat area. Keeping to the side where they were afforded some cover by bramble bushes, McFeeley took stock of the situation. Straight ahead of them the open area came to an end as the lush green of the downs closed in to have the valley resume. To their right was a narrow path that led up a steep gradient between wooded slopes. Checking the position of the late afternoon sun, McFeeley selected the narrow path over the valley, as the latter would take them too far to the north if it continued in the way it began.

In a precautionary move, McFeeley, his musket held at the ready, had Lady Sarah walk behind him, with Rachel coming next in single file, and Jonathan Piper bringing up the rear.

'Did you ever attend any of the theatres in Shoreditch?' Rachel was asking Piper when McFeeley silenced her.

'No talking, please,' he ordered in a half whisper.

Seconds later he held up his right arm to stop them, making a gesture with a forefinger against his lips for them to stay quiet. McFeeley heard it first, then Piper brought his musket up as he caught the sound. It went silent once more but the two soldiers knew that they hadn't misheard as again the jingling of a horse's harness came to them. Taking Sarah by the arm, McFeeley assisted her up the bank and into the trees, while Piper did the same for Rachel. It was difficult for the two women, who slipped and slid. Keeping up the pressure on them, McFeeley was able to get his little group up to a vantage point.

Partially concealed by the trunk of a tree, McFeeley peered up through the narrow pass. The wood had thinned up ahead so that the trees were sparser than where he was standing. With a good view of the track, he waited.

A sharp intake of breath by Lady Sarah told him that she had seen the soldiers heading their way down the track at the same time as he had. A mounted captain, sitting his horse upright and alert, rode ahead of a sergeant who led a squad of twenty men. The sight had McFeeley's body tense. These were rebel troops, but not the poorly armed rustics that the duke had collected about him since landing at Lyme. This was the elite of Monmouth's forces, each carrying a musket; each with the soldierly bearing that announced they could use the firearms expertly.

Aware now that he hadn't climbed high enough, McFeeley knew that it was too late to move. Gesturing behind him with his right hand to have the other three crouch down, he resigned himself to hoping that the Monmouth troops would pass by without noticing them. A strange sound disturbed him, having him put his head on one side to gauge the direction from which it came. It was Rachel's breathing. Laboured by fear, her breath left her with the sound of a panting dog. Leaning close to Lady Sarah, his lips actually touching her tiny ear, McFeeley whispered urgently, 'Calm her.'

Sarah put her arms round her companion, hugging her as the soldiers came on, the captain now so close that McFeeley could see the steely-blue of his ever-watchful eyes. Himself wearing a Monmouth tunic, McFeeley considered signalling for Piper to take off his uniform. That way, if the worst came to the worst, they might save themselves in these conflicting times by stating that they were serving with the rebel duke. But it was a stupid idea, McFeeley suddenly realized. If Piper divested himself of his tunic now his movements would catch the restless eyes of the captain.

Initially, McFeeley could not tell what was happening. A soldier ran up from the rear of the column to the captain, who reined up and leaned sideways in the saddle to hear what the man had to say. Sitting back upright, the captain issued orders to the sergeant with movements of his arms. Dismounting, the captain led his horse up the bank, going high to conceal the animal in a cluster of trees. The rest of the squad had dispersed to go up the banks on both sides and take cover in a way that only veterans knew how. Within the space of a minute the track had been cleared so effectively that it was diffi-cult to credit that it had contained twenty-two men and a horse so short a time ago.

McFeeley waited, wondering. Then he saw what had brought about the change. Coming down the track, walking with easy unconcern, was a squad of about a dozen king's men. Mentally cursing their carelessness, McFeeley watched them sauntering like a family out on a Sunday stroll. McFeeley saw a young lieutenant at the head of the party, musket on his shoulder, parade-ground fashion. At his side was a sergeant. From the dark hue of his skin McFeeley knew that it was Jack.

Though not one given to comradeship, McFeeley had shared so much danger with Jack that they had tacitly become close. The number of Monmouth soldiers and the fact that they were strategi-cally placed made the situation hopeless. Behind McFeeley

Jonathan Piper muttered a foul oath. It wasn't a word a gentleman would say in the presence of ladies, but McFeeley felt that the soldier could be excused as the squad came ever onwards.

A petulant Lady Henrietta stood beside her husband in the Taunton street. The spectacular sunrise did nothing to lift her spirits. A little way along the street opposite to Lord Grey of Werke and his irritated wife, outside the front door of Captain John Hucker's house wherein the rebel duke had spent the night, stood Miss Blake, headmistress of Taunton's Academy for Young Ladies. Henrietta glared at the school-teacher, who stood in front of her young students. To the practised eye of Lady Henrietta, Miss Blake's veneer of a blending of education and respectability couldn't conceal a smouldering inner fire. Neither had this escaped the experienced eye of Monmouth, which was why Henrietta was denied her place in his bed the previous night.

A hush greeted the opening of the door. With the panache of an actor coming to the front of the stage, confident of acclaim, the Duke of Monmouth stepped out into the street. He was at his most stylish. At the sight of him the adoring people of Taunton cried out in a rapturous chorus:

'A-Monmouth and the Protestant religion!'

Ordering her charges to remain where they were, Miss Blake moved toward Monmouth bearing gifts, a Bible in one hand and a drawn sword in the other. Lady Henrietta murmured bitterly to Grey from one side of her mouth, 'It was neither a Bible nor a sword that she had in her hand last night.'

There was an orgasmic flush to the schoolmistress's cheeks when the duke's eyes met and held hers as he graciously accepted the gifts. They stood for a moment; aware only of each other as they both did a parting lover's sexual re-run through their memories. Then the rebel duke took one quick step backwards to snap the silver cord of intimacy, freeing himself from the teacher to make a brief speech. Then he escorted Miss Blake back to her pupils, kissing each of the young girls in turn. Led by a red-faced mistress, they marched off with little arms swinging and heads high. It was an example of discipline that Monmouth's untaught soldiers could never hope to emulate.

As the children went on their way, a distinguished-looking horseman rode up to dismount in front of the duke, dropping to one knee, reaching for the hand of Monmouth and kissing it.

'Whence came you, my good sir, and what is your business with me?' the duke inquired when the man came up off his knee.

'My name is John Whiting, Your Grace,' the rider said humbly.

'Another courageous recruit to my colours, eh?'

'I come to be with you and the Protestant religion,' Whiting explained, 'but it is contrary to my persuasion to appear in arms, for I am a Quaker, sire.'

'You are heartily welcome, John Whiting, and you may serve in whatever capacity you deem fitting,' Monmouth said, shaking the man by the hand.

Watching the little scene, Henrietta muttered sardonically, 'What a rebellion! He takes a dried-up spinster into his bed and a gutless Quaker into his army.'

'The taste of sour grapes is distorting your beautiful features, my dear,' remarked Lord Grey of Werke, who had once resignedly condoned his wife's relationship with the Duke of Monmouth, but had actively encouraged it of late.

'I could tend the injuries of your wounded, Your Grace, and satisfy the spiritual needs of both them and your dead,' the Quaker was offering.

'Then that is how you must serve me, John Whiting,' the rebel duke clapped a friendly hand on the Quaker's shoulder, 'for I ask of no man that he goes against his conscience.'

'And what of a woman and her conscience, James?' Henrietta asked archly and softly when the duke had moved away from the newcomer.

'My sweet Henrietta,' Monmouth replied for her ears only. 'I know every part of you, most intimately, but for the life of me I can't recall having met your conscience.'

Wanting to hurt him, she replied, 'It would seem to be as elusive as your legitimacy, Your Grace.'

The further they went down the track the uneasier Sergeant Jack became. From the top of the downs they had glimpsed McFeeley, the two women, and another soldier making their way through the trees up the hill. He had agreed with Tonge at the time that if not sighting a Monmouth patrol, they should walk openly to meet the others so that there would be no mistaken firing of muskets. It was a reasonable idea, but now he could practically feel an increasingly potent danger in the atmosphere.

In the days he had spent with Lieutenant Tonge Sergeant Jack had come to regard him as a capable officer who could be relied on in a showdown. Once the lieutenant had learned that Jack's taciturny was a character trait rather than a personal reaction to him, they had got along well. Sitting by their night fire the lieutenant had talked to him of combat in Poland, of his recent marriage to Nancy, his childhood sweetheart from his home town of Chatham, and his pending promotion to captain, which Tonge hoped would result in a desk job so that he could spend maximum time with his beloved Nancy.

'Do you feel the same as me right now, Jack?' Tonge asked as they went round a bend in the track and the hills rose steeper than ever on each side of them.

'If you're feeling that something just ain't right, sir, then I'm with you.'

Sliding his musket down from his shoulder, Lieutenant Tonge said, 'It seems likely that it's too late to do anything about it. I'd welcome any suggestion from you, Sergeant.'

Inclined to agree with the officer that they had passed some invisible point of no return where the hazard, whatever it was, was concerned, Jack was disappointed that McFeeley and the women, together with the end of the mission he was on with Tonge, had come so close but now looked very much in doubt. Scanning the hills up ahead, Jack, knowing that the men behind followed in two ranks of five, put his idea to the lieutenant.

'See that crag just up ahead there, sir?' he asked, continuing when Tonge nodded. 'Well, what if we split – you to the right, taking your five with you, and me to the left?'

Tonge quickly checked out the plan. Where the rocky crag was protruding, the trees on the hills were closer spaced, thereby offering them more cover. Not only was Sergeant Jack's plan sound, it was the only possible one.

'Five more paces, Jack, and we'll split,' he told the sergeant, turning over his shoulder to tell the men in a low voice, 'On my command. You five men behind me make it to those trees up on the right. You men, follow the sergeant up to the trees on the left.'

Jack found himself counting the paces – one, two, three … That was when the first crack of a musket, ear-splittingly loud as it shattered the silence, came from up on the hill to their right.

'The avoidance of criticism, Colonel Kirke,' Lord John Churchill said flatly, 'requires one to say nothing, do nothing, and therefore become nothing.'

'I am distressed that you consider I would venture to level criticism, my lord. My purpose was to bring to you a consensus of military opinion in the campaign against James Scott. It is not, I assure you, my personal opinion,' said Colonel Percy Kirke toadingly, making a qualifying statement.

En route to Bristol where the first major confrontation with Monmouth's army was anticipated, Colonel Kirke and his notorious regiment of 'lambs' had joined Churchill at Shepton Mallet. Coming up from Ilchester, eager to push on and get into the fight, Kirke had been frustrated to learn that Churchill had received orders to halt his column and await the arrival of Lord Feversham.

These orders had also annoyed Churchill while at the same time he welcomed them. He was aware that Feversham, disabled by trepanning, was putting on a display of power when it was safe to do so – before the event. When the armies of the king moved on from here, the responsibility and any blame would be Churchill's but the kudos would go to Feversham. The delay pleased Churchill, who was still hoping for news of Lady Sarah. With Critchell's favourite, Lieutenant McFeeley, seemingly having failed in his rescue mission, Critchell had ridden out to learn what he could. Churchill accepted what the captain would do if it became necessary, but he was petrified by contemplation of what it would do to a man to turn the guns on his commanding officer's wife and friend.

Feversham arrived just before noon, sitting on his horse with the vacant look that everyone except Churchill now regarded as normal. Having known Feversham as a brilliant soldier, tutor and mentor, Churchill found himself continually and unhappily comparing the man of yesterday to the walking dead figure of today. Coming with Feversham was a troop of Life Guards and sixty Horse Grenadiers. Riding at his side was stern-faced Colonel Oglethorp of the Household Cavalry.

Studying the maps put before him, nodding and shaking his head in agreement with whatever Churchill or Kirke put forward, Feversham, Churchill was sure, was neither seeing nor hearing anything. The sleepiness that was characteristic of his injuries was overtaking him, and Churchill spoke urgently to get his request across before Feversham's consciousness drifted into the regular coma in which his body worked reasonably well, providing it gorged itself on food, but his mind did not function.

'My ideal would be to move on to Keynsham,' he told Feversham after explaining that his wife and companion were still possibly in the hands of Monmouth, and that Captain Claude Critchell was at that very moment attempting to establish the situation regarding the two ladies. He added, 'There would be nothing lost if I remained there until Captain Critchell rejoined me.'

Taking the line of least resistance, Feversham was nodding his plated head in easy agreement when Percy Kirke butted in.

'While deferring to the superior rank and ability of my lord Churchill, my Lord, I request permission to speak,' Kirke said.

'Go ahead, Colonel Kirke,' Feversham said, fading in and out of the conversation.

'While recognizing and sympathizing with my Lord Churchill's dilemma concerning Lady Sarah,' Kirke began, 'I am of the opinion that any further delay will give James Scott an advantage from which we may never find it possible to recover, my lord.'

'I can understand that, Colonel Kirke, but you will agree that Lady Sarah and Rachel must be given our consideration,' Feversham said, impressing and encouraging Churchill.

'Absolutely, my Lord Feversham,' Kirke said with an open-eyed yet bogus sincerity, 'but I am convinced that I will be able to make a strategic advance and take up important ground without endangering the ladies further.'

Feversham turned this over in his head for some time, an exercise that rapidly tired him. Voice slurring, he gave his consent to Kirke's project. 'As long as I have your assurance regarding the two unfortunate ladies, Colonel Kirke, then you must go ahead.'

Less than an hour later a despondent John Churchill watched Colonel Percy Kirke ride out ahead of his regiment. The concern Kirke had expressed over Lady Sarah and Rachel, together with his assurance that he would do nothing to cause the two women more difficulties, rang hollow for Churchill. Kirke and his whole regiment, the infamous 'lambs' were murderers who used a uniform to excuse their foul deeds.

Although expected, the shot that rang out gave McFeeley's body an uncomfortable start. From behind him came concerted gasps from Lady Sarah and Rachel, then Piper cursed under his breath as the columns behind and the lieutenant split to run up the banks. The first shot from the rebels had brought down the soldier who was immediately behind the officer. Watching the man writhing as he lay on the trail, his body jerking backwards so that he was almost doubled grotesquely with the back of his head against his buttocks, McFeeley assumed the soldier's spine had been snapped by a bullet.

A volley of shots followed, bringing down yet another king's man before he could reach cover. Then Jack and the lieutenant were behind the trees, proving what good soldiers they were by taking the fight to the enemy.

'Can't you do something to help?' Lady Sarah inquired now that the noise of battle permitted speech.

'We can't take the risk,' McFeeley told her, wishing that it wasn't so. Had it just been Piper and himself here they could have come up behind the Monmouth patrol to use surprise to have them run.

The exchange of fire became more intense. Despite being outnumbered, the king's men were giving a good account of themselves. Seeing a Monmouth man come into sight as he pitched sideways from behind a tree to roll head over heels down the bank, McFeeley felt certain that his comrade had shot the man.

A king's soldier suddenly shrieked out, the gurgling that came at the end of his scream of pain a sure sign that he was mortally wounded. This acted as some kind of unofficial signal for the Monmouth soldiers. Moving expertly from tree to tree, confident in their superior number, they started a relentless advance. The soldiers of the king were forced to pull back. The Monmouth soldiers' tactics were plain to McFeeley. Behind Jack and the others the banks comprised just grass and a few low bramble bushes. The king's men would very soon run out of trees and would be exposed fully to enemy musket fire.

Recognizing this, and that the only hope for what remained of his men was for them to escape over the tops of the high hills, the lieutenant gambled everything on a personal act of bravery.

Stepping out from behind a tree, firing as he came, he ran towards the enemy. Dropping to the ground, he adopted a half-sitting position to reload and ram his musket as bullets flew around him. McFeeley didn't doubt that what the lieutenant was doing was courageous and brought about by desperation. It failed in its aim. Before any of the king's men could take advantage of the diversion and get away, the lieutenant was coming up with his musket reloaded when a Monmouth bullet hit him in the head. It caused the lieutenant to spin on his heels like a top for several revolutions, before he flopped to the grass and rolled sideways down on to the track below.

Keenly aware that now Jack and the other soldiers were doomed, McFeeley had to do something to help. Moving Lady Sarah and Rachel into a place among the trees where they were concealed by bushes, he told them what was to happen.

'Piper and I have got to join in the fight,' he told them tersely. 'If we don't, then once Monmouth's men have finished off the others they are certain to find us. I think we can make it, and I want you both to stay here and stay quiet until I come back for you.'

'What if you don't come back?' Sarah asked the question McFeeley had been dreading.

'I'll be back,' he said because there was nothing else to say, even though the two women and he knew that he couldn't be certain. After he had checked that Piper's musket was loaded and that the soldier had shot, powder and his ramrod with him, they were about to move out when Lady Sarah reached out to put a hand on McFeeley's arm. His whole system jangling at her touch, he looked into her face that was upturned to him. Lips moving as if she was going to say something, they then began to quiver. Remaining silent, she snatched her hand back as if his arm had become scorchingly hot. Then she turned away from him.

Moving off with Piper, the two of them dashing from tree to tree, McFeeley wondered what Sarah had intended. The contact between them when she had touched him had been sensual, but there was much more to it than that. For McFeeley there had been a reminder in it of what he had felt when with Rosin. He pushed as much of it as he could from his mind. In his time he had run considerable risks in his assignations but even to think of dallying with the wife of Lord John Churchill was enough to have him thrown in the Tower.

Nevertheless, when he caught sight of his first Monmouth soldier, who stood facing a tree with his musket aimed at where Jack and the others were and with his back to him, McFeeley said a little prayer that he wouldn't die before knowing what had moved Lady Sarah as he was leaving her.

There was no time for chivalry, for introducing sportsmanship into warfare. McFeeley fired, hitting the soldier in the back. As he watched his man go down like a felled tree, he heard Piper's musket fire. McFeeley knew that now the Monmouth men were aware of others behind them, speed was of the essence.

With no time to reload his musket, he saw a soldier turn from where he had been using a nearby tree for cover, The Monmouthian was bringing his musket round towards McFeeley, who lifted his weapon high and ran with it, stock first, at the soldier. The soldier was young. There was both shock and fear on a face that was made ugly by an oversized chin. As always when in battle, McFeeley had to contend with and quell the strange feeling that came the moment an enemy came out of anonymity and into a body made of flesh and blood. This boy in front of him wanted to go on living, deserved to go on living just as he did, but a situation that was not of their own making decreed that one of them must die. Disciplining himself, McFeeley drove the musket forward into the young face. Feeling the stock connect to squash flesh and splinter bone, he rammed harder. The Monmouth boy's head was banged back against the tree and the force of McFeeley's blow cracked open the skull like a coconut.

Seven

PIPER HAD HOLD of his musket with both hands close to the muzzle and was swinging it round and round over his head, The stock clumped against the head of a Monmouth soldier, dropping him. McFeeley made the most of the break to reload his musket.

Sergeant Jack had realized that something was happening to the rear of the Monmouth party and had begun an assault of his own. The Monmouthians, no longer sure how many guns they were facing, began an immediate withdrawal. McFeeley wounded one who was able to keep lamely going and was out of sight by the time he had reloaded. Piper killed a Monmouth man who had clambered down from a tree hoping to flee, while Jack or one of his men brought down another.

Now the guns had fallen quiet. In the new silence that followed the only disruption was an occasional long and low moaning from a wounded man who lay among the bodies strewn across the track or lying awkwardly against the banks with that distinctive flatness of the dead.

'Check that out!' McFeeley ordered Piper, who stepped carefully among the bodies, his musket pointing downwards in readiness.

Satisfied, McFeeley hurried back to where the two women anxiously awaited him, telling them, 'It's over, and the party sent out to meet us is here. Come along.'

They went with him down the hill, turning away in revulsion as they passed each body. Up ahead Sergeant Jack was kneeling beside the dead lieutenant. As they approached Jack he took something from the officer's pocket and stood up to put whatever it was inside of his torn tunic.

'It's for his wife ...' Jack started to explain, showing no reaction to McFeeley being in a Monmouth uniform. Then, obviously referring to the dead, he asked, 'What do we do, sir?'

It was a problem. They couldn't carry the bodies with them, and the remaining six men of Jack's squad looked to be exhausted, with one of them trying to staunch the blood flowing freely from a wound in the upper part of his left arm.

'Let the dead bury the dead,' Jonathan Piper suggested laconically from his seat on a rock.

Taking a look at him, Jack turned to McFeeley, one eyebrow raised in question, which McFeeley answered. 'Private Jonathan Piper of the Queen Dowager's Regiment of Foot.'

'That was a Biblical quotation, Sergeant,' Piper said blandly.

'The Bible don't answer my question, soldier,' Jack replied. 'What do we do, sir?'

'Where is our army now, Jack?'

'If they've called a halt they'll be at Shepton Mallet, sir.'

There was a lot of distance to cover and there was every chance that along the way they would encounter more of Monmouth's soldiers. A lack of time and the fact that they didn't have one shovel between them ruled out burying their men here. Yet each one of them was so deserving of a funeral with full military honours. McFeeley chose a compromise, a half-lie that would be a salve for his conscience and, hopefully, the consciences of his companions.

'We'll have a burial detail sent out as soon as we make contact with headquarters,' he declared, seemingly satisfying the others, with Jack being the exception. He was looking worriedly at the body of the lieutenant.

Piper didn't bother with tact when putting the situation into perspective for Jack. 'There isn't anything that'll gnaw at them above ground that won't do just as much chewing on them under it, Sergeant.'

Ignoring this, Jack made a request. 'I'd like permission to bury Lieutenant Tonge, Sir.'

'What would you use to dig a grave?' McFeeley questioned the idea.

'My hands, if necessary, sir,' Jack replied resolutely. 'If you move out I'll catch up with you.'

Granting permission, McFeeley then led Lady Sarah and Rachel away, with the men of Jack's squad next, and a watchful Jonathan Piper bringing up the rear. They made good time through what was left of the afternoon, wading across the River Brue while the sun was still high, and climbing into the Mendips, where they made camp as twilight dimmed the world.

Jack rejoined them by the time McFeeley had chosen a wide plateau as their resting place for the night on which there would be a moon making it possible for a single sentry to see any Monmouth men trying to come up the wide, treeless slopes. The meal they ate was an austere one. What rations Sergeant Jack and his men had brought out with them had long been exhausted, and the supper consisted of fruit picked along the way. McFeeley had Jack post two guards, then he sat, relaxing as best he could.

He heard Rachel questioning Piper about the theatre. 'You spoke earlier of *The Mulberry Garden*, Jonathan, so I assume that you are an admirer of Sir Charles Sedley. I admire the way in which he maintains a boundary between the just bawdy and the blatantly indecent.'

'As I writer I believe that he has no equal, but as a man it is to be regretted that he does not recognize in his private life the boundary you refer to,' Piper replied, causing McFeeley puzzlement and consternation as to how so erudite a man came to be serving in the army as a private soldier.

The topic of their conversation had Rachel and Piper straddling two worlds which distanced them from the others. Lady Sarah sat quietly, lost in her own thoughts. Jack sat alone staring, as he always did when at rest, at a scene that wasn't visible to the others.

'What if I inquired as to your favourite, Miss Rachel?' Piper said.

'Then my answer would come without the slightest hesitation,' Rachel trilled. 'My favourite character has to be Wycherly's *Lady Flippanta*.'

'Indeed you do surprise me, Miss Rachel,' Piper exclaimed.

'That is because you don't know me, Jonathan,' Rachel said.

Aware that Jack had selected Piper for the second watch on the wooded slope, McFeeley was determined to stay alert. Yet he had made no allowance for how tired he was. No sooner had all of them, with the exception of the two soldiers on guard, bedded down for the night than he had drifted into a deep and restoring sleep.

He was awoken, coming fully alert but lying perfectly still, by the feeling of something tickling over his hand. At first he suspected an insect at best, an adder at worst, but then slim fingers entwined with his. His hand was being tugged at tenderly, and then Rachel's voice came to him, her words enticing: 'Please come with me, Colm.'

Partially refreshed by sleep, unable to resist an invitation made to the only weakness in his character, McFeeley let her guide him up onto his feet. He tensed as a dark figure loomed up at them in the night, musket projecting aggressively towards them. It was Piper.

McFeeley ordered. 'Stand steady, soldier. It's me, McFeeley.'

Without a word, Piper did a silent quarter turn on the grass and walked tactfully away. With his arm round Rachel his intention was to go some way into the trees. But Rachel had different ideas. As lithe and ferocious as a tigress, she leapt at McFeeley gasping. 'I can't wait!'

It was an hour later that they came back up to the level area of the camp. Jonathan Piper was still on guard but he didn't approach them. Remaining in the shadows, he softly quoted: 'Unfortunate lady that I am. I have left the herd on purpose to be chased—'

'*Lady Flippanta*!' a giggling Rachel whispered close to McFeeley's ear.

Then she was gone, half tip-toeing across the grass to where she had left a space beside Lady Sarah. McFeeley was stabbed by an unrelenting guilt when noticing Sarah's open eyes sparkling in the moonlight.

Even so, the fact that Sarah was now definitely aware that Rachel and he had been intimate weighed heavily on his mind. For a long time it prevented a return to sleep for him when he lay down. He had at last managed to slumber when someone shook him awake by the shoulder. For a moment he feared the insatiable Rachel, but it was a grave-faced Jack.

'There's something happening, sir.'

'What is it, Jack?' McFeeley inquired.

Jack's care to be quiet would seem to have been wasted. Something had disturbed the two women, who were walking to where McFeeley had got to his feet to stand beside the sergeant.

'This way, sir,' Jack said.

McFeeley walked with Jack to the crest over which Rachel and he had recently gone. The two women both followed nervously close behind them. Initially McFeeley could see nothing when Jack pointed down below and out past the woods. Then he saw a deep, glowing red that occasionally altered hue as yellow flames flickered. It was a fairly large fire for an ordinary camp-fire.

'The sentry heard a shot, and then voices down there,' the sergeant reported.

Turning his head, McFeeley saw that Piper had been relieved by one of the mullato's party. He was a clumsy fellow who would have fitted better behind a plough than he did a musket, and his round rustic face registered apprehension over what he had observed down below.

'We'll be going that way in the morning,' McFeeley said, 'so we can discover what it is then.'

Barely had he finished speaking when an unearthly and protracted scream came to them. Distorted by the distance it had travelled, clearly having come from the area of the fire, the scream had lost none of its terrifying content when it reached them. Another shriek joined the first one before it had died away.

'Oh, my God,' Lady Sarah exclaimed, aghast.

'Those poor women,' Rachel moaned.

'Those are not the screams of women,' Jack said curtly.

'Are you saying…?' Lady Sarah began.

Having half come to the conclusion before Jack put it into words, McFeeley answered Sarah, knowing that Jack wouldn't do so. 'It's men screaming down there, Lady Sarah.'

'But what…?' Rachel began, to fall silent as the screams were replaced by a howling.

The screaming went on and on, so eerie that even the hair on the back of the neck of the tough McFeeley started to prickle. McFeeley ordered everyone but the sentry back into camp. Once there, although they took a memory of the screaming with them, they had distanced themselves so that it was impossible to tell whether a faint howling was real or imagined.

Yet there was no further sleep for any of them that night. They were heading out of camp before the sun had chance to even slightly lighten the eastern sky. McFeeley was aware of Lady Sarah studying him when she felt he wouldn't notice. He wondered what was on her mind. She had not expressed disapproval of Rachel and him that morning either verbally or in any other way.

They went down the hill through trees and started out along flat ground beside the river. It was an idyllic morning that was warmed comfortably by a sun not yet at full power. As they forked left away from the river to cross a lush meadow they seemed to be in a golden land in which the terrible sounds of the previous night could not possible have taken place.

There was a hint of burning on the unmoving air as they rounded a hill and started across undulating grassland, its troughs and peaks so deep and high that it was impossible for them to see very far ahead. But the unmistakably pungent smell of a dead fire was stronger now. A feast must have been held close by for there was also an aroma of cooking meat. McFeeley tried, and failed, to equate a feast with the ghoulish screaming they had heard.

Ahead of the others, he topped yet another corrugation to find that it was the last. An expanse of flatland stretched ahead of McFeeley, and what he saw had him turn to signal for the two women to stay where they were. For an agonizingly long moment, McFeeley looked at a makeshift gibbet that had been erected some fifty yards in front of where he stood. That the gallows had been extensively used in the night was evident in the broken bodies lying around. They weren't *bodies* but what was left of soldiers who had been hanged, drawn and quartered. Only a few green patches showed through over a wide area. The grass looked as if a lunatic artist had painted it red. Controlling a gagging urge to vomit, he turned and went back down the slope to where the two women and the men were clustered together, waiting.

'What is it, Lieutenant?' Lady Sarah asked tentatively, as if she was aware that she wouldn't welcome the answer.

But McFeeley was unable to reply. It would have been cruel to tell her and Rachel the truth. So he said gruffly, 'I will explain later, Lady Sarah. I want you and Miss Rachel to remain here. Sergeant Jack and Private Piper will go with me, but the soldiers will stay to protect you.'

Studying the soldiers, McFeeley selected a sandy-haired man who looked to be the eldest and most responsible of them. He told the man, 'You, soldier. I am putting you in charge until we return. You're in a small world here, the boundary being that crest behind us. See that you keep a close watch on that ridge at all times.'

McFeeley left then, flanked by Jack on one side and the mysterious Jonathan Piper on the other. The latter ripped out a curse as they went over the ridge and he saw the scene of butchery in front of them.

'This explains the screaming in the night, sir,' Jack said.

'And the fire that we saw,' Piper nodded to a charred area at the far side of the gallows. 'They tried to burn some of the bodies.'

'To hide the evidence,' McFeeley nodded.

Having moved a little way from the other two, Piper looked down at a mutilated body. Whoever it was had been disembowelled. Face twisting in revulsion he forced himself to take another look. Lying close to the grisly remains was part of a torn uniform. Identifying the clothing, Piper called to McFeeley. 'These are the Monmouth chaps we fought with yesterday, sir. Who could do something like this?'

'Only one man,' McFeeley muttered.

'Colonel Kirke,' Jack filled in, 'and his "Lambs".'

'Ah!' Piper's memory worked well. 'I've heard of him. He's best known for what he did in Tangier, isn't he?'

'He's best known for being a brutal bastard,' McFeeley said. 'Kirke must have taken these poor fellows as prisoners. We'd best get back. To avoid the ladies seeing this means making a wide swing that is going to cost us a lot in time.'

Keen to get moving, and eager to get away from the macabre slaughter, they hurried over the ridge – only to stop and stare in shock at the sight before them. Lady Sarah, Rachel, and the soldiers McFeeley had left to guard them, were standing among a large party of troopers. These were men of the king's army but, nevertheless, the menace in the air was a tangible thing. McFeeley was able to identify its source then. Sitting in the saddle of a white stallion, staring stonily at McFeeley and the others, was Colonel Percy Kirke. Beside him, mounted on a far less impressive horse, was a young lieutenant who spurred into action when Kirke bellowed an order.

'A man of Monmouth, by God! Complete with uniform. Take that man and hold him, Lieutenant.'

It was a farce, a charade put on by Kirke, McFeeley knew, because hatred for him had the colonel recognize him immediately. Even so, he was seized and bound. Separated from the others, the anxious eyes of Jack and Jonathan Piper on him, both Lady Sarah and Rachel looking totally bemused, he was at the rear of the troop when it moved out, being pulled along by a rope tied to the saddle of the young lieutenant.

McFeeley had hoped that Captain Allenby would be present. Had he been so there would have been hope, for the quick-minded adjutant was an oasis of sound sense in the huge desert of insanity that was Kirke.

They journeyed for what McFeeley estimated to be two hours. It was a tough time for him. Not only had the burning sun reached its zenith, but the lieutenant, either under orders from Kirke or because of his own cruelly vicious nature, would at short intervals pull on the rope so that McFeeley sprawled headlong into the dust. With his wrists bound behind his back he would find himself dragged along the rough ground each time before he was able, with great difficulty, to regain his feet.

Colonel Kirke's camp, just outside Wells, was a hive of activity when they reached it. His 'lambs' were cleaning muskets, loading ammunition onto carriages, grooming horses. Everything was taking place with the disciplined efficiency that can be achieved only by a totally sensitive commander.

Kept separate from his earlier companions, not even getting a glimpse of them, McFeeley was taken to and confined in a small tent on the perimeter of the camp. His arms remained bound and the length of rope attached to him was tied to an iron stake that a soldier drove into the ground just outside of the tent. When the lieutenant was satisfied that McFeeley was securely held, he walked off, leaving two sentries posted each side of the entrance to the tent.

Throughout that afternoon the heat built up intolerably inside the canvas. Wet through with sweat, McFeeley soon found that he was parched, his tongue adhering to the roof of his mouth. But he was brought neither water nor food. As evening eased in, bringing a modest but very welcome drop in temperature, the lieutenant returned. McFeeley had his first real opportunity to look at the officer. He was chubby of body and face. A turned-up nose and a puffy-lipped mouth that was pulled down at each corner imparted a pugnacity that related more to that of a lap dog than a bull terrier.

Accompanied by an armed escort he introduced himself. 'I am Lieutenant Riglar and I am here to take you before Colonel Kirke.'

With one member of the escort of four holding the rope that was McFeeley's leash, and the remaining three keeping him covered with their muskets at all times, he was taken through the camp to a large tent in which Kirke sat alone. Along the way McFeeley looked unsuccessfully for Lady Sarah, Rachel, Jack and Piper.

Riglar entered the tent with McFeeley while the escort was left outside but far enough away to guarantee that they wouldn't over-hear what was to be said in the tent. Colonel Kirke stood and paced up and down. In addition to his bald pate he was a man who was ageing long before his time. Wizened by his own toxic bitterness, Kirke could only look another man in the eye when he was bullying him into abject terror. Aware that he would never succeed in intim-idating McFeeley, he kept his eyes away from him as he began to speak.

'You are an officer, and as such, even though you serve James Scott, I would treat you with due respect had we met under battle conditions and you had become my prisoner,' Kirke said in his piping voice. 'But you are a spy, Lieutenant, a disgrace to the uniform that you wear or, indeed, army uniform.'

Riglar addressed McFeeley then, after receiving a signal from Kirke to do so. His pouting lips gave him the peevish look of a baby as he asked. 'Do you have anything to say?'

'I am a lieutenant with the Kildare military.'

'Indeed!' the colonel stopped his pacing and mockingly held out a hand to McFeeley. 'Your papers, please, Lieutenant. Your identification.'

McFeeley, aware that he was being baited, replied. 'I carry no papers with me.'

'How unusual and, indeed, unfortunate,' Kirke permitted himself a humourless smile.

'Lady Sarah will vouch for me,' McFeeley said with confidence.

Shaking his head, Riglar replied. 'We have spoken to Lady Churchill, who admitted that you were wearing a Monmouth uniform when she first became acquainted with you, and that you have worn the same uniform ever since.'

'Then ask Sergeant Jack; he has served with me in the king's army.'

'Sergeant Jack and the other soldiers you brought with you are at this very moment on their way to Lord Churchill at Shepton Mallet, together with the two ladies,' Riglar informed him.

'Bring the sergeant back and he will confirm who I am,' McFeeley protested.

Kirke snorted angrily. 'Disrupt the king's army in the hope that a sergeant will tell lies to save your valueless skin?'

'You know who I am!' McFeeley hissed angrily, leaping towards the colonel but being stopped by Riglar who rammed the muzzle of a pistol into his throat, forcing his chin up, his head back. Hampered by this, McFeeley still managed to speak. 'You want to punish me because your spineless brother in-law blew his brains out because he couldn't face becoming a soldier!'

Although Riglar's face registered consternation when he heard this, he kept the pistol against McFeeley's throat. Kirke pushed on past McFeeley's provable statement by thrusting his face close to grind out, 'You deserve nothing, you cur, but, above all else I am a fair man, so I will give you a choice. Do you wish to die now with a bullet in your head, or would you prefer the gallows at dawn?'

'Tell him to squeeze the trigger,' McFeeley answered, indicating Riglar.

A sinister chuckle came from the colonel. 'I only asked which you would prefer so that I could deny your request. Take him away, Lieutenant Riglar. He will be hanged at dawn as a Monmouth spy.'

McFeeley was taken away and doubled back to his tent where he was once more tethered to the stake. An hour later, as the sun did a multicoloured retreat for the day, McFeeley walked on his knees to peer out of the tent when he heard hammering. To his left, back-lit dramatically by the sunset, a crude gallows such as he had come across earlier that day, was being constructed.

Resigned to his fate and cold now that night had come, McFeeley slept. He was awoken by the movements of someone entering the tent. Opening his eyes, McFeeley's spirits soared instantaneously as he saw Captain Allenby peering at him in the half light of the moon.

'Just in time, Captain,' he said, huskily due to the heat of the day having reduced his bodily fluids. 'A few hours later and you would have found me swinging from Colonel Kirke's gibbet.'

McFeeley plunged into an abyss of despair as he saw the look on Allenby's face. The captain said listlessly, 'I returned to the camp by chance, Colm, and once I learned of your fate I wanted to see you. But I am simply the adjutant and cannot countermand an order given by my commanding officer, Colonel Kirke.'

'All I ask is that Claude Critchell is informed of what is happening here,' McFeeley pointed out.

'That is not possible,' Allenby shook a sad head. 'I left Lord Churchill's headquarters at Shepton Mallet earlier today, Colm, and Captain Critchell had left there a day or two before to go on some reconnoitre. I gained the distinct impression that he is not expected back for some time.'

This was very bad news for McFeeley. Without intervention from Critchell his life would end on the gallows at dawn. There would seem to be only one hope left for him, and he broached it to Allenby. 'I would say that there is just enough time to get a message to Lord Churchill at Shepton Mallet, and his order saving me from execution brought back.'

'There is time, Colm,' an unhappy Allenby agreed, 'but Colonel Kirke would never permit it.'

'You could do it, Captain Allenby,' McFeeley urged.

With an emphatic nod, Allenby said, 'I could do it, but if I did, then I would receive a bullet in the back when the first chance presented itself. I am not proud of myself, Colm, but when it comes

124

down to being a case of my back or your neck, I find myself becoming very fond of my own back.'

Head bowed, the captain went to the flap of the tent, turning to ask with a tremor in his voice. 'Would you find it in your heart to forgive a coward, Colm?'

'No, but I could easily forgive an honest man, Captain,' McFeeley said.

Going outside, Captain Allenby called back into the tent.

'Goodbye, Colm, and may the Lord bless you.'

Lady Henrietta looked across the table at a morbid Miss Blake. All the other Taunton dignitaries were saddened by the imminent departure of the Duke of Monmouth, whereas the schoolmistress appeared to be in deep mourning for her virginity. Draped on the wall behind her were the twenty-seven banners made by her young pupils for Monmouth's army to march with. The material used had been the schoolgirls' petticoats. What did that imply? wondered Henrietta, who was a self-taught student and graduate in human sexuality. The most auspicious banner was the gorgeously fringed one, embroidered with the initials JR and topped by a crown, which was the creation of senior girl Mary Mead. The girl was fortunate not to be here at the last meal in Captain John Hucker's house, Henrietta thought wryly. If Monmouth could collect military victories the way he did hymens he would be king of England within a week. He was making a mistake by lingering in Taunton. Monmouth claimed he had agreed to host this meal to repay the townsfolk for their support. Henrietta believed that he was unwilling to move on and face whatever military force James II might have waiting. She had witnessed Monmouth's nervousness on learning of the Earl of Argyle's invasion of Scotland petering out mainly due to desertions, and the non-starters that the promised uprisings in London and Cheshire had proved to be. Had there been a chink of a way out with honour, then she was in no doubt that Monmouth would right now be squeezing through it.

Edmund Prideaux and John Trenchard were sitting further down the table, the latter with a cut, bruised and badly swollen face, having brought more bad news for Monmouth. Ignorant of it up to that time, Henrietta had learned of the failed plan to apply pressure on John Churchill by holding his wife and Rachel as hostages. Prideaux had linked the escape of the two women with McFeeley, but Monmouth had refused to believe it. Mention of the untamed McFeeley had awakened arousing memories in Henrietta.

'When teaching future generations, Susan,' Monmouth smiled across the table at Miss Blake, 'may I ask that you be kind to me in the history of our great land?'

The schoolmistress's face blushed deep red, causing Henrietta to mutter to her husband, 'For heaven's sake, you stupid woman, he's asking you to open your heart this time, not your legs.'

'Keep your voice down, Henrietta, or you will cause great embarrassment,' Lord Grey cautioned her sotto voce.

Henrietta gave him a sideways smile. 'Since when have my little indiscretions worried you?'

'Only when they are likely to cause problems, Henrietta,' he replied tetchily.

Her husband was in a worse state of anxiety than Monmouth, Henrietta realized. This didn't surprise her, as, for all his faults, Monmouth had courage, whereas Lord Grey of Werke could not be relied upon even to protect her against anything but a mediocre threat. It had been agreed between Monmouth and her husband that she would remain here in Taunton when they rode out. Being a sensitive person underneath her flippancy and philandering, Lady Henrietta was made miserable by her inner conviction that she would never see either of the two men alive again. Perhaps what she felt for Monmouth was love, while her relationship with her husband was habit. Was there any difference between those two things, she was pondering when Monmouth drained his glass with a finality that said his sojourn in Taunton was coming to an end.

Standing, Monmouth told his fellow diners, 'It is time. First I must speak again to the loyal people of this town and then I will lead my mighty army away to fight the good fight. A fight that will not cease until we have successfully defended and vindicated the Protestant religion and have delivered the kingdom from the usurpation and tyranny of James, Duke of York.'

Dr Robert Ferguson jumped to his feet, mouth open, prayers ready to tumble out, but he was pre-empted by John Whiting, the Quaker unexpectedly made a guest by Monmouth.

'Now let us pray,' John Whiting said in a quiet, humble way. 'Let us pray for the man who will be king, and pray to the cities of our God and that the Lord will seemeth it fitting to aid and protect the Duke of Monmouth, protector of our people, a warrior for our faith.'

As the 'amens' went on around her, Henrietta walked between her husband and Monmouth out into the street. Hers was a position of privilege. Others were pushing, struggling, even fighting to get close to the duke. She noticed that Whiting was near. Like her, the Quaker was to stay here in Taunton. His task was to form a team of medics who would then go behind Monmouth's troops into battle. Uncertain as to what would be asked of her, Henrietta was soon to learn. In the doorway Monmouth lightly took her arm to move her close to him.

Not knowing what to expect, Henrietta needed to strain to catch Monmouth's low-spoken words as the crowd outside built up a tumultuous greeting for the duke. He asked. 'Do you remember the man named McFeeley, Henrietta?'

A cautionary voice in Henrietta's head spoke urgently to her. Had the duke while at White Lackington either noticed or had been told of her romp in the garden with the rugged McFeeley?

'I'm not sure. Was he a rough sort of fellow who was at George Speke's home?' she asked coyly.

Monmouth nodded with a smile of reminiscence. 'That is the man, Henrietta. A rough diamond, that is for sure, but I have this feeling that he will be coming to Taunton to join me.'

'But …' she was a little confused. 'I heard both Edmund Prideaux and John Trenchard denounce him as a traitor, James!'

'Balderdash, Henrietta. McFeeley is worth five hundred Edmund Prideauxs and a thousand John Trenchards. If I am to have any chance I must have men like him fighting at my side. I want you to remain here and send him after me to Bridgwater, Henrietta. I have your promise?'

'I promise,' she vowed, and they permitted themselves a furtive, brief, but nevertheless stirring touching of hands.

Eight

SADDENED BY THE duke's departure, and full of shame because of the warm anticipation of the possible arrival of McFeeley, Henrietta turned with the intention of going back into Captain Hucker's house, but she paused to listen to a conversation between a group that had formed since having given the rebel army a rapturous send-off. A tall man with an expensive tricorn hat was addressing an audience of eminent persons who were nodding and murmuring, 'Yes, yes, quite right, quite right!' all through a speech that was delivered both guardedly and, contrarily, fervently.

'There is no time to be lost,' the tall man warned. 'If we hesitate or delay in any way then we will sacrifice every man, woman, child and building in this town. He must not be allowed to return here. Should he do so, then the king's army will burn Taunton to the ground. A deputation must be arranged immediately to ride out and plead with him, beg him and, if necessary, demand that he does not return. Are you with me?'

There came a shouted chorus of, 'Aye!'

Realization came to Henrietta, sickening her as she was walking in through the door of the house. They were discussing Monmouth, the man the townsfolk had minutes before unreservedly acclaimed. Now they were adopting measures to ensure that he would never return to Taunton. Having suspected that it could happen; now she knew it for sure. The Duke of Monmouth was doomed.

As she went up the steps to the door of the house, some clouds, strangers in the sky this long, hot summer, darkened the sun to deepen her depression. Moving away from where he had been standing just inside the lobby, eavesdropping on the speakers outside, John Whiting saw her despondency and placed a consoling hand upon her arm.

'These people and their fickle loyalties distress me as they do you, dear lady,' he told her with a weak smile. 'But take heart, for I have good news. I hear from a most reliable source that at this very moment a Quaker is riding to acquaint His Grace the duke with the fact that the club-army that now comprises ten thousand well armed men is soon to join him.'

'I don't understand,' a bemused Henrietta said.

'It is magnificent news, Lady Henrietta, for the country is rising for Monmouth.'

'But what is the club army?' Henrietta asked.

Seemingly uncertain, Whiting replied, 'It is a gallant band of men who originally gathered together for mutual protection but will now lend their strength to the Monmouth cause.'

'I see,' Henrietta said walking up the stairs, heading for the room Monmouth had secured for her.

What the Quaker had said did nothing to lift her spirits with regard to Monmouth, yet she guiltily felt warmth and slipped into a much brighter mood as she anticipated the arrival of McFeeley in Taunton. At White Lackington they had rolled in the grass like a pair of wandering gypsies, whereas here in Taunton she had a comfortable room and a luxurious double bed for them.

A slight sound that he couldn't identify brought McFeeley fully awake. Until he realized that it was still dark outside of the tent, he was convinced for one blood-freezing moment that the execution party had come for him. The barely audible noise was coming from the rear of the small tent that was his prison. Blinking his eyes, he saw the tip of a knife slicing up through the canvas of the tent.

Guessing at first, that Captain Allenby had decided to risk everything to free, him, McFeeley dropped the idea when a much younger, far more agile figure than that of Allenby, came quickly into the tent on all fours. Without even a whisper likely to alert the sentries outside the figure came silently to McFeeley's side. One hand feeling for the ropes that bound McFeeley's wrists, the newcomer used his knife to slice through that rope and also the one by which he was fastened to the stake.

A long length of hair brushed against McFeeley's face, tickling so much that he had to lift one of his arms to rub at the itch. Romantic ideas raced through his mind. Perhaps Rachel or Sarah had come to rescue him. Then the true and less exotic identification came to him. It had to be Jonathan Piper.

Starting to follow Piper to the long slit the soldier had sliced up through the back of the tent, McFeeley found himself temporarily but severely disabled by cramp from having been too long in one position. An urgent Piper reached back with one hand to grasp McFeeley's jerkin and pull, which had a psychological effect that got McFeeley moving painfully, but moving.

A pale moon gave enough light for McFeeley to read the question on Piper's lean face, and he gave a nod. He was ready to go. Building up his strength to force his body upright, McFeeley was about to move when he saw Jonathan Piper tense and bring his musket up. A shadow fell across McFeeley and he looked up to see one of the sentries, his feet astride and his musket aimed at them.

The sentry represented a serious problem, but McFeeley was thankful that it was Piper beside him. They would both be thinking alike. While the sentry's musket covered them, Piper's musket was pointing at the sentry. Yet there was no option other than to shoot the sentry and make a run for it. Piper should have fired! Then he put himself in Piper's position and the truth dawned on him. The sentry was a comrade, serving in the same army, was wearing the same uniform.

The sentry was equally as reluctant to shoot. But his eyes went into their corners to keep a watch on them while he turned his head, opening his mouth, ready to shout to the other guard. Something had to be done, but what? McFeeley was aware of Piper, but only to lay down his musket. Still turned from them, the sentry's shout of warning was rising up out of his throat.

'You have been through a most traumatic time, Sarah, and it is I who should be begging your forgiveness for being so thoughtless.'

John Churchill spoke out of the shadows at the far end of the tent that served as his military headquarters during the day and their home at night here at Shepton Mallet. Sarah knew that she had failed him as a wife yet again. A patient man, her husband had tried many times to coax out the other her. There had been a few times when her sexuality had been tantalizingly close, but it had always escaped before John and she were able to embrace it.

For a short while Sarah listened to the sound of activity outside: the sharpening of swords, the filling of powder flasks and the cleaning and oiling of firing pieces. When they were still infants their families had decided that they would be man and wife. Sarah didn't envy hard-working serving girls their lot but she was jealous of their relative freedom of choice in relationships. John was kind, considerate and protective, but did she love him? That was impossible to answer, for Sarah didn't know what love was. Her confusion over this had been added to by the strange feelings evoked in her by McFeeley.

Striving to sound casual, she inquired; 'John, is the man who rescued me back in camp?'

'I have yet to have word of him. Why do you ask, Sarah?'

'I feel that I owe him so much. My life, in fact!'

'That's true,' Churchill agreed, standing upright and stamping both feet to complete the fitting of his boots. 'I am most mindful of that. I am waiting for the return of Captain Claude Critchell, to have him seek out the man. Lieutenant McFeeley is a very special soldier, Sarah.'

Sarah was pondering on how different her life would have been had she belonged to the world that McFeeley inhabited, when a call came from outside of the tent.

'Are you awake, sir? I have an urgent message from Captain Allenby.'

Going to the flap of the tent, Churchill took a letter from a young soldier, ordering him. 'Remain there, soldier.'

As Lord Churchill read the missive he had been handed, Sarah watched his face darken and a frown crease his brow. Churchill then turned to the tent opening. 'Return to Captain Allenby and advise him that, though it fills me with regret, there is no action that I am able to take.'

Her husband was so agitated that he needed to confide in someone. She was the only available listener. 'Colonel Kirke has captured Lieutenant McFeeley and will execute him as a spy at dawn.'

She asked, 'Is he a spy, John?'

Churchill shook his head, 'No, not against the king.'

'Then Kirke must be stopped,' she said, more vehemently than she had intended.

'I am afraid that it is not that simple, Sarah,' Churchill said gravely. 'I suspect that Claude Critchell could, in his devious way, find a way to have the man freed, but Claude is at Bristol.'

'Then you must take immediate action, John,' Sarah half-ordered her husband.

'There is no opportunity open to me,' he said, suspicious Sarah thought, of her intense concern. 'I need Feversham's permission, and McFeeley will be long gone before I can contact him.'

That was Churchill's final word. He went out of the tent then, leaving behind a tormented Sarah. Dressing swiftly, she knew that she had to do something, hoping that an idea would come to her. It did. Putting her head out of the tent opening first, checking that the immediate area was clear, she slipped noiselessly out into the night. She needed a horse to take her to Colonel Kirke's camp. In the past, his advances had disgusted her. To repay the rugged lieutenant for rescuing her, she was now prepared to sacrifice herself to save him.

Coming quietly up behind a sentry she made a low hissing sound to attract his attention. The soldier spun on his heel, bringing up his musket.

'I need a saddled horse, soldier,' she told him, aware that she had at her command the forceful manner to swear him to secrecy once he had done her bidding.

'Yes, my lady,' the guard stammered.

Gambling on the quick-witted Piper to catch on, McFeeley did a fast twist on his buttocks to sweep his legs round to knock the sentry's legs out from underneath him. Quick as a flash, Piper dropped on to his back and reared up his legs to slam both feet together hard into the falling soldier's chest. It should have been perfect had not the musket discharged as the guard had fallen. The explosion it made in the night was shattering, alerting the whole camp.

A shout of, 'Call out the guard!' was reiterated so that it rose and fell in the darkness.

Springing to their feet, McFeeley and Piper ran, neither slowing nor ducking as a bullet, fired by the second sentry, passed with a sibilant hiss between their heads. Leaping a stream they ran across a meadow, the sounds of a pursuit being organized adding speed to their feet.

They went over the top of the hill and were pounding down to where a meandering river waveringly marked out the nadir of a valley. Wading across the shallow river they went up the far bank and took a meandering route that Piper gaspingly assured McFeeley would lead them to Shepton Mallet.

'Where's Jack?' McFeeley inquired when they slowed their pace.

'He was on duty and couldn't get away,' Piper replied, pointing to a small wood to their left. 'Through those trees,' he said, 'and then just half a mile along a stony track and we're there.'

'Good. Whose orders were you acting on when you came to get me? Captain Critchell's?'

'Captain Critchell's not at the camp,' said Piper.

This puzzled McFeeley, who could not imagine Lord John Churchill ordering any kind of rescue party, one-man or otherwise. Piper now had an evasiveness about him.

'Who gave you the order to come and get me, soldier?'

'Nobody,' Piper answered, shrugging. 'It was just my idea.'

'You knucklehead, Jonathan! They'll lock you up when we get back,' McFeeley exclaimed.

Tilting his head to look up at the steadily brightening sky, Piper observed, 'I don't know about me being locked up, sir, but they would be stringing you up about now!'

'You know that I can't argue against regulations,' McFeeley warned. 'But I owe you my life and will do everything I can in mitigation.'

'I understand the position I have put you in, sir,' Piper said. 'I hesitate to advise an officer, but you're going to have to get out of that Monmouth uniform before we approach the camp, sir.'

About to agree, McFeeley stayed quiet and gestured Piper back into the bushes as approaching hoof beats could be heard. Whether it was friend or foe, McFeeley was taking no chances. Climbing up a tree trunk he waited, ready to spring. The rider came on steadily, allowing the horse to pick its way through the tangled undergrowth. At the right time, McFeeley launched himself through the air.

Colliding with the rider, he wrapped his arms round him and the two of them crashed to the ground on the far side of the startled horse. Slightly winded by the fall, McFeeley lay still for a moment, his captive lifeless in his arms. Then he found himself looking down on the white face of Lady Sarah Churchill. Eyes closed, she was unmoving, and McFeeley was mortified. But her eyelids first flickered and then lifted. There was not only consciousness but the shock of recognition in the eyes looking up at him.

'Oh, dear God, have I hurt you, Lady Sarah?' McFeeley groaned.

'Let us turn to Joshua, chapter twenty-two, verse twenty-two,' said the Reverend Robert Ferguson, who had laid down the sword he had waved at Taunton to don a gown and clergyman's staff as he preached to a congregation that packed Bridgwater Castle.

In the front pew Monmouth was ecstatic. Bridgwater, a town of dissenters, had given him a royal reception. Backed by an enthusiastic town council, the mayor had read his proclamation at the Market Cross, and hundreds of men had come forward eagerly to serve in his army. He employed blacksmiths who toiled day and night converting scythes into hand weapons. He then formed a scythe company for each of his regiments, using his experience and innate talent as a military commander to give them regular battle-drills and daily training.

Now Ferguson had used matins to turn this huge audience into a holy crusade. His stirring words had every person there ready to fight for God and their 'king', Monmouth.

In that congregation, but not a part of it, was Kathleen Nerney. Kathleen had just celebrated her sixteenth birthday as she had many of her anniversaries that had gone before – fatherless. Michael Nerney was a Catholic recusant, an honest God-fearing man who was imprisoned indefinitely for refusing to attend Church of

England services. Angered by the double standards of Charles II, who had refused to grant a general pardon for Catholics, but had sneaked a priest into his chambers to administer the last rites, Kathleen had faith in James II and saw Monmouth as a menace to people like her father. There were many of them rotting in prisons solely because of their religion.

Sickened by the euphoric mood here in the castle, she fumed with impotence. What could a young girl do to harm this fast-expanding rebellion? If there was any action she could take, no matter how small and ineffective, Kathleen was determined to do it. Glowering with hatred at Monmouth, resplendent in princely purple and with the Garter star prominent, the young girl regretted that she possessed neither the courage nor the ability to carry out the assassination of the rebel duke.

Kathleen looked at those around her, desperately in need of a kindred spirit. There wasn't one. These were the people of Bridgwater who constantly harassed and persecuted her and her mother. Blinkered by their own selfish aims they didn't even have an inkling of how much good folk such as her father had suffered and for how long.

When the Reverend Ferguson had ranted his final rant and the congregation had cried out its last response of loyalty to Monmouth, the huge audience crushed together in a move towards the exit. Kathleen found herself abused because of her pretty face and shapely body. Pressed claustrophobically from all sides, she shrivelled in disgust as she felt a determined hand groping her.

Turning she saw leering faces all around her. Tears streamed down her face as she ran all the way home, promising herself that she would play a significant part in any local opposition to Monmouth. Bursting in through the door of her home, and into her mother's comforting arms, Kathleen was sure that the invasion of her physical privacy she had just experienced would be the worst ever time in her life. The heavy curtain draped between Kathleen Nerney and the immediate future mercifully spared her from much greater trauma.

*

'I'm not conversant enough with the facts to invoke criticism, Lieutenant, but I wager that you were ill-advised to return to the camp where Lady Sarah, the Lady of Brigadier-General Churchill was,' Captain Claude Critchell said, fixing McFeeley with a watery-eyed stare.

Despite Critchell's disclaimer, McFeeley recognized that he was being criticized, and unfairly so. Lady Sarah had, fortunately, not been unhurt to any real extent when he had knocked her out of the saddle. He'd had no way of knowing who the rider was, or that it was a woman in the saddle.

Although it must be plain to Churchill, and excitingly clear to McFeeley that she had ridden out that night with the purpose of helping him, Lady Sarah had not confessed to this. All that she would say was that she had been unable to sleep so had decided to take a horse ride. Churchill hadn't believed her but had made no accusations in front of others, and McFeeley felt sure that neither would he do so when he and Lady Sarah were alone. Even so, the brigadier-general had a controlled but barely concealed anger towards McFeeley.

It was purely the fact that he, McFeeley, was needed for further espionage work that saved him from being buried under the boredom of some mediocre duty. Jonathan Piper was put under arrest while McFeeley was requested to await the return of Captain Critchell, who would give him his next assignment.

'I asked for none of this to happen, Captain,' he explained to Critchell. 'Not for one moment did I suspect it would be Lady Sarah riding through the woods at that hour of the night.'

'I accept that,' Critchell nodded, treating each of his nostrils separately to a sniff of an orchid that he delicately carried. 'It would seem that you have a drastic effect on females, Colm, and Lady Sarah would not seem to be immune. You reap the wild wind of what you sow.'

'Yet I cannot be held responsible, Captain,' McFeeley insisted.

'Not in a moral sense, no. But, militarily, someone has to be deemed responsible for everything,' Critchell said with a sad shaking of his head, 'and the brigadier-general is unhappy with you at the present time.'

'Are you telling me that I am to be relieved of special duties, Captain?'

'Not at all, not at all, Colm,' Critchell seemed stunned by the suggestion. 'We have a new king ruling, Lieutenant, and I think you'll agree we all have to do our utmost for His Majesty.'

'I wouldn't get carried away,' McFeeley shrugged. 'Even when they're perched on the loftiest throne in the world they are still sitting on their own arse, Captain.'

'Perhaps that is not a view you should express to anyone but me, Colm,' Critchell gave an insincere smile. 'Now, these are dire times and there is a mission for you to undertake. When you left James Scott, was he aware that you were really a lieutenant in the king's army?'

'I don't think so.'

'Then you could rejoin him without arousing his suspicions?'

'I can't say that he wouldn't be suspicious,' McFeeley said, 'but he would accept me.'

A pleased Critchell slapped his booted thigh in delight. 'That is what I wanted to hear, Colm, exactly what I wanted to hear. You see, we have the might to crush James Scott and his army of sod-kickers but to do that it is essential that we know where he is. We want you to go back to him, taking a few men with you who you can send back to us as messengers.'

'For someone who is constantly ridiculed, Scott would appear to have you all worried, Captain,' McFeeley said with a trace of sarcasm.

'He may be leading regiments with straw in their hair, Lieutenant,' Critchell acknowledged before going on with an admission, 'but it must be borne in mind that he is known to be a superb commander with an absolutely brilliant grasp of strategy. Strategy, Colm. It is his strategy that has us concerned!'

'Which is where I am needed,' McFeeley said.

'Urgently needed, Colm. You can have your pick of the men, regardless of rank,' Critchell offered. 'I have authority to make available to you every man up to and including the rank of major!'

'All I need are Sergeant Jack and Private Jonathan Piper,' McFeeley announced.

Critchell did a dubious pursing of his lips. 'Piper is under close arrest, as you know, so that could present a difficulty.'

'You said you had the authority to make any man available to me,' McFeeley reminded the captain.

'That's true,' Captain Critchell assented, 'and you shall have the two men you request.'

After making that promise, Critchell went quiet for a time. In his last few minutes of silence he studied McFeeley intently. With a deep sigh he then said, 'Where you are heading now, Colm, the Bristol/Gloucester area, is a Monmouth stronghold. If there are one or two Royalists there, which I doubt, you are not likely to meet them.'

'Is this another of your attempts at giving a concealed warning, Captain?'

'It is just that,' Critchell nodded. 'Once you leave here, Colm, you will be isolated, completely alone.'

'I didn't have a lot of support last time,' McFeeley complained. 'I was used to shoot one of our own men, who was himself being used—'

'That was dictated by circumstances,' Critchell interrupted.

'In addition to that, I would have been executed by Colonel Kirke if Piper hadn't—'

'Again, there was good reason for that unfortunate event,' Critchell came in once more. 'Had I been nearer then I would have had you released immediately.'

'Would it be uncharitable of me to expect a hidden agenda of treachery in this new mission?' McFeeley inquired.

'I am of a mind that it would be most foolish of you, perhaps fatally so, not to protect your back at all times,' was Critchell's wry comment.

'You're a man who lives dangerously, Colm McFeeley. Perhaps too dangerously!'

Lady Henrietta made the comment from where she stood by the bedroom window, naked. Lying on the bed, arms up with his hands behind his head, enjoying the special relaxation that comes in the wake of uninhibited lovemaking, McFeeley studied her. Did a man and a woman who had been intimate ever part completely? He mused. Although he couldn't clearly remember them all, the women in his life were still attached to him in some way, as if joined by some slender and invisible umbilical cord of love. Sun came through the window to show Henrietta's firm, bare breasts back-lit, the fine, fair, soft down on the skin erect and sparkling. They were twin hills of flesh over which Monmouth had oft sensually wandered. In his dreamy, contemplative state McFeeley wondered if with their acts of love, had Henrietta, the rebel duke, and himself woven threads in an unseen and parallel world. Threads that would forever bind the three of them together.

'Why do you say that?' he asked.

'Well …' she thought on what she should say, running a tongue lightly over full lips that took only a split second to become charged with passion. 'This is the house of Captain Hucker, who is possibly James's closest friend! The Captain will, I am sure, regard it as imperative to acquaint Monmouth with the fact that you have shared my bed.'

'I would imagine Monmouth has more on his mind than the possibility of your infidelity,' McFeeley said, being kind.

He doubted if Monmouth had given Henrietta a thought since he had ridden out of Taunton. The rebel duke had both an ample heart and a roving eye. Among his many conquests was Eleanor Needham, the most celebrated of all the Court's beautiful women. McFeeley had glimpsed her just once, when he had been serving in London, and had, ever since, been haunted by the vision. Eleanor was perhaps at the head of Monmouth's list of female priorities, for she had taken less than four years to bear him four children. Maybe McFeeley was being unduly cynical, but he was of the opinion that if Monmouth was thinking of Henrietta at all, then it would just be to compare her performance with that of the woman who would, right then, be supplying his needs at Bridgwater.

'I wouldn't like to think that James wasn't thinking of me, as I am of him, no matter what he has to contend with.'

McFeeley did a mental shaking of his head in wonderment as he got up from the bed. Having just lain with him, and not mentioned her husband even in passing, Henrietta was speaking of Monmouth as if they were a faithful husband and wife who owed one another total loyalty. Never one for illusion, McFeeley was disturbed when encountering it in others.

Going to the washstand he poured water from the blue china jug into the matching bowl. Scooping it up with his hands to dash it against his face and chest he was brought fully awake and felt invigorated by the cold water. Satisfied with his new alertness, he knew that he had to keep moving, to join Monmouth at Bridgwater without delay. Jack and Piper, both of whom had rooms in the nearby Red Lion, would be waiting for his call.

Aware of his urgency, Henrietta, moved by a woman's need to cling for as long as possible to a man after loving, asked, 'You will take breakfast with me, Colm?'

Wanting to refuse, knowing that he should refuse, that his duty as a soldier demanded that he refuse, McFeeley was moved by the fear of rejection that was so evident in her soft eyes as she looked at him. He nodded his assent, but when they were seated at the table downstairs he discovered Henrietta had slipped into a pensive mood.

'You must be the most enigmatic character I have ever come across, Colm,' she commented as they ate. 'To be truthful, I am far from sure which side you are on.'

'Does it matter, Henrietta?' he countered. 'When this is over, when the last cannon falls silent, it is unlikely that we will ever meet again.'

'I know, and it saddens me. Do you feel nothing, Colm?'

'On the contrary,' he began, but said nothing else. All the good-byes he had ever said in his lifetime had accumulated to become a permanent ache in him.

Her eyes were on him intently, and the little catch in her voice evinced that she was shaken by an inward revelation. 'You're far from being as tough as you make yourself out to be.'

'You are being fooled by my temporary weakness caused by you upstairs,' he said as a cover. McFeeley didn't like the post-coitus inquisitiveness of women. It was a time when there were chinks in the personality armour that he was always wore.

'I don't think so,' she expressed dissatisfaction with his answer, biting lightly on her heavy lower lip before going on. 'How would it be, Colm, if life were different? If you and me went on together from this moment?'

'Within days you would be longing for James Scott,' he told her.

Inclining her head a little, she mused. 'Perhaps so. And who would you be longing for, Colm?'

Not knowing the answer himself, he couldn't reply to her. Rosin came instantly into his mind, but she was a ghost and Henrietta was dealing in flesh and blood. None of the others had registered with him, even the golden-haired Rachel, as fiery and skilled as Aphrodite herself, had been nothing but an appeasement of hunger. Rachel and those who had gone before her had satisfied an appetite in him without touching his soul. Conversely, Lady Sarah Churchill had bypassed his appetite to touch his soul.

'The army is all I would miss,' he replied, and could tell that Henrietta knew that he was lying.

When they were outside, both delaying the final farewell, and with Jack and Piper waiting for him at a respectful distance, Henrietta had become even more melancholy. McFeeley gained the impression that she had something to say but lacked the resolve to say it.

She finally managed to speak, with her face away from him, her eyes absently going out to the Market Cross. 'Although I am unsure as to why, Colm, before you leave I want you to know that I am carrying James's child.'

The announcement stunned McFeeley for a moment. Then his mind was racing with the possibilities opened up by her statement. There was the time they had spent together in the garden of the manor at White Lackington. Then there was her husband, Lord Grey of Werke, who had to be a contender where fathering the baby was concerned.

'Are you sure that Monmouth is the father?' he asked, hoping that his question didn't imply that he regarded her as a slut.

'I am absolutely certain,' she told him with a conviction that only a woman, who has more access to intuition than a man, can muster.

Before telling him that she was pregnant, Henrietta had confessed that she didn't know why she was doing so. Now it was

McFeeley's turn to wonder why she had told him. He would rather that she hadn't. Though it neither concerned nor affected him directly, having this knowledge strangely disturbed him.

'Does your condition please or displease you?' he asked, not sure what he should say, really wanting to get away, to take Jack and Piper with him to Bridgwater so that they could begin the work the army required them to do.

'I am delighted,' she replied, although McFeeley could see no real sign in her that could vouch for the truth of what she claimed.

'I must go,' he said, kissing her long and lingeringly, with Henrietta clinging to him unashamedly, despite the fact that they were on the street in full public view.

McFeeley had taken just a few paces from her when Henrietta called. He stopped and turned back to her.

'Colm! Please don't tell James about the baby,' she said wistfully and pleadingly. 'I want to tell him myself when he comes back to me.'

Her delusions, which would eventually fall away to leave her devastated, ravaged McFeeley there and then. It was a tragedy that he was leaving her behind at Taunton, and it was made a thousand times more distressing for him by the belief that he was on his way to a far greater disaster.

Nine

L ARGE AND IMPRESSIVE but not of mansion dimensions, the house stood high on a hill with a sweep of superbly colourful countryside in front of it running down to Bradford on Avon. As the day drew to a close Lady Sarah and Rachel sat on a balcony. Brigadier-General John Churchill had just left to return to his army at Westonzoyland. The strain of the Monmouth campaign had begun to show on John Churchill. He had lost his temper that morning with Colonel Percy Kirke. Although unable to hear what was being said, Sarah had recognized the name 'McFeeley' that was spoken many times.

Rachel walked to stand with her hands placed wide on the horizontal rail that ran along the balcony. Her hair was pure glistening gold in the falling sun. With her back to Sarah, she said, 'You probably are aware that I envy you, Sarah.'

'Why on earth would a girl like you envy me?' Sarah gave a genuine gasp of astonishment.

'Lots of reasons,' Rachel replied, turning to rest her back against the rail as she looked at Sarah. 'You have John, a good, solid marriage, and a secure future to look forward to.'

Compared to her vivacious companion's energetic, to say the least, social life, Sarah's existence was a dreary one. For many years to come John Churchill would remain much more of a soldier than he was a husband. When the time did come for the roles to be reversed, then it would be too late, far too late.

'Security could sometimes be interpreted as suffocation, Rachel.'

Sarah hadn't really intended to say the last sentence. She certainly hadn't wanted to say it with such feeling that Rachel immediately scrutinized her face. This was a disturbing experience because Rachel had a perception that could better be described as a sixth sense.

'You know, don't you, Sarah?' Rachel made it more of a statement than a question.

Standing, Sarah went to the rail beside Rachel, looking out over the balcony so that they were facing in opposite directions. Rachel could read a face easier than other people could take in a page of a book.

'What do you believe that I know, Rachel?'

'You pretend not to know that I am talking of our bold Lieutenant McFeeley,' Rachel chided.

'The men you play your games with are so numerous, Rachel,' Sarah smiled, completely devoid of acrimony and criticism, 'that I cannot keep track.'

'This is different,' Rachel plucked a dandelion in seed and made a kissing 'O' with her lips to blow at it. 'He loves me, he loves me not, he loves me not. This is different, dear Sarah, because in this instance you wished many times that you had been in my place.'

'How can you say such a thing, Rachel?'

'That's irrelevant, Sarah. Nature does not recognize marriage, and I doubt that God does.'

'That is a terrible thing to say, Rachel!' an aghast Sarah objected.

'The truth is often terrible,' Rachel smiled. 'We must assume that if the Creator had planned monogamy, he wouldn't have it so that every male sword will fit into any female scabbard.'

'You deliberately try to shock, Rachel,' Sarah objected.

'I deliberately try to be candid,' Rachel corrected. 'There was something between you and Colm McFeeley that a blind man in a dark alleyway could detect. Deny it at your peril.'

'I can't think what you mean, Rachel!'

'You suppress what is natural in you,' Rachel said firmly. 'Just like those silly old spinsters who go to bed with two candles but only ever light one of them.'

'You are simply disgusting, Rachel,' Sarah protested, stifling a laugh.

'Fine, fine!' Rachel surrendered. 'Accept that you and Colm were fashioned for each other.'

'What would you have me do – abandon John?' Sarah cried.

'Good Lord, no,' Rachel exclaimed. 'You don't jump in the river because you are thirsty!'

'The whole idea is totally ridiculous, Rachel!'

Giving her a one-armed cuddle, Rachel at first chastised her gently. 'You sweet little fibber! You deserve some fun, Sarah, so I will arrange for you to meet Colm McFeeley.'

Lowering the spyglass, a downcast Monmouth turned to McFeeley. They were standing in the squat tower of Bridgwater's St Mary's Church, the highest point for miles around. The rebel leader had been looking out across the King's Sedgemoor Drain to where the little stationary white squares of tents and the moving red pinheads of soldiers could be seen. James Scott had welcomed him back effusively, but there was a reserve in him, nevertheless. McFeeley put this reserve down to suspicion, and both Jack and Piper had confirmed this by reporting to McFeeley that they were being watched at all times. This was bad news because it meant that when McFeeley had gathered intelligence of Monmouth's movements he couldn't use either of his two men to take it back to Captain Critchell.

'They are out there, in force, as I suspected,' Monmouth told McFeeley.

From outside there came to them a joyous chorus of a song soldiers were singing in praise of their rebel commander:

The Duke of Monmouth's at Bridgwater town,
All a-fighting for the Crown,
Ho, boys – Ho!

McFeeley commented, 'They are full of admiration for you, sir.'

'Half full of admiration, the other half is local cider,' a cynical Monmouth said. Then relenting, he added in a softer voice, his eyes misted, 'No, that is unkind. They are loyal, Lieutenant, and loyalty has become a rare commodity. I was promised a club-army ten thousand strong. When they joined me, Colm, there were just one hundred and sixty of them. My uncle has issued a proclamation undertaking to pardon all, at this stage, other than those who sailed with me from Holland. As Uncle James had planned, this has led to mass desertions.'

Monmouth had painted a true but gloomy picture, and McFeeley felt that it would soon become worse. The fine weather showed every sign of breaking, which would give the king's men, all but a few of whom were tented, yet another advantage over Monmouth's soldiers, who would be exposed to the rain. The rebel duke suddenly brightened.

'Yet, *nil desperandum*, Lieutenant, if as a Protestant I may be permitted two Latin words,' Monmouth said. 'I have a surprise or two to spring on the enemy.'

'I have never doubted you as a commander, sir,' McFeeley said sincerely.

'In all modesty, Colm, those who underestimate me do so at their folly. This very evening I am calling a council of war.'

Monmouth was as good as his word. The meeting with his senior officers was arranged to take place in an unoccupied farm labourer's cottage not far from St Mary's Church. Monmouth's new mistrust of him was confirmed for McFeeley when he received no order to attend.

Yet it was vital for McFeeley to know the full details of what was decided at the rebel duke's council of war. Timing it right, he set out in a dusk brought on early by heavy cloud and a drizzling of rain. Making his way through a series of meandering lanes, he paused a little way off from the building in which the rebel hierarchy was to assemble.

McFeeley made his way closer to the cottage. Just as he thought, the Duke of Monmouth had not considered it necessary to post sentries in this totally partisan town. Able to get to the back of the building, McFeeley pressed himself tightly to the wall as he slid along it until he reached the edge of a window.

'This morning, gentlemen,' Monmouth was saying, 'I was informed that a Sedgemoor peasant by the name of Godfrey sought an interview with me. I granted the fellow time, and was highly rewarded for doing so. My observation of the Royalist lines led me to believe that Feversham's horse are situated some considerable distance from his foot, and this fellow Godfrey says that this is so.

'It is possible for us to pass through their artillery unnoticed to make an incursion through enemy lines in strength by night. If we make two separate and simultaneous attacks on Feversham's infantry and cavalry, we can hit the enemy severely before he can be reinforced.'

'You are speaking of avoiding the Royalist guns on the Bridgwater road, Your Grace?' a voice McFeeley couldn't identify, asked.

'Exactly, Colonel Wade. You have a question, Colonel Fowke?'

'Not a question as such, Your Grace. I see that we would be presented with considerable difficulty at night in crossing Sedgemoor.'

'Ordinarily I would share your perturbation, Colonel,' Monmouth replied. The listening McFeeley noted how strong was his voice, and how buoyant he had become since they were earlier together in the church tower. 'But this Godfrey knows Sedgemoor like the back of his hand, and has agreed to guide us. We will complete the surprise by making a detour north of Chedzoy.'

This information had to be relayed to Critchell at once, McFeeley knew, but if Jack, Piper or he tried to leave Bridgwater with it they wouldn't get past the soldiers who would already have orders to shoot them down.

It was raining harder now as he heard Grey raise the question of a possible danger. 'My only reservation is the possibility that the redcoats are entrenched.'

'That likelihood occurred to me earlier,' Monmouth replied, revealing what a reliable strategist he was. 'I sent Godfrey back to Sedgemoor on reconnaissance. There are no trenches, no parapets. Feversham had posted neither guards nor piquets. What is more, gentlemen – many of Feversham's men are drunk on cider or are sleeping. In recommending this plan, gentlemen, I want it to have the unanimous support of you, my regimental commanders. Now, those in favour!'

A chorus of 'Aye' boomed around inside of the small cottage, and when Monmouth offered. 'Those against?' there was total silence.

'Thank you for that vote of confidence in me, gentlemen,' the duke said. 'I will ask you all now to come with me to St Mary's tower, where you may all use my glass to determine the deployment of the enemy and to learn the route that I intend us to take.'

A sense of urgency hit McFeeley, only to be knocked back by his frustration. Monmouth would be moving out soon, perhaps within the hour. There wasn't even time to seek out Captain Critchell. A direct message detailing the Duke of Monmouth's intentions had to go immediately to Feversham! But how?

Moving away from the window, McFeeley heard a scampering just a yard or two from him. It came to him that he hadn't been the only one spying on Monmouth. Some other person had been only feet from him, yet the two of them had been oblivious to each other.

Not prepared to leave any loose ends, McFeeley abandoned caution to spring through the darkness after whoever it was scurrying away at speed. Seeing the figure, small but speedy, was in his reach, McFeeley leapt to wrap both arms around it, slamming the light body against a dry stone wall and pinioning it there. It shook him to find that his captive was a young girl with an ashen but very pretty face. Made big by fear her eyes stared up at him.

'No, please, don't!' she pleaded.

'I intend you no harm, girl,' he assured her. 'What were you doing back there?'

'I could ask you the same thing, sire,' she retorted, having recovered her nerve now that she was free, and looked pointedly at his Monmouth uniform. 'If you are with James Scott then why do you need to spy on him, sire?'

'What has you say that I was spying, girl?'

'Well,' she looked at him defiantly. 'I was, so you must have been doing the same thing.'

'You have just made a dangerous admission,' McFeeley warned the girl.

'It don't make much difference now, sire. I would do anything for the Catholic King James – even die with his name on my lips if you intend to kill me.'

Impressed by her courage he asked. 'Do you have a name?'

'Kathleen Nerney, if it's anything to you.'

'Would you believe me if I told you that I am really an officer with King James's army, Kathleen?'

'I'd say I believed anything to have you let me go,' she replied frankly.

'I don't want to let you go. There is something you can do for the king, but it will put you at great risk.'

'Whatever it is, I'll do it,' she said from self-assurance and not bragging.

'How much did you hear back there?' McFeeley jerked his head back towards the cottage.

'Everything.'

'But how much do you remember of it?'

'Would you have me recite it word for word, sire?' she offered confidently.

'No.' McFeeley was made hesitant by the enormity of what he was about to ask of her. 'Tell me, do you think that you could find your way across Sedgemoor to the Royalist lines and back?'

'With my eyes closed, sire,' she said, again without a trace of boasting.

'Would you go in all haste to ask for an officer and tell him everything that you heard planned back there?'

'I will go, sire, with great speed, but they will not believe what a girl tells them, surely?'

This was a real possibility that he had overlooked, and McFeeley told her. 'You have to tell them that Lieutenant McFeeley sent you, Kathleen.'

'Is McFeeley your name?' she said with a pleased smile, girlishly more interested in finding this out than she was in the danger she would soon be facing.

'Yes. Now, tell them that I sent you, and that my credentials can be checked out with Captain Critchell at Brigadier Churchill's headquarters.' McFeeley said. 'Do you think that you can remember that, Kathleen?'

'My body is thin because we can't afford to buy food, sire, but do not judge the size of my brain by it,' Kathleen rebuked him.

McFeeley gave her bony shoulder an affectionate squeeze. 'I could never misjudge you.'

'Except for my father, Lieutenant McFeeley, you are the only man I've ever met and liked,' she told him in her forthright way. 'Where will I find you when I come back?'

Looking round him, McFeeley pointed to the graveyard that was at the far side of the church. The now steadily falling rain blurred the night a little. 'Do you see that bent tree at the corner of the grave-yard? I will be waiting there for you.'

'It's a bit spooky!' the girl giggled. Then she said. 'My father told us that it's the living we should be afraid of, not the dead. Is that what you think, Lieutenant McFeeley?'

'These days I don't know who or what to be frightened of, Kathleen,' he replied, looking at her concernedly. 'You are wet through, child.'

'I'll soon dry out when I start me running. I'd better be off. I'll be back very soon.'

Reluctant to let her go, McFeeley watched her trot off as easily as a schoolgirl late for class. Calling her name guardedly, he stopped her.

'Kathleen!'

'Yes?'

'I'm proud of you.'

'I'll make you more proud of me,' she promised with one of her little giggles before the night swallowed her up.

Lieutenant Bryan Riglar sat on grass that was still soaking wet even though the rain had stopped. Swigging from a bottle of cider, he wasn't even aware of the discomfort of the damp seeping through his clothing. This Somerset brew was powerful. It first hit the legs. That was a distressing experience. Paralysis set in and you first walked stiff-kneed and awkwardly before falling over. But when the cider spread up to your head it gave you back your legs while taking away your cares and your boredom. He lay back on the grass, spilling drink over his face and tunic, chuckling inanely as he heard Lieutenant Poore complaining.

'Not one damned sentry, not one piquet,' Poore moaned. 'Every damned man either drunk or asleep. What game is Feversham playing with us, Riglar?'

It was true about no guards having been posted, but not every soldier was either asleep or drunk. Over from where they sat drinking, a battalion of Dumbarton's regiment, strictly disciplined and distinctive with their white breeches and deep white cuffs, were going about their duties in the way that soldiers should.

'Our French commander does not consider James Scott's peasant army capable of instigating any kind of attack on us,' Riglar informed Poore. He moaned. 'I want more drink, and a woman.'

Unsteady on his feet, a third officer, a lieutenant named Fielder, came over to stand looking down at the piggish face of Riglar that had been given a sheen in the night by sweat and spilt drink.

'There's more cider, but the only female within miles is a cow, Riglar,' Fielder said in the grave way of a drunk.

'Then bring me a cow,' Riglar spluttered, then specifying, 'but it must be a black and white one.'

Flattened by his own wit, Riglar lay on his back, arms spread wide, howling with laughter. It was the toe of Fielder's boot in his side that slowed him down to a chortle.

'Shust!' Fielder hissed to silence him. 'I saw something moving down by the brook.'

All three of them were on their feet then, swaying as they made their way shoulder to shoulder down the gradual slope. The trio had been made both courageous and stupid by the cider and they went on further than they should have done. A slight movement of a shadow up ahead had all of them halt abruptly, turning back a little, ready to run. But the shadow straightened up to become the silhouette of a person, who was moving toward them.

'Who are you?' Riglar croaked hoarsely.

The figure came on, stumbling to its knees, calling to them as it got up. 'I have come from Lieutenant McFeeley.'

The name meant something vaguely to Riglar. Any possibility of him making something of it was finished by the fact that it was a girl's voice that had called.

All three officers rushed forwards, and as Riglar reached out to grab the thin figure with both hands to pull it close so that he could peer into the face, he exclaimed excitedly. 'By the Lord Protector! We have a comely wench here for our pleasure, my friends. Identify yourself!'

'I am Kathleen Nerney,' the girl fought to get out of Riglar's grip. 'I have been sent to give warning that Monmouth is to attack this very night.'

This made Riglar chuckle heartily, and his three companions joined in, chortling more when he said, 'The message is balderdash, boys, but the messenger is just what we need!'

'But Lieutenant McFeeley—' the girl tried to insist, her words altering to an incipient scream that was stifled by Riglar pulling her even closer to him and covered her mouth with his open one.

'Someone is coming, Riglar,' Poore gave a sibilant warning.

Approaching them down the slope, his gaitered legs twisted as he turned both feet to keep from slipping on the damp grass, was Dr Peter Mews, the Bishop of Winchester, who was staying in the camp for the night. As he came closer, Riglar clapped his hand hard over the girl's mouth and the other two officers moved so as to conceal her presence from the bishop.

'Is all quiet here, young sirs?' the bishop inquired, staying a little way off from them.

'Nary a sign of Monmouth, m'lord,' Lieutenant Poore, the least drunk of the three of them, replied.

Tilting his head back, Mews looked up at a full moon that had now shouldered its way through the earlier cloud to bring something similar to an inferior daylight to the night, and commented, 'The duke would be most unwise to attempt an assault this night.'

'We would see him clearly from twenty miles off, m'lord,' Poore agreed.

'Well then, all that remains is for me to bid you all a good and peaceful night, young sirs,' the bishop said, turning to struggle back up the slope on spindly legs.

As he went, Poore whispered anxiously to his two companions. 'Methinks we should convey to Captain Mackintosh what the girl has said.'

Mackintosh was in command of a company the Dumbartons, and was a diligent, efficient officer who would know whether or not to alert Colonel Douglas, the regimental commander.

'It is balderdash, Poore, forget it,' Riglar retorted angrily. 'Let us enjoy this gift sent to us by the god of soldiers.'

With that, Riglar wrenched at the girl's clothing. There was a ripping sound that carried on the night air, and the girl began a scream that was abruptly shut off as Riglar's meaty fist clipped her jaw.

Up on the crest Dr Mews paused, puzzled by two short sounds that had travelled through the night to him. Considering going back down to investigate, the bishop took a couple of steps back in the direction from which he had just come. Pausing again in indecision, he listened, heard nothing, told himself that he had imagined hearing something, turned again and carried on toward the Earl of Feversham's headquarters.

Decent, honest and a brave man of God, the bishop would have been mortified had he known what he had just walked away from.

Hidden in the shadows of the graveyard wall, McFeeley witnessed great activity all around him. Rural men, farmers one day and now soldiers the next, tumbled out of unfamiliar billets, obeying the call to action, but frightened now of the unknown that battle was to them. Monmouth's army was on the move. The clatter of horsemen's boots along cobbled streets became an orchestrated symphony of war as the jingle of spurs and a rattling of scabbards joined it. McFeeley, who had been part of many such assemblies of militia, could smell fear in the air as was to be expected, but it was diluted by the smell of cider. He thought for a moment of how fast and high the fear would soar if the effects of cider waned before no more than a musket's range would separate the two sides.

Listening and watching the road, he wanted to warn Kathleen Nerney of the presence of so many Monmouth men. His anxiety for the safety of the girl, acute when she had left him, was raging like the effects of a fever in his head now, when he had expected her to be back. Crossing Sedgemoor in the middle of the night would be hazardous enough for a girl in times of peace.

Once Kathleen had left, McFeeley had gone to Jack and Piper to tell them what was happening. They had agreed that their only course was to be a part of the Monmouth assault, then cross to their own lines as soon as it became possible to do so.

'We're going to have to make a show of fighting, sir,' Jonathan

Piper commented in his cool detached way, 'so who do we point our muskets at – our men or theirs?'

'Ours, soldier,' McFeeley had replied, 'but you aim high.'

To do that would be to satisfy the Monmouth men around them. Even so, getting safely to their own lines while wearing rebel uniforms would be a high-risk move. Yet it had to be done. Sergeant Jack had what would possibly be the best answer.

'If Feversham doesn't have a broad front,' Sergeant Jack had suggested, 'we'd probably stand a better chance if we flank our lines and come in from the rear.'

'A good tactic, as long as Monmouth's men don't shoot us in the back when we leave,' Piper had observed.

McFeeley had ended it there, for the time being. 'We'll make our plans on the spot when the time comes. We'll need to know the deployment of both sides before we decide. What is essential is that we stay together. We can only look out for each other if we don't become separated.'

Thinking back on that conversation with his men had McFeeley fully grasp, perhaps for the first time, the bizarre situation they were heading into. In his time he had operated behind enemy lines. He had been on patrols to snatch prisoners in the night, and had even allowed himself to be captured to gain entrance to an enemy camp, but this would be the first time he would have to pretend to actually be a member of, and fight with, the opposing side.

Stilling his mind then, he tuned in his ears to pick up every sound around him. Believing that he had heard Kathleen's furtive return, but prepared to believe that he was wishfully fooling himself, he peered out into the lane she would come down. It was deserted! McFeeley pulled back into his hiding place, reaching for his knife as he heard a slight sound from the gravestones behind him.

There was someone back there, McFeeley was sure of it. While he had been concentrating out ahead of him he'd been crept up on from behind. Carefully and silently placing his musket on the ground, McFeeley placed his knife sideways in his mouth, gripping the blade with his teeth and leaving his hands free to feel his way through the gravestones in the dark. He was moving off when he heard his name called softly from behind him.

'Lieutenant McFeeley?'

It was Kathleen, and in his relief McFeeley blurted words louder than he intended. 'Kathleen! Thank God! Did you get the message through?'

'They wouldn't believe me,' she told him from out of the darkness, her voice breaking up so that it was barely audible.

Assuming that she had been running hard, McFeeley asked. 'Who did you speak to?'

'Lieutenant Rig … lar,' she told him shakily.

Instantly placing the ugly young officer who had imprisoned him at Colonel Kirke's camp, McFeeley silently cursed the bad luck that had the girl find such a pig of a man. Though disappointed McFeeley called fondly to the girl. 'You did well, Kathleen. Come out now, I'm here by the wall.'

'I can't, I can't,' the girl began to sob.

'It is all right, Kathleen,' he said coaxingly. 'Come to me, child, I am your friend.'

She stepped out from behind a tall angel carved out of stone. The full power of the moon illuminated her clearly, and McFeeley swung an anxious head towards the street. They were safe for the moment. Turning back to the girl, McFeeley, a man of steel, shrank back when he saw the state of her. He couldn't bear to look at the child, but knew that he must force himself. Her pretty face was swollen so badly that she was barely recognizable. Her hair, carefully combed back and tied with a ribbon when he had last seen her, was as unruly as that of a witch at the cauldron. Torn and hanging in shreds, her clothes were a mess, and she was splattered all over with what could have been mud, or might have been blood. Of the opinion that it was both, but unable to tell, McFeeley stepped out and extended his arms to her.

Cringing away from him Kathleen let out a mournful little howl that was like that of a small, wounded animal. 'Oooh, sire, they had me! They had me and treated me real cruel, sire!'

'You poor child,' McFeeley groaned, reaching out for her.

Avoiding him, the girl staggered past McFeeley. Out in the lane she did a reeling run. He called after her, 'Kathleen!' as loud as he could risk. Either not hearing or ignoring him, the girl went on. He saw her falling this way and that on thin, unsteady legs.

When she first blended with the shadows and was then snatched away by the night, McFeeley had to brush his right forearm across his eyes, angry with himself for being a soft fool.

As it formed up on the Eastern Causeway, the old Bristol road, it wasn't the kind of army that McFeeley was used to. There was more enthusiasm than he had known in soldiers before a battle, but far less discipline. The Duke of Monmouth was up ahead, a strange look to him in the night due to having exchanged his beaver for a helmet. His Light Guard of Horse attended him, while next came the Blue Regiment, of which McFeeley, Jack and Piper were members. Behind them were White, Red, Green and Yellow Regiments, with the Lyme Independent company bringing up the rear. Lord Grey of Werke looked a superb cavalryman at the head of his six hundred horse. Accepting that quantity was no substitute for quality where warriors were concerned, McFeeley estimated as he looked down the columns that they would outnumber the king's men.

'Hang me, if I am not pleased extremely with this new-fashioned caterwauling, this midnight coursing in the park,' Piper said, obviously making a quotation.

'What are you talking about, Piper?' McFeeley asked edgily, still morose from his sad encounter with Kathleen Nerney.

'Wycherley,' the soldier told him brightly. 'His *Love in a Wood*.'

'Save it for the ladies, Piper. Me and Jack don't speak theatre.'

'I was merely making a point, sir, as Wycherley was. He spoke of London's nightlife, which I once knew so well. Wycherley's character, Ranger, was referring to the unlit walks of St James's Park where the scented women of the night paraded in masks, exchanging badinage and making assignments with the men who accosted them.'

'I have tried, Piper,' McFeeley said, finding that the soldier was lifting his spirits, 'but I'll be damned if I can detect your point.'

Nodding at the raggedy rows of men around them, Piper said, 'You surprise me, sir. I thought it plain that what we see here is much more reminiscent of that parade of ladies than any line-up of militia I have ever witnessed.'

Judging the estimation to have been an accurate one, McFeeley gave a short laugh and was about to tell Piper so when he saw some kind of diversion taking place a little way off. Two men were down by the banks of the River Parrett, calling excitedly up to their comrades and waving their arms in animation.

Curiosity had McFeeley follow those who broke rank to go down to the river-bank, Jack and Piper going with him. They saw one of the men knee deep in water, tugging at something.

'It's a sheep,' one of the men on the bank shouted. 'Pull it out, William, and if it ain't been in the water over long then we'll roast 'er later and have us'selves a feast later this night.'

There were more men splashing into the river now to assist the first man in dragging his find to the bank. Then a startled shout went up. 'Land sakes! 'Tis not a sheep at all, but a body! Give I a hand here, my boyos!'

Ten

DISINTERESTED, ANXIOUS FOR the battle to begin so that they could get back to their own army, McFeeley and his two companions stood a little way off. They heard a shout. 'It's a lad! Do any of you know who 'tis?' Then came an awed gasp. 'T'ain't a lad. T'ain't a lad. Look, the clothes is all torn and you can see 'tis a young maid we got 'ere! Pull 'er out onto the bank, my boys.'

McFeeley startled Jack and Piper by springing forwards. When they caught up with him he was peering between the heads of those standing in front of him, trying to see what was happening. He shoved his way through with a shoulder just as one of the men looking down at the body on the bank made a crude remark.

There was total mayhem then. McFeeley felled the man with a rabbit punch to the back of the neck, then bent to pick up the thin little body of Kathleen Nerney. A friend of the man McFeeley had struck was swinging a pikestaff at him until the sergeant back-heeled him in the groin. Another Monmouth soldier drew his sword, ready to deal with McFeeley, who now held the dripping corpse in both arms. From a couple of yards away Jonathan Piper drew a small knife from a sheath at the back of his neck, throwing it all in one swift movement. The blade thudded into the swordsman's chest, rasping against ribs as it went. Coughing out an eruption of thick red blood, the man dropped his sword and pitched head first into the river.

'You men,' Sergeant Jack ordered. 'Get back to your places.'

They meekly obeyed, helping the man McFeeley had hit, who was rubbing his sore neck, and leaving behind a former comrade who was now no more than a spreading patch of blood on the surface of the water. Piper stood looking anxiously at the back of McFeeley who, still carrying the body of the girl, was walking away into the night, climbing a fairly steep hill. When the young soldier started to go after the lieutenant, Jack stopped him.

'Let him go, Jonathan, let him go. Never go uninvited to McFeeley,' Jack advised.

They moved back to stand with the others, waiting for the command to move out. Coming back down the hill, free of his burden now, McFeeley walked along the columns, pausing to call, 'Is there a preacher here?'

'Perhaps I could help,' a tall, dignified man with long, prematurely grey hair offered, stepping out of the ranks of militia.

'Are you a clergyman?' McFeeley inquired hopefully,

'Of a sort, if I am not being unduly immodest,' the tall man replied. 'I am John Whiting, sir, a Quaker.'

'Do you know some burial prayers, John Whiting?'

'A prayer, sir, should be from the heart, not from the memory,' Whiting advised McFeeley.

'You'll do for me, John. Let us walk to that hill,' McFeeley said, going off with Whiting at his side.

'Is it a comrade?' Whiting asked solicitously as they climbed the hill together.

'No, John, the deceased is not a soldier, it is a she. A brave maiden from Bridgwater who was superior to all of us, including Monmouth and King James II,' McFeeley said. 'Yet she was nought but a child.'

'Then forever cherish her memory,' John Whiting advised when they reached the small grave, which McFeeley had dug to bury the girl in. It was at the top of a hill that in daylight would overlook the town of Bridgwater. 'Let her live on in your heart, my friend, as she will wish to do. I don't have your name...?'

'Lieutenant McFeeley. Colm McFeeley.'

'Then bow your head and empty your mind of all thought, Colm, and I will offer up a plea to the Lord for your little friend.'

As he stood respectfully still as the Quaker said prayers, it seemed to McFeeley that Kathleen Nerney was somehow present in the ground-clinging fog that swirled around their legs. It would not have surprised him to hear her voice, so full of life and quick wit when he had first met her; so shattered and full of suffering when she had walked away from him for the last time.

When the two of them went back down the hill it was to find that Monmouth, protected by his own Life Guard of Horse riding fore and aft of him, had given his makeshift and furtive army the signal to begin its night march. Shaking each other's hand, McFeeley and John Whiting parted then to join their respective units. They marched northwards for the first mile or two; McFeeley was flanked by Jack on one side and Piper on the other. The latter had gathered information in McFeeley's absence, and gave his report as they marched.

'What route are we taking?' McFeeley wanted to know.

'I only learned the first part, sir, which is to keep that village over there, Chedzoy, to our right. The people there are loyal to the king, and Monmouth's scouts believe there could be a patrol of Lord Oxford's regiment located there.'

'Sir Francis Compton's lads,' McFeeley commented. 'They are good!'

The sergeant spoke for the first time since they had set off, to complain. 'Better than this lot we're with. Look at them, sir! They should be muck-spreading not fighting.'

The column forked right then to slip and slither down muddy Bradney Lane, heading for Sedgemoor. McFeeley saw Monmouth, confident that surprise would bring him victory, leave the baggage wagons, more than forty of them, at Peazy Farm. He also left a guard detail complete with one of the cannon with the wagons, with orders for them to move north once the Royalists had been defeated.

McFeeley's opinion of the Duke of Monmouth, which waxed and waned according to circumstance, was boosted now as the rebel duke, his civilian scout, Godfrey, at his side, led his army over the first drainage rhine, the Black Ditch, with great skill. However, a confused muddle, not the fault of Monmouth, followed when he paused to have Earl Grey of Werke bring up his horse to form a parallel column. A watching McFeeley immediately identified the problem as being caused by inexperienced horsemen and unschooled horses.

'They should never have left the farm!' Jack groaned.

When some kind of equine order had been restored, Monmouth rode back to the Blue Regiment to summon McFeeley. 'Lieutenant McFeeley!'

'Your Grace,' McFeeley responded, stepping forward.

Dismounting, Monmouth led his horse away from the soldiers, beckoning McFeeley to follow until they reached a position where they could have a conversation without fear of being overheard.

'It seems that I owe you an apology, Lieutenant,' the rebel duke said.

'Why should that be, Your Grace?' a puzzled McFeeley asked. Now that engagement of the enemy was close, Monmouth wore the calm mantle of a true military commander.

'Because I doubted you, Colm, which I confess,' Monmouth replied. 'A man in my position, a position that is possibly unique in the history of this country, must be prudent when placing trust.'

'In what manner did you mistrust me, Your Grace?' McFeeley inquired, wondering if they were speaking of Lady Henrietta, but pretty sure that Monmouth referred to his campaign.

The rebel leader permitted himself a wry smile, 'I am given to understand that we share a mutual interest in a lady now in Taunton, Colm, but I do not view that as a contentious issue! Your long absence from my command caused me to doubt your allegiance. It was remiss of me. Please forgive me, my friend, and tell me if you are prepared to carry out a special duty for me?'

'What would you have me do, Your Grace?' McFeeley reasoned that a special duty may well facilitate a return to their own lines for his two men and himself.

Monmouth explained. 'We will shortly be crossing the next drainage channel, the Langmoor rhine. That will bring us within some three quarters of a mile of the enemy camp, Lieutenant. Once over that ditch I will be sending Earl Grey and his cavalry on ahead, together with Godfrey, my guide. What I am about to say now, Colm, is for your ears only. The truth is that I cannot put any dependency on Lord Grey when he is under pressure. I want you to choose thirty good men to move up tight behind Grey. I want you to be close behind Lord Grey so that you can force him to accept that it will be less frightening for him to advance against the enemy than it would be to turn and face you.'

'To what extent can I go to so as to achieve that effect, Your Grace?'

'There is no limit, Colm,' Monmouth said, eyes averted. 'We are going into a fight that I must win. You can take any measure necessary to have the cavalry continue to advance.'

This was a golden escape opportunity, McFeeley recognized. He had even been granted a licence to blast Earl Grey of Werke out of the saddle if necessary. Monmouth's willingness to sacrifice his second-in-command also made McFeeley feel easier about his eventual betrayal of the rebel duke.

'I will do what I have to do, Your Grace,' he replied in what sounded like a solemn promise although the words meant nothing.

Grasping his saddle-horn, Monmouth prepared to mount, but he paused to reflect. 'If only we knew what the next few hours hold for us, Colm! This is not what I anticipated. My army is weak and inefficient but I was led to expect strength and proficiency, my friend. I was content in my Netherlands home, Colm, really happy, possibly for the first time. I had no wish for this, whatsoever. Yet those who wanted a revolution involved me. Now that the hour has come for battle to be done, they are in their homes, cringing like the cowards they are.'

Feeling sympathy for the duke, McFeeley made no response as Monmouth swung up into the saddle. Though he accepted what the duke had said about being induced to take up arms against his uncle, McFeeley didn't doubt that the rebel leader had omitted to say that he had dreamed the dream of being king, a dream that would shortly become an awesome nightmare.

Leaning down out of the saddle, Monmouth stretched his right hand out to McFeeley. 'I pray that we shall stand together in victory at dawn. If not, and you should survive me, please hold a memory of me in a small corner of your heart.'

'I will never forget you, Your Grace,' McFeeley truthfully replied.

Returning to Jack and Piper he explained that they were to make up a special group to follow the cavalry when it moved out.

'How am I going to select thirty good men from among this collection of dolts?' the sergeant complained.

'The idea is not to select good men, Jack,' McFeeley corrected his sergeant. 'If we are going to get away we need to have thirty of the most stupid Monmouth soldiers with us.'

Understanding, the sergeant grinned as he moved among the troops making his careful selection. There was some kind of chaos up ahead now. McFeeley gathered that Godfrey, who 'did know Sedgemoor better'n any other man,' had become lost in the fog and missed the giant boulder, the Langmoor Stone, that marked the crossing place of the Langmoor Rhine. At last, to the relief of everyone including McFeeley and his two king's men, the plungeon was located and the silent Monmouth army crossed the drainage ditch.

Up ahead of them Monmouth was sending Grey out, Godfrey at his side and eight troops of cavalry behind him.

McFeeley had Jack move his men off, tight behind the horse, when a single shot behind them shattered the stillness of the night. Listening to the sounds going on to the rear, McFeeley gathered that one of Compton's blue-coated troopers had ridden out of the fog to stumble upon the Monmouth army. As surprised as the men he had almost collided with, the trooper had fired a shot to raise the alarm.

As the drummers set up a steady pounding, McFeeley could imagine the activity taking place in the camps of the king's army. Perhaps it would be too much to say that the Compton trooper blundering on his army in the fog had sealed Monmouth's fate, but it had drastically reduced his chances of success.

'Lord Grey! Lord Grey!' a mounted messenger was calling through the fog.

'Here, soldier, here!' Grey called back.

McFeeley led his men towards Grey's voice, able to see the misty outline of the messenger ride up to the cavalry commander.

'Compliments of the Duke of Monmouth, my lord,' the messenger began. 'His Grace commands that you take advantage of what surprise remains. You are to attack and fire the village of Chedzoy immediately, my lord!'

Then Grey was leading his cavalry forwards at a dash. Running behind although losing ground, McFeeley had Jack and Piper beside him, all three of them calling back to exhort their squad to follow. It was cruel, but when they eventually faced their own lines they would have more chance if they presented thirty Monmouth men for the king's soldiers to shoot at.

Moving at a steady trot, McFeeley brought his musket up to cover a stocky figure that came looming out of the mist towards them. A civilian, he had a chubby face that was quivering animatedly as McFeeley demanded to know who he was. McFeeley shouted, 'Hold fast, stranger.'

'I am Godfrey,' the scout gasped out his identification then said, 'It's a disaster, it's a disaster.'

'What's happened?' McFeeley grabbed Godfrey's jerkin, shaking him violently.

'Lord Grey dismissed me. He's gone on ahead. Oh, my God, sir, it's a disaster,' Godfrey moaned, his eyes rolling in his head. 'They'll be at the Bussex Rhine by now. 'Tis dreadful broad and there's only one way across. My lord don't know the way, sir, and the foe's waiting on the far side.'

'The man's a fool,' McFeeley cursed Grey.

McFeeley's squad came upon Monmouth's cavalry, which was in complete disarray. They were milling around, riding up and down the bank, seeking a way across the ditch, colliding with each other, having the horses panic. It was a sight that distressed McFeeley. Notwithstanding the need of him and his two men to rejoin the king's army, he couldn't stomach the mass slaughter that Grey was setting his horsemen up for.

'Lord Grey!' he yelled, spotting the cavalry commander and running up to him.

Swinging his head to take a look at McFeeley, Grey ignored him from then on. Pointing an arm to where lights were sparkling on the far side of the Bussex ditch, Grey informed his senior officers who were gathered round him, fighting to control their horses. 'There before us, gentlemen, are the lights of Weston!'

He was mistaken, horribly mistaken, McFeeley knew. What Grey was observing was not the lights of a village, but the matches of the Dumbarton regiment, which McFeeley knew was the only regiment in Feversham's army to still use matchlocks. What Grey believed were harmless illuminations were muskets ready to deal out death.

'Who are you?' a shouted challenge came from the other side of the wide, deep and soft-bottomed ditch.

One of Grey's officers showed a much greater presence of mind than he did. The officer called back. 'We are horse with the militia of the Duke of Albemarle!'

This quick-thinking answer satisfied this challenger, but the challenge was repeated further down the bank. 'Who do you ride with?'

Stay cool! Stay cool! McFeeley did a mute pleading. The sound of the rebel duke's columns of foot soldiers behind told him that they were fast coming close. When the king's men opened up, as they surely must before long, Monmouth would suffer horrific losses at a stroke. 'Do you think the three of us could cross further down, sir?' Piper whispered close to McFeeley's ear.

Shaking his head, McFeeley cancelled out the idea. The Bussex Rhine that was defying Monmouth's cavalry would bog Jack, Piper and himself down if they tried to cross it. They would be sitting ducks for the musketeers of the king's army, who would regard them as rebels.

'Who do you ride with?'

The challenge was repeated, suspicion in the voice of the officer who was calling. Doubting that Grey's officers would be successful the second time by claiming to be with Albemarle's militia, McFeeley hadn't predicted just how swiftly things would go wrong.

One of Grey's officers broke under the strain that had been building up. 'We are for Monmouth, and God with us!'

Everything, including every movement of men and horses, seemed to be held in suspension for a longish period after that proud but crazy shout. Then life restarted and pandemonium reigned as the first volley of that night rang out. Monmouth men toppled from their saddles. The dead fell heavily with no more than a feeble groan, but the wounded shrieked as loud as the screaming of their terrified horses. Soldiers turned and ran off into the night, and deserting horsemen who were gradually regaining control of their mounts followed them.

'What a mess!' Piper exclaimed in disbelief.

'Stay out of it,' McFeeley warned, speaking only to Jack and Piper because the thirty men they'd had with them had run away from the terrible scene.

'Are you with me, Lieutenant McFeeley?' Monmouth's shout came to pull McFeeley's attention to where the duke stood holding an infantry officer's half-pike.

In the grip of conflicting loyalties, McFeeley hesitated initially. He was aware that he owed allegiance to King James II, but he couldn't push Henrietta from his mind. Thinking of her waiting with the child she was carrying back in Taunton, he spoke sharply to Jack and Piper.

'You two wait here!' he ordered. 'Keep yourselves safe by staying clear of the fighting.'

'Why help him, sir?' Jack questioned.

'Monmouth is finished, sir,' Piper called to McFeeley, who was moving away. 'You can do nothing to save him!'

'I'm doing it for the unborn!' McFeeley called, aware they wouldn't know what he was talking about.

He was up beside Monmouth then, who, seeing him arrive, spoke bitterly through the noise and acrid smoke of battle. 'Lost by the cowardice of my Lord Grey, Colm!'

Having determined a strategy of affording Monmouth what protection he could while at the same time not firing on his own men, McFeeley had misgivings at first when Jack and Piper disobeyed orders to join him. The rebel duke had come into his own. Full of courage and vitality he led his column of foot from the front. Exposing himself to the fire from across the Bussex, he kept tight control of his Blue Regiment, deploying them along the bank of the rhine, holding their fire as they settled in so as to be effective when the order came. But the situation was made additionally hazardous by the following White and Red Regiments. Nerves shattered, they were discharging their muskets without waiting for an order to fire. Consequently, as they gathered round the rebel duke to shield him, he, McFeeley, Jack, and Piper were in a precarious position with a fusillade of fire coming from the foe in front and the friend behind. Bullets were whistling by them, passing close.

Yet from the absolute chaos, Monmouth displayed his genius by restoring an order that astonished McFeeley and must have caused great concern to the king's men at the other side of the ditch. Twisting this way and that, as if he could sense the trajectory of every bullet, the rebel leader, with McFeeley and his two men at his heels, ran to where his cannon had been brought up. From their accents McFeeley judged the two artillerymen to be Dutch. They were certainly fine soldiers and experts at their job. Staying calm as mayhem went on noisily and dangerously around them they obeyed Monmouth's order and fired their three small iron field-pieces.

The result among the king's men across the rhine must have been devastating. The heavy balls must have cut swaths through the tightly packed ranks of Dumbartons, and McFeeley's heart went out to his real comrades. From the Royalist side of the ditch the staccato, nervy shouts of officers struggled to be heard above the anguished yells of wounded men, the neighing and snorting of frightened chargers and the occasional blood-curdling scream of a mortally wounded horse.

Again the cannon fired to inflict great damage among the king's men. Monmouth, seeing his chance and recognizing it as probably his last hope of victory, was an inspiration to his foot soldiers as he risked his life over and over again to rally their commanders.

'If he moves his foot across right now,' Piper said to McFeeley and Jack, 'following up on the opening blasted by his artillery, we may not have an army to go back to.'

'A single musket shot would end Monmouth and his campaign,' McFeeley observed.

It seemed impossible to get the rebel soldiers under control. Striding up and down, ordering, pleading, cajoling, threatening, Monmouth looked capable of achieving such a miracle at any moment. This put McFeeley into a quandary. Now that his subversive work, which had been unsuccessful, had come to an end, his duty was to do whatever he could to halt or impede the rebellion. He could finish it by putting a bullet into the brave rebel duke.

Unable to fire the shot himself, McFeeley would not order either Jack or Piper to do so. Yet he was tormented by guilt as he listened to the cries of his comrades at the far side of the ditch, and saw Monmouth's foot take heart from the damage done by their artillery, and begin to make preparations to advance.

*

Brigadier-General John Churchill was alive to the serious situation that his Royal army was in. Having made his priority the silencing of Monmouth's miniature cannon he'd ordered three of the guns along the Bridgwater road to be brought up. But when this superior artillery was close to the Bussex rhine the wheels sank deep into ground so soft that it was impossible to manhandle the guns into position.

'I see your problem, my lord,' Bishop Mews said as he looked out to where soldiers unsuccessfully fought to move the guns. Then Mews went on to have Churchill become ashamed of his thoughts about interference from the bishop. 'Have your men use my carriage horses, my lord. They are more than capable of bringing your guns forward.'

Rapping out orders after offering Mews brief thanks, Churchill had the guns pulled into position by the bishop's horses. Soon they were in action, roaring as they returned the rebel cannon fire something like tenfold.

With this taken care of, Churchill moved swiftly and cleverly. His right flank had taken the brunt of Monmouth's attack, and the brigadier reinforced this with the Queen Dowager's under Colonel Percy Kirke, and Trelawney's who were commanded by his brother Charles Churchill. He had these two units move up behind and to the right of the three Guards battalions he already had in action there against the rebels. This done, Churchill then personally led a troop of his dragoons across the rhine to hit Monmouth's tiny artillery section, having a company of foot follow him to take care of the mopping up after he had hit the Monmouth cannon hard.

When Churchill had left, the mostly comatose Lord Feversham came angrily to life, vowing. 'By God, I'll make these rebels pay for their effrontery!'

He ordered the main body of Life Guards and Horse Grenadiers, together with four troops of dragoons across the ditch. At the same time more Royal Cavalry returned from patrol work on the Bridgwater road to back up the infantry that was moving up onto Monmouth's left.

Despite their huge numbers and superior equipment, the king's men were repulsed on many fronts by stiff opposition from the rebels. The Monmouth scythemen had no respect for the king's cavaliers. Standing their ground they swung and slashed at the Royal Cavalry, keeping them at bay.

The night was filled with a mixture of noises – there was musket and pistol shot, the metallic clang of sword against scythe, the bell-like jingling of bit and bridle and the thunder of hoofs on rushy ground. It was a fight to the finish, and John Churchill was in no doubt over whom the victor would be.

'From what you say, Critchell, I'm to be deprived of the chance of confronting James Scott's army,' the Duke of Calvert's face registered regret as he poured sherry for Captain Critchell and Lady Sarah and Rachel, who were guests at his Bristol home.

'My regret is that I am unable to be there at the finish,' Critchell said. 'When I left Lord Churchill he was confident that this night would see an end to the rebellion.'

Listening, Lady Sarah felt that she was expected to inquire after her husband, but she was afraid that her words would come out jumbled if she attempted to speak. She was terribly confused, and filled with remorse, because she had been worrying over the safety of McFeeley rather than being concerned about her husband. Rachel had said nothing on the subject since they had left Bradford on Avon, but Sarah suspected that her astute companion was aware of the turmoil she was in. It was Rachel who filled in for her now as she sweetly made an inquiry.

'And what word of my John Churchill, Captain Critchell?' she asked. 'Both Lady Sarah and myself have been worrying about John. Is he in any peril?'

'No military commander, particularly an actively involved leader such as the Brigadier avoids danger, Rachel. But you can both rest assured that he will come to no harm putting down this revolution,' Critchell smiled at them both as he gave the message, forgetting his prominent tooth for a moment, pulling a peculiar face as he quickly covered it with his top lip.

There was no reason to feel shame, Sarah told herself, for she had been most concerned about her husband, although worry over the rugged McFeeley had taken precedence. It had been frightening coming here. Thousands of the king's soldiers had lined the road ready to defend Bristol, and they'd had to be escorted across the Avon because the Keynsham bridge had been broken by Royal command, although it was still well guarded.

Then Sarah was unable to believe her ears as she heard Rachel questioning Critchell further, and she knew that Rachel was really asking on her behalf.

'That officer who brought Lady Sarah and myself away from White Lackington, Captain, Lieutenant McSweeney, wasn't it?' Rachel asked, deliberately getting the name wrong to disguise real interest.

'McFeeley,' Captain Critchell corrected. 'Yes...?'

'We were much impressed by his resourcefulness and compe-tence,' Rachel said vaguely. 'I, that is, we, imagine that so efficient an officer will be in this battle you report to be going on at Bridgwater.'

'To the best of my knowledge, yes, Lieutenant McFeeley is at Sedgemoor,' Critchell replied, adding mysteriously, 'but I much regret, ladies, that I am unable to give any further information about that particular officer.'

Why not, Lady Sarah wondered. During the time of her marriage, which had involved her with the army, she had never known an officer performing his duties with the autonomy permitted to Lieutenant McFeeley. It was as if he did not belong fully to the army as the other officers and men did. That was fitting, for McFeeley had a definite air of independence about him.

I am thinking of him again, she rebuked herself. There was no point in doing so. Not only were she and the tough lieutenant on opposite sides of the social charm, but, in spite of Rachel's vow that she would fix her up with a meeting, Sarah had accepted that she would never again clap eyes on McFeeley. She and Rachel had been sent here to the security of Bristol to await the quelling of the rebel-lion. Then they would enjoy a leisurely journey through the West Country and back to London.

'Would I be out of line to inquire as to your brief, Captain

Critchell?' the Duke of Calvert asked with a smile that was apologetic in advance. 'Only I would have thought that an officer of your calibre and experience would be invaluable in this Sedgemoor business.'

Going thoughtful, Critchell gave a wry smile. 'Once upon a time perhaps, Your Grace. I suppose it is right due to my advanced years, but of late I have been more and more of a shadowy soldier with assignments that are conducted clandestinely, as it were.'

This interested Sarah. Whenever she had heard McFeeley's name spoken, either Captain Critchell was there or his name was included in the conversation. It seemed to her that both of them belonged to a branch of the army she knew nothing of.

'Espionage, old boy?' Calvert raised a questioning eyebrow.

'Perhaps it occasionally comes close to the dramatic,' Critchell gave a modest smile, 'but my present mission is much more mundane, although some might say it would best be described as macabre.'

'My word, you do have us intrigued, Captain,' Rachel prompted him to go on.

'It is not something that should be discussed with ladies present, my dear Rachel.'

'We have been close to the heart of James Scott's rebellion from the start, Captain,' a piqued Rachel pouted, 'and I doubt that anything remains that could shock us.'

'As you wish,' Critchell shrugged. 'I carry orders to the commanders of loyalist troops. Orders, incidentally, that come direct from his majesty the king. They are to capture as many fugitive rebels as possible and hand them over to the civil authorities for trial in due course as traitors.'

'Oh, my God!' Sarah gasped. 'But treason carries a most frightful penalty.'

'Hanging, drawing and quartering,' the Duke of Calvert confirmed for her, increasing Sarah's anguish before he turned to Critchell. 'But that would be an enormous task for the civil courts, Captain. Surely it wouldn't be workable?'

'On the contrary,' Critchell answered. 'Arrangements are already in hand to facilitate the trials of an expected huge number of rebels.

For this purpose a special Commission of Oyer and Terminer and General Gaol Delivery is to be issued to Lord Chief Justice Jeffreys and four of his brother judges.'

Up to that time Lady Sarah Churchill had been ill at ease with Englishman fighting Englishman, a king opposing a king, nephew at war with uncle, but now the whole web of intrigue had become terribly sinister. What Captain Critchell had just revealed bore no relation to magnanimous victory or gracious defeat. It smacked of pure vengeance.

'I can't see my husband being party to so vindictive and gruesome a process,' Sarah exclaimed.

'Brigadier Churchill will not be involved, Lady Sarah,' Critchell assured her. 'When the soldier has fought the war the politician takes over.'

'The war will come to an end but the killing won't stop for many a long day,' added the Duke of Calvert.

'Surely the defeat of James Scott will suffice,' Rachel opined.

Shaking his head sadly, Critchell told her, 'The king would probably be satisfied had James Scott and his army collapsed when the shooting started, Rachel, but he came close to snatching success. For that neither Scott nor anyone who supported him will ever be forgiven.'

Eleven

'AMMUNITION!' THE CRY went up in the hard-pressed rebel ranks. 'For the Lord's sake, ammunition!' Monmouth's men were desperately short of ammunition, and as McFeeley and his two men stayed close to the rebel duke, who still gamely roused and inspired his men, they knew the end had to be close. The able Brigadier Churchill had brought three companies across the rhine to fight the rebels head on in hand-to-hand fighting while engaging them with musket fire on their flank. Then the Household Cavalry joined the fray. They rode in hard, two lines abreast as they charged into pistol range. Firing their volley, the order was yelled to, 'Draw swords!' and what followed was better described as slaughter rather than warfare.

With the Duke of Monmouth standing his ground, McFeeley's position was becoming more untenable as each second dragged by. Had Jack, Piper and he been fully involved they could have adapted to the situation. But they were in a state of limbo that could only end badly.

'My Lord! My Lord; our ranks are broken, my Lord, the time has come to flee!' came a cry that was soon drowned out by the sounds of battle, as Monmouth's personal servant came dashing up with his clothing spattered with the viscera of others.

McFeeley watched the rebel leader made into a statue by indecision. He stared ahead at the advancing Royalist hordes, saying to McFeeley in a croaking voice, 'With all the world behind me these fellows could not be stopped now, Colm!'

Grey, accompanied by several men, one of whom McFeeley recognized as Dr Oliver, Monmouth's surgeon, came running up shouting, 'All is lost, James, all is lost! We must fall back.'

Slowly the rebel duke came alive, pulling off his helmet to cast it aside. Then he ripped off his breastplate and threw it on the ground before taking to his heels and running off with the others through his men, who were dying all around him. It was an awesome scene of carnage. McFeeley realized the duke would find no sanctuary anywhere. His enemies awaited him all over the country.

Bringing himself back to the plight this left his two men and him in, McFeeley beckoned them and they ran together, going down to the basin of the Bussex. A decision had to be made, but McFeeley couldn't bring himself to make it. All three of them carried muskets, which they well had need of to defend themselves. But if they approached the lines of the king's army while armed and wearing rebel uniforms, then they were likely to be shot on sight.

'Disband arms,' he gave the order as they stopped in a dark hollow to regain their breath. Jack and Piper looked at him hesitantly, not immediately obeying the order.

'Who be you?' a voice barked the question from above them on the bank of the rhine.

A big man appeared in a scarlet coat, the three ostrich feathers in his beaver, two white and one red, telling them he was with the Life Guards. He held a musket prepared to fire, aiming at McFeeley.

There was time for McFeeley to get the Life Guard, but he couldn't kill one of his own. Beside him Piper was muttering curses of frustration. This is it! With his death imminent, McFeeley felt strangely calm. It was a calmness that ended abruptly when a musket exploded.

As McFeeley looked up at him the big Life Guard let the weapon drop from lifeless fingers, clutching his ample belly with both hands, and pitched forwards into the ditch.

'I had to do it!' Sergeant Jack said, to no one in particular.

'Let's get moving,' McFeeley said urgently.

Piper was already at his side, eager to be away, but McFeeley had to grab Jack by the shoulder to pull him along a few steps before he would move under his own volition. A volley of musket fire came from further along the ditch. Turning to look, they saw a row of king's infantrymen standing on the bank of the ditch in line, having just shot down the rebels who had recently passed McFeeley and the other two.

'We retain our muskets,' McFeeley said firmly.

It was raining, heavily, as they set off at a trot, the sounds of the rout of Monmouth's army going on at a distance behind them, the muffled sound of gunfire and men shouting orders that mingled with the cries of distress. Appreciating the comparative peace around them, it was suddenly shattered by a group of panicking Monmouth horse coming over the bank, heading straight for them. In close pursuit was a troop of Household Cavalry. The marshy floor of the Bussex was the undoing of the Monmouth Horse. Wheeling this way and that, causing McFeeley, Jack and Piper to split up, they were bogged down just long enough for the Household Cavalry to cut them to pieces.

It was every man for himself now, and McFeeley ran off the way they had been heading, confident that his two companions would follow to join him later. McFeeley had built up a steady pace and was rounding a curve in the rhine when a shadowy figure leapt from the bank to slam against his back. McFeeley was sent sprawling on his face by the impact. His musket had been knocked from his hand, but he groped successfully for it in the darkness. He had the impression that whoever had jumped on him had also lost his balance to fall into the mud.

Pulling his face up out of the water that had gathered in the ditch, McFeeley quickly pushed himself up onto his hands and knees.

'Do not move another inch!'

McFeeley saw a lieutenant with the Queen Dowager's Regiment. He was sitting up, back propped against the side of the ditch, a pistol held rock steady, pointing at McFeeley, who was at a disadvantage. Seated uncomfortably in water, the lieutenant, lowering his pistol, sighed out the words, 'It's you, McFeeley! Thank the Lord!'

Just for a moment this latest incident in an eventful night had McFeeley dumbfounded. All he could appreciate at first was that the pistol no longer threatened him. Taking an intent look at the lieutenant, who was smiling up at him as he came to his feet, McFeeley instantly recovered his faculties. Bringing his musket up he took two steps forward to prod the muzzle hard into the chest of the other man. Recognition had McFeeley gripped by a rage that was all the more terrible because of its icy coldness. The man he was half-skewering with his musket was the swine-featured Lieutenant Riglar.

'Get hold of yourself, McFeeley. For God's sake man, we're on the same side!' Riglar protested.

Not speaking, McFeeley could see Riglar in front of him, but between him and the obese lieutenant was an oddly glowing vision of a pretty young girl, Kathleen Nerney, who was smiling in that slightly impertinent way she had been when McFeeley had first met her.

Turned into a quivering mess by the stark message in McFeeley's eyes, Riglar started to beg. 'For pity's sake, McFeeley. I beg of you in the name of the Lord—'

McFeeley wanted to make sure the lieutenant died in agony. Easing pressure on the musket away he lowered the muzzle to dig it hard into Riglar's belly. A gut shot was the most painful wound of all.

'Nooo ...' Riglar opened his mouth wide to scream, but McFeeley fired; the powder from the musket set the lieutenant's coat alight while the bullet tore through his intestines. With no medical help to hand Riglar would suffer a protracted and extremely painful death. McFeeley looked down at Riglar before walking away and climbing up out of the Bussex.

McFeeley went on at a steady pace heading due south; a direction which he hoped would eventually reunite him with Jack and Piper. The three of them would then go back to the ranks of their own army. The rain had stopped and as the sun came up a rise in temperature joined the heat generated by walking to dry out his clothing. He was puzzled at having covered a considerable distance over moorland without having a sight or sound of either of the two armies – the winners or the losers. Meditating on this he was alerted by the sound of distant hoof beats. They moved closer until he saw five backlit horsemen coming towards him out of the sun. With no cover available within miles, McFeeley could do nothing but stand and wait, musket held at the ready.

As the horsemen neared he identified them as king's men. Ripping off his Monmouth tunic he threw it to the ground, trampling it into the peat. Turning to face the horsemen, his heart sank as he recognized first a white charger and then the bulky figure on its back. Riding at the head of the five cavalrymen, Colonel Percy Kirke was coming towards him.

'No chance at all, my Lord?' Captain Critchell checked with Brigadier-General Churchill, having drawn him away from his wife, Rachel, and the Duke of Calvert.

Churchill shook his head. 'I'm afraid not, Claude. You will have heard that there was some confusion at Sedgemoor, which I presume, prevented Lieutenant McFeeley and the other two men from getting back to us. It grieves me to say that McFeeley must have perished.'

'Did I hear the name of McFeeley mentioned?' Rachel inquired.

'Only in passing,' Critchell lied to be kind.

'I would gladly have missed Sedgemoor,' Lord Churchill said feelingly.

'Nonsense, Brigadier, total nonsense!' Critchell scoffed.

'What I would willingly miss,' Churchill began fervently, 'are the true bills to be presented against the Monmouth prisoners by the Grand Juries of Somerset, Dorset, Devon and Hampshire.'

'Having the misfortune to know George Jeffreys, I imagine that he is already preparing Jack Ketch, the executioner,' Calvert said unhappily.

'Surely these people rose up against the king so they must expect to be brought to justice,' Rachel gave her opinion.

A morose Churchill said, 'Vengeance, not justice. Catholic vengeance administered by a Protestant on Protestants at the behest of a Catholic king.'

'Whatever,' Sarah said brightly. 'I trust that you will see that those deserving of reward are recognized, John.'

'As you well know, Sarah, I will, as always, act on recommendations made by my regimental commanders. Those reports will be with me in the next few days.'

'The lieutenant who saved us both at White Lackington merits recognition for his bravery.'

'McFeeley,' Critchell, much more sensitive than Churchill and suspecting that one or both of the women were interested in McFeeley, tried to convey a need for caution to the brigadier.

'I am grateful to you for pointing that out to me, Sarah, Rachel,' Churchill said. 'I will arrange an award for McFeeley. Of course it will have to be awarded posthumously.'

There was great consternation then as Lady Sarah Churchill folded to the floor in a faint. Rachel and the three men rushed to her.

'It is simply an attack of the vapours,' Rachel explained.

Gently helping his wife into a sitting position, Churchill accepted fully what Rachel had claimed. But Captain Claude Critchell, standing a little way off, believed that he could see the situation in total, and it worried him greatly. A scandal within the Churchill family was something that the new King James II administration just couldn't afford.

Consequently, when Critchell caught Rachel alone he asked, 'Did anything take place between McFeeley and Lady Sarah, Rachel?'

'No, I give you my word,' Rachel assured him, and her word couldn't be questioned.

This should have been enough for Critchell, but he couldn't drive a nagging worry from the back of his mind.

Brought back as a captive to the area of the Bussex rhine, McFeeley had been unable to believe his eyes. There had been a wholesale erection of gibbets and the bodies of executed rebels swung and gently twisted this way and that in the stirring of a summer breeze. Although it had been plain that Colonel Kirke recognized who he was, he was regarded as a rebel and stood now among Kirke's 'lambs', hands bound behind his back and ready for execution.

A short distance from him a boy, no more than fifteen years of age, who had marched proudly with the Monmouth army, was crying and wailing as soldiers dragged him towards a gibbet. McFeeley recognized a weeping figure kneeling beside the gibbet, wringing his hands as he pleaded for the life of the boy to be spared. It was John Whiting, the Quaker, crying not for himself but for all those about him who were either dead or about to die.

A well-aimed boot of a king's soldier knocked Whiting from his kneeling position, pitching him flat onto his face. The boy was hoisted up, struggling and kicking, while the Quaker scrambled to his feet, shouting his objections, only to be knocked down once more by one of the brutal 'lambs'. The whole terrible scene was disrupted as a carriage was driven in fast, causing Kirke's soldiers to dive out of the way to avoid being run over. It swung round to pull up beside Colonel Kirke and the small group of officers around him. Almost tripping in his haste to scramble out of the carriage, Dr Mews, the Bishop of Winchester, waddled towards Kirke on legs stiffened by anger and disgust.

'In the name of God I command thee to cease this outrage, Colonel!' the bishop yelled in a shrill voice.

'The king commands me, Bishop,' Kirke replied.

'Stop!' Dr Mews screamed out the word.

The hanging detail halted in their work, and the cry from the bishop had been so vehement that even Kirke turned to him, as if accepting the shout as an order and awaiting further instructions. Taking full advantage of his attention-getting, Mews addressed Kirke in a firm voice. 'I will not accept that His Majesty, an Englishman, knows of this barbarity. King James would not condone it, let alone have it carried out in his name.'

'My orders came not from an Englishman, Bishop, but a Frenchman who understands this kind of punishment. You must take up your argument with Louis Duras Feversham, Dr Mews,' Colonel Kirke countered.

'There is no time for me to contact the Earl of Feversham. The decision must be yours.'

Kirke looked at the bodies swinging from the gibbets, and to where others had been taken down and stacked in a gruesome but orderly fashion. He then scanned the bound prisoners; McFeeley included, then studied the sun exaggeratedly before at last speaking to the bishop.

'We have hanged one hundred and twenty rebels so far, Dr Mews, and there's many times that number still to go. But now the sun is on the final part of its journey so I will content myself with executing that group there,' Kirke indicated a group of prisoners in which McFeeley stood.

McFeeley found himself being herded towards the nearest gallows, while Dr Mews stood red-faced but speechless. One of the Monmouth men was weeping as he staggered along, another gnawed on a chunk of vegetation that he held, squirrel-like, in both hands, his eyes wide as he peered at an approaching insanity. It was difficult for McFeeley to see these dejected, terrified captives as the zealous would-be soldiers who had in concert sung Monmouth songs.

The executioners grabbed the crying man, who died on the gibbet as silently as he had wept. John Whiting was still actively pleading, on his feet now, wandering this way and that in his anguish, protesting to no one in particular. An ashen-faced Bishop of Winchester stood by in abject misery as the man who had been eating was led docilely to the foot of a gibbet. Still chewing, he gave his executioners an inane and crooked smile. Then, as they clustered around him to carry out the final tasks, rationality suddenly returned to have him explode into action. A blow from the doomed man's elbow felled one of the king's men. This success had him fight with the ferocity of a lion. Blood flew as noses were smashed, but then the 'lambs' got the upper hand, clubbing the man to the ground and then taking revenge with their boots.

'Stop it, you men!' Kirke commanded loudly. 'Desist, I say, desist. Do you want to kill the poor fellow? Stand him up and hang him.'

The contradictions in what Kirk had said confirmed for McFeeley his earlier formed belief that the colonel was mad. Consequently they hadn't seen a bulky but distinguished figure ride slowly up, but his authoritative inquiry, delivered from horseback, had every head, including that of Colonel Kirke, turn his way.

'What is going on here?'

Kirke walked slowly to the horseman, asking truculently. 'And who might you be, sir?'

'I am the Duke of Calvert, Colonel, and from your appearance and this disgraceful scene, I take it that you are Colonel Kirke.'

'A man could consider that to be an insult, my lord,' Kirke protested.

'Please consider it so, for that was my intention, Kirke,' Calvert said.

'Thank God!' the Bishop of Winchester exclaimed hurrying over to stand by Calvert.

'I am simply obeying orders, sir,' Kirke complained, his florid face still registering how miffed he had been by Calvert's comments.

'Then you will now obey my orders, Colonel, and begin by putting a halt to what is murderous behaviour on the part of an army,' Calvert replied.

'With respect, my Lord, I am answerable only to the Earl of Feversham.'

Dismounting, Calvert said. 'You will not need reminding, Colonel, that Feversham himself is answerable to His Majesty King James II. You will cease this mass slaughter at once; otherwise I shall acquaint King James with your refusal. Is that understood?'

'Yes, my lord,' Kirke replied, not bothering to conceal his ire.

'These people are to be handed over to the civilian authorities for processing through the courts,' Calvert said to Kirke, then, speaking to the Bishop of Winchester, 'I wonder if I could presume upon you to regulate what happens here.'

At this Colonel Kirke broke in angrily. 'My lord, you cannot expect me, a colonel with the militia, to put myself under the jurisdiction of a clergyman!'

'Dr Mews will, through me, have the authority of the king, Colonel,' Calvert replied coldly. 'Now, Your Grace, I must be on my way. I will rely upon you, possibly with the assistance of this gentleman here,' he indicated John Whiting, 'to have a head count and ascertain that not one single captive is harmed in any way.'

'Colonel Kirke,' the Duke of Calvert was saying as he placed a foot in the stirrup, 'you will inter every body before leaving here, and submit a list to the Earl of Feversham giving the name and every available detail of each man executed here.'

'My word, sir, it is you!'

The incredulous words had come from the right and a little behind McFeeley. Jonathan Piper, his thin face showing the effects of suffering and physical abuse.

'It is great to see you, Jonathan!' a delighted McFeeley blurted out. 'What of Jack?'

As a reply Piper used a movement of his eyes. Following them, McFeeley saw Sergeant Jack dangling from a nearby gibbet. It was plain that he had been dead for several hours.

'He was a great soldier, a loyal friend, and a mystery. He didn't know where he came from.'

'I hope he knows where he's going,' Piper expressed a profound wish.

Brigadier-General John Churchill and Captain Claude Critchell waited in Whitehall to be brought to the king in Chiffinch's room, where the Duke of Calvert was first having a meeting with His Majesty.

'How thorough was the check you had made on McFeeley, Claude?' Churchill asked.

'As thorough as the circumstances would permit, sir. He did not die at Sedgemoor.'

Churchill let his eyes wander round the room that was once the lodgings of Will Chiffinch, page, secretary and spy for King Charles. Gaining a feel of history always made the present more tolerable for him. He tried to conjure up an image of the hard-drinking and devious Chiffinch, but failed, and returned to the perplexing problem of Critchell's anxiety over McFeeley.

'Then where could he be, Claude?'

'I cannot think, my lord,' Critchell admitted. 'But I am convinced he would never desert.'

'It upsets me, Claude, to think that though you are free and welcome to approach me on any army subject, you resort to inference,' Churchill chided the captain in a kindly fashion. 'It would seem to me that you are implying that he may be held among the rebel prisoners taken at Sedgemoor.'

'I regard that as the logical conclusion, Brigadier. I would respectfully suggest that we owe it to McFeeley to investigate this possibility.' Critchell said.

Churchill gravely replied. 'There are two thousand six hundred captives, and we as soldiers have neither the time, the expertise, nor the authority to make a search for the lieutenant.'

'Surely my lord is not saying that we should abandon McFeeley,' Critchell said tentatively.

'Our only option is to turn the matter over to the politicians and their fellow illusionists.'

Relieved, Captain Critchell said, 'You will initiate an inquiry, my lord? At once?'

'Immediately, Claude, but I must caution you not to expect too much,' Churchill warned. 'I promise you that I will broach the subject to the king.'

As good as his word, Churchill raised the subject of McFeeley as the interview of Critchell and himself with the King drew to a close. The response of James II was not encouraging.

'You will appreciate my position at this very moment. The death of my dear friend Lord Keeper Guildford means that I am myself forced to be Chancellor. You of all people, my Lord Churchill, will be fully conversant with the fact that despite one threat to my throne having been swiftly dealt with, another looms large on the horizon. My nephew will soon pay for his ill-advised and misguided attempt at rebellion, but my son-in-law is a threat which increases daily.'

Conditions had deteriorated fast in the three days that McFeeley had been held in the overcrowded Dorchester Prison. The reek of the decaying dead had now overtaken the foul stench of the unwashed living. Smallpox, at first a rumour, was now a grim reality. Cruel coincidence had placed Thomas Yates close to McFeeley. The few prisoners who had not surrendered to their own misery spoke of the drunken despot, Judge Jeffreys, who would conduct the coming trials. Talk of the court was so daunting that, when promised leniency if they pleaded guilty, a large number, including Thomas Yates, volunteered. This was a ploy to get more than two and a half thousand prisoners through the Assizes in the five weeks left before the Michaelmas term began in London.

Yates, who was among the first prisoners being taken to the court, proved that justice definitely wouldn't be done. A couple of hours later, the jailers threw Yates back into the prison. Weeping uncontrollably he fell onto his knees, holding his head in both hands and swaying wildly from side to side. A prisoner who had been brought back with Yates, who had pleaded not guilty, explained that he was to be transported for seven years.

'And him?' McFeeley inquired, gesturing towards the distraught Yates.

The prisoner, a slow-witted country fellow, replied, 'He did do as they asked and pleaded guilty. They did showed him mercy, right 'nuff. He's going to be hangded, drawndid, and quartered!'

When they came for Yates, he didn't go quietly. They half carried him out, kicking, screaming and pleading. On the gibbet he did not call on God. Over and over again he howled his wife's name. 'Lucy! Lucy! Lucy!'

This harrowing event was on McFeeley's mind as he was moved into a batch of prisoners due to go to court. He was experiencing an advancing melancholia which was eased as Jonathan Piper was pushed into the line some three places from him. Separated after being saved from execution by the Duke of Calvert, they had not seen each other since.

Under armed escort and in single file, they were taken outside. Heads twisting away from the bright sunlight, eyes rapidly blinking to screen out at least some of the brightness after having been kept in the semi-dark, they started up the sloping road to the centre of the town. Each side of the road was lined with spectators, some jeering and shouting abuse at the prisoners, all wanting to prove themselves to be loyalists now that the ill-fated rebellion had been smashed. Thinking that he had glimpsed a familiar face in the crowd but unable to put a name to it, McFeeley risked punishment by staring in that direction. The man concerned, aware that McFeeley was looking hard at him, moved backwards into concealment in the crowd, but not before McFeeley had recognized him as Edmund Prideaux.

Up ahead of him there was some angry muttering among the prisoners. This brought shouts for them to remain quiet, but these orders were largely ignored because a little way ahead of them a boy was being whipped through the street.

'That's young Billie Wiseman,' a prisoner with a local accent identified the youth on the receiving end of the vicious lashes.

'He read out Monmouth's proclamation at Weymouth,' another man said.

'No talking,' one of the escort shouted, this time being obeyed.

A coach was lumbering slowly down the slight hill towards them. The coach pulled over to one side and came to a halt. This caused more discontented muttering from the file of prisoners. The well-to-do passengers in the coach were going to have their fun in watching the shattered remnants of Monmouth's army pass by in chains and humiliation.

Until they had reached the outskirts of Dorchester it had been a pleasant excursion through the sunlit delights of autumn. Nearing the county town they had clutched at each other as they shrank away from the sight of gibbets erected around the countryside. Although covering their faces with both hands, the compulsion that the horrific holds had caused both Lady Sarah and Rachel to peep through their fingers at the grisly parts of bodies, the entrails and the blood that had dyed green grass into a rusty brown.

Entering the town, relieved to have left the gory scenes behind, they found a new horror waiting for them as their coach eased its way down the gentle slope of the main street.

'Oh, Rachel!' Sarah cried out in anguish as they entered the town and saw a boy staggering towards them; the clothing ripped from his back by the whip was now lashing his bare, bleeding flesh.

The scene was shut off for the two women then as a line of prisoners, dirty, bedraggled and cowed, filed up the road between them and the arguing clergyman and gaoler. Sarah Churchill's heart first fluttered and then her heartbeat accelerated as she recognized one of the prisoners beyond a doubt as Colm McFeeley.

'That's Lieutenant McFeeley,' she said to Rachel in a voice that she didn't recognize as her own.

'It is, and, look, there's Jonathan just a little way back from him!' Rachel cried excitedly, then leaned out of the coach to call, 'Come, gallant, we must walk towards the Mulberry Garden.'

Both Piper and McFeeley turned their faces to the coach, the countenance of the former brightening as he called back across the street.

'I'm afraid, little mistress, the rooms are all taken up by this time.'

Wincing as she saw a guard catch Jonathan Piper a heavy blow to the aide of his head with a musket for his impertinence, Sarah knew that her irrepressible companion and the soldier had exchanged lines from the play *Lady Flippanta*.

'Sarah, we must do something at once!' Rachel exclaimed urgently, agitation having her move about inside of the coach.

'What can we do?' a despairing Sarah sighed, looking out at a street in which the undercurrents of violence were alarmingly detectable. The line of prisoners had passed on, and if Rachel hadn't shared the experience with her, Sarah would now be wondering if she had really seen McFeeley and Piper.

What was happening now was merging into the nonsensical, shadowy existence that the past few weeks had become for Sarah. On the surface Rachel seemed to be coping far better than she was, yet Sarah suspected that further down Rachel was every bit as uncertain as she was herself.

'We must go to the authorities and report that McFeeley and Piper are soldiers of the king and not rebels!' Rachel declared with much determination.

'How would we have them listen? What proof have we to substantiate that claim were we to make it?' Sarah pointed out. 'Lord Stawell is expecting us, Rachel, and he has been a good friend to John over the years. He will know what to do.'

Leaning out of the coach, Rachel called up to the coachman. 'Take us on to Stawell Manor, driver.'

Twelve

JUDGE GEORGE JEFFREYS studied McFeeley in the main, and Piper occasionally saying, 'I have been subjected to stories and excuses at this Assize that for sheer invention would put William Shakespeare to shame. Having said that, I must confess that the tale you tell me regarding yourself and the prisoner Piper stands out as by far the most ingenious. However, you can offer nothing to support your assertion that both of you are members of the king's army.

'In contrast, McFeeley, the evidence against you is as full and plain as can be. Therefore I have no alternative but to find you both guilty of high treason. For this heinous offence each of you must suffer the prescribed penalty of being hanged, drawn, and quartered. When I left His Majesty he was pleased to remit the time of all executions to me: that wherever I found any obstinacy or impenitence I might order the executions with what speed I should think best.

'In this instance you have introduced to the court a bizarre story of His Majesty stooping so low as to have his soldiers pose as rebels. Therefore, take notice that I shall order the sheriff to prepare for your executions this afternoon.

'But withal I give both of you prisoners this intimation. You shall have pen, ink and paper brought to you in your place of confinement, and if, in the time left to you, that pen, ink and paper is employed well by you it may be that you hear further from me in deferring the executions.'

When they had been taken back to the prison and the writing materials promised by Jeffreys had been produced, Jonathan Piper looked glumly at the clean sheets of paper, and asked McFeeley,

'What does this mean, sir?'

'It would seem that he is suggesting that our only hope of mercy lies in petitioning the king.'

'Will that work, sir?'

'No. The rebellion has been put down, so we are expendable, Piper.'

An expression of hope grew on Piper's thin face. 'Lady Sarah and Rachel, sir! They saw us! They know what's happening and they can help!'

'I will give petitioning the king a try, Jonathan,' McFeeley said to pacify the young soldier.

At Stawell Manor on the outskirts of Dorchester, it was taking some time for Sarah and Rachel to recover. The two gibbets that had been erected on the estate, and the pieces of bodies scattered around among entrails and blood had once been two human beings. Lord Stawell, getting on in years, was trembling as he explained that Judge Jeffreys deliberately had the two executions carried out in the grounds of Stawell Manor because he, Lord Stawell, had refused to accept Jeffreys's invitation to take a drink with him.

'You could apply for an interview with Judge George Jeffreys,' Stawell said when they had told him the story of seeing the two wrongly imprisoned king's soldiers, 'but I can't guarantee that he'll see you. The whole Assize is a reprehensible thing.'

Hearing this did nothing to lift Sarah's spirits. She had hoped that Lord Stawell, whom she had first met at her wedding, might have been able to intervene on behalf of McFeeley and the other man, and it was a blow to learn that he was at odds with Jeffreys himself.

'The judge has no better nature to appeal to, my lord?' she asked.

'Most definitely not,' Stawell replied. 'But I'm told that he has a pocket that is accessible!'

'Bribery!' Lady Sarah breathed the word contemplatively.

'Exactly. There was a young fellow at the club two evenings ago actually boasting of having eluded a charge of high treason by paying Jeffreys a sum of £15,000,' Lord Stawell shook his head in disbelief at such corruption. 'It was the drink talking, and we advised the young fellow to keep his mouth shut. But then he started bragging of how he had been given a discount of £240 by Jeffreys for prompt payment. Foolish fellow, I pity his poor father, Sir Edmund.'

An animated Rachel breathlessly asked Stawell, 'Do you speak of Edmund Prideaux, sir?'

'That's the young bounder,' Lord Stawell exclaimed, surprised that Rachel knew the man.

'Listen to me, Sarah,' Rachel began excitedly. 'Leave this to me, I will first make an appeal to the judge, and if that should prove to be fruitless I will find Edmund and have him arrange for us to pay for the release of McFeeley and Jonathan.'

'But I must come with you, Rachel!'

'No, my dear Sarah, it is best that I go alone,' Rachel was adamant.

'No,' Lord Stawell corrected Rachel, 'it would be best for neither of you get involved.'

'We have to, my lord,' Sarah said, her face serious.

'Are these two men worth it. You must take that into considera-tion,' Stawell advised.

'One of them saved our lives, my lord, several times.'

Accepting this from Sarah as sufficient cause, Lord Stawell told Rachel, 'I will have you taken to George Jeffreys' lodgings, young lady, but my man will have instructions only to guide you there. He will not be able to assist you further.'

'I do appreciate that, sir,' Rachel said with a smile, keen to start out on her mission.

Her enthusiasm hadn't waned when she was helped out of the carriage in Dorchester and Lord Stawell's driver pointed across the road to a covered alleyway. In the fast thickening dusk it had a sinister appearance for Rachel but she didn't let it deter her.

'Go into the archway, my lady,' the nervous carriage man instructed, 'and ask at the first door on the right for the judge. I will return to the carriage, my lady. The instructions given me by my master is to wait one hour for you, but no longer.'

'Thank you, I shall be with you in that time,' Rachel told the driver, feeling some trepidation for the first time as she started off across the road. There were few people about. Two begging children accosted her at the centre of the street. Three ruffians, young men given licence by the turbulence of the post-rebellion period, loitered by the entrance to the alleyway. They leered at Rachel through the growing darkness, and she felt they would have caused her trouble had it not been for Lord Stawell's footman standing watchfully beside the carriage across the street.

Passing them by, she went into the archway, a little unnerved and disorientated by stepping into the dense blackness of the alleyway, She was making her way to the entrance when a door opened and closed on her left as someone stepped out into the alleyway. The size and shape of the silhouette told her that it was a man, and she was relieved as he started to pass with no more than a glance at her.

Then her nerves jangled as the figure paused, head thrust forwards as he peered at her, saying politely, 'Forgive me should I be mistaken, madam, but are you perchance Rachel?'

'Edmund!' Rachel was uncertain whether this unexpected meeting was for good or for bad.

'My dear, sweet Rachel!' he cried, taking both of her hands in his. 'The good Lord has answered my prayers and sent you to me. What in the world are you doing here in Dorchester?'

'That is a very long story, Edmund, but I will tell you my reason for being in this place at this very moment,' Rachel replied before going on to explain about McFeeley and Piper and her proposed audience with Judge Jeffreys.

Not interrupting, Prideaux listened intently. When Rachel had finished, he offered his help. 'I have met the Lord Chief Justice, Rachel, and must caution you that unless a particular approach is made to him he can be a most obstinate and unhelpful fellow.'

'Then will you assist me, Edmund, possibly even come with me to the judge?'

'I would be unwise to accompany you, but I give you all the help that I can,' Edmund assured her. 'I have a room here, so let us go there and plan the right approach to make to Judge Jeffreys.'

Initially, the room Prideaux took her to gave Rachel a feeling of security after having been out alone in a strange town. She was relieved to think that her path to Judge Jeffreys was to be eased by

Edmund. The Lord Chief Justice was a man with a formidable reputation.

Everything went wrong immediately after Prideaux had lit two candles that showed the room to be a small but pleasant one. A small dresser stood against one wall on the left of the door, and a single bed was positioned against the opposite wall. A poorly executed portrait of King Charles II adorned the wall above a small grate in which a fire was retreating into grey and barely glowing, embers.

'It's been so long, too damned long, Rachel!' Prideaux complained, taking her into his arms, becoming rough when she tried to struggle.

'My frock, Edmund,' she said, a trace of anger in her voice as his fumbling became violent and a tearing of material bared her bosom. 'Will you please stop!'

'You've never wanted me to stop before,' he told her mockingly, striving for a kiss, but Rachel avoided his mouth by twisting her head vigorously from side to side. Prideaux caught and held her chin in a vice-like grip between the thumb and forefinger of his right hand. Rachel, unable to move, kept her lips tightly closed and stiff when he lowered his mouth onto hers.

A moment later she began to respond and she knew that she was going to lose. As he held her tightly and manoeuvred her towards the bed, Rachel spoke to him pleadingly around their unbroken kiss. 'I have to see Judge Jeffreys, Edmund.'

He replied in a muffled murmur. 'In the morning, my sweet Rachel! In the morning I will go with you, Rachel.'

'Do you promise, Edmund?' she asked worriedly.

'I promise.'

Reassured, she gave way to her passion. Closing her eyes, Rachel relaxed against her lover, her arms going round him.

A boot nudging into his ribs awakened McFeeley. It wasn't really a kick, but a toe-twisting covert move of torture delivered by an expert. The pain brought him round angrily. Jerking himself up into a sitting position, ready to spring onto his tormentor, he was halted by a muzzle of a musket being pressed against his forehead. In the dim light of a dawn filtered through a small window, he saw that Piper was already on his feet, a gaoler on each side of him.

'On your feet!' McFeeley was ordered, and he had no choice but to obey.

'We didn't buy a lot of time, sir,' Piper made a laconic comment.

A few hours, McFeeley thought grimly. Had they not petitioned the king it would have been all over now. Never a coward, McFeeley had always expected to die on a battlefield.

There was just the two of them. Their unsuccessful petition to the King had separated them from others to be executed. They walked along the street which they had taken to the court. There were no crowds as there had been then, but they drew glances from towns-folk made curious by the unusual sight of just two men being escorted to the gibbets.

Trudging along a street that was given an illusion of length by the tall buildings that stood on either side, they came out into open ground. A gentle slope ahead led up to some kind of earthworks dating back to the Romans. Grassed over now, the area had three closely grouped gibbets on it.

McFeeley saw that they were now collecting would-be specta-tors at a fast rate. McFeeley breathed in the aroma deeply. A sideways glance at Piper, impassive, lean-faced, he was proud of the young soldier. Both of them had much to endure in the minutes to come, but he knew that Jonathan Piper would be just as determined as he was not to afford their executioners or their audience one iota of pleasure by giving any sight or sound of fear or weakness.

McFeeley was fortified on his last walk on earth by the possibility that he might well be re-united with Rosin. His thoughts turned to his foster mother, the huge-hearted Philomena O'Driscoll. Unable to find out what had happened to her in this world, McFeeley hoped he would in the next.

'What wouldn't I give to snatch a musket and go out fighting!' Piper said softly but longingly.

'They'll make sure that we'll never have the chance,' McFeeley said, knowing how Piper felt.

There were two men by the gibbets. From the talk heard in prison

McFeeley identified the executioner Jack Ketch. His assistant Pascha Rose was, fittingly, a local butcher.

As they neared the gibbets the now considerable crowd was held back into what was judged to be a reasonable viewing distance. Piper had a sardonic smile on his face as he asked McFeeley a question: 'Do I have to address you as *sir* when we say goodbye, sir?'

'Colm will do, Jonathan,' McFeeley answered easily, adding, 'but if I still have my rank when we get to the other side, go back to calling me sir.'

The escort halted them and Jack Ketch stepped forwards to give them a look over with a cold and professional eye. He had the appearance of a man you would be happy to take a drink with if you served together. At that very moment he was displaying a state of nerves that made him seem like the condemned rather than the cool McFeeley and Piper. The jittery executioner signalled to Rose, who brought a noose and dropped it over Piper's head.

'Do you have any religion at all, Jonathan?' McFeeley inquired in a light tone.

'No,' Piper shook his head inside of the noose 'but I was at the funeral of Oliver Cromwell. Do you think the angels might take that into consideration?'

'I would not risk mentioning it,' McFeeley advised dryly. 'I am told that none but the dogs cried!'

'No more talking,' Ketch ordered in a surprisingly high voice.

'These two prisoners made a similar claim to me, Lady Churchill,' Judge Jeffreys said in a surprisingly gentle tone.

Sarah was worried about Rachel who had failed to return to Stawell Manor the previous night. The wayward Rachel at the mercy of her own sexual needs, had probably spent the night with a man, she thought. In contrast, McFeeley had no control over his destiny, so he was Sarah's major concern this morning.

'You will reconsider this case, my lord?' she inquired.

'Good Lord, my dear Lady Churchill, we most assuredly will. The gentleman you first approached,' Jeffreys indicated the grey-haired man who had brought her to him on her arrival, 'is Sir Henry

Pollexfen, the Crown Prosecutor. We have delayed the court sitting in deference to you.'

There were impatient sounds from the court that reached the anteroom to make Jeffreys agitated. Even so, Sarah wanted some firm commitment from the judge before she left. She inquired, 'Now that I have vouched that the two men are soldiers of the king, my lord, will they be released?'

'Of course, of course,' Jeffreys shuffled some papers, selected one and picked up a pen. 'You will be happy to sign for the release of the two men per pro Brigadier-General Churchill!'

This was something that Sarah would not do. With a new king and unrest throughout the land, there was much intrigue and jostling for high positions. She didn't trust Jeffreys, whose words of a fair administration of justice were cancelled out by the grisly scenes now evident throughout Dorset.

To sign anything on behalf of her husband now could well mean having it used to the detriment of Lord Churchill in the near future, so Sarah said, 'I will not give my signature in Brigadier Churchill's name, my lord, but I will sign anything to you that the two men are soldiers of the king.'

Unable to conceal his annoyance, Jeffreys gave a grudging nod, screwed up the sheet of paper he had been writing on, replacing it and writing rapidly. 'If you so wish, Lady Churchill.'

A stocky man appeared in the doorway, and Jeffreys issued an order that had Sarah filled with relief. 'Mr Sheriff, I want you to take this immediately to the executioner. It countermands the order which has the two men taken to the Rings this morning.'

'I'll do as you command, my lord, but I fear that I will be too late!'

'Then you must go in all haste, Mr Sheriff,' Jeffreys urged.

When Sarah stepped back out into the covered alley the area was crowded by sightseers ready for the first batch of prisoners of the day to be brought along. The sound of a door opening on the opposite side of the alley attracted her attention. Looking casually in that direction she was startled to see a frantic Rachel come rushing out to fall tearfully into her arms.

'Oh, Sarah!' Rachel wailed mournfully, 'I've let you and them down so badly!'

*

They were both in position under separate gibbets. Their farewells had been in the form of a short but firm handshake. Ketch and his assistant were busy with Piper, who was to be executed first. Both executioners were pulling on the rope around Piper's neck when McFeeley, who had averted his gaze, heard a shout and looked back to see a stocky man running to the gibbets, waving a document.

'Hold on, Mr Ketch, hold on! I have orders with me for the two men to be released!'

Releasing the rope they were holding so that Piper's feet came unsteadily back down onto the ground, Ketch and Pascha read the paper held by the sheriff then slashed the bonds holding McFeeley and an ashen-faced Piper, freeing them.

Giving the shaky Piper support, McFeeley hurried with him out to the road, running until they were clear of the crowd and had become anonymous and of no interest to anyone. Piper, who was rapidly regaining his strength, made a comment through a sore throat, 'That was close – too close!'

'So close that I want to get away from here in case our luck changes,' McFeeley replied.

'Which could be right now,' Piper said ominously as a pony and trap came towards them.

The driver was an elderly man with a heavy, lined face. Dressed in the livery of a servant, he reined in beside them. The driver asked, 'Would one of you gentlemen happen to be Lieutenant McFeeley?'

'I am,' McFeeley volunteered.

'I bring the compliments of Lady Sarah Churchill, Lieutenant. 'My lady asks that you and your companion be kind enough to grace her with your presences at Stawell Manor.'

The miracle that saved them had been wrought by Lady Sarah, McFeeley realized. He questioned the elderly driver. 'Where is Stawell Manor?'

Raising up a little on his seat, the servant used his whip as a pointer as he gave instructions. 'Go back down through the town, sir, past the court, then turn right and go down to the river. Don't cross over the bridge, but turn left, walk along the river-bank and you'll come to Stawell Manor. That is the shortest way on foot, Lieutenant.'

'Thank you,' McFeeley said, waving a hand as the trap was pulled round and driven away.

They walked at a steady pace, finding it odd that none of the people they passed took any interest in them. Passing the court caused neither of them the trauma they had anticipated, but they were saddened and stood quietly and reverently as a line of wretched creatures passed by on the way to execution.

They were on the river-bank when a woman accosted them. Straggly hair awry, her clothing was dirty and dishevelled in a way that said she had been living rough. She beseeched, 'Could you spare a coin or two for a poor woman seeking her man, young sirs? He was with Monmouth and I have not seen—'

Stopping her talk she stepped closer to peer up at McFeeley. She clasped his hands, crying, 'I know you, don't I? You were a soldier, sir! You came to my home! We lay together, sir!'

'Lucy Yates!' McFeeley recognized the woman, pulling his hands from her grasp. There was a wafting of alcohol around her that rode on a stale, unwashed smell. It didn't seem possible she was the same desirable woman he had known. 'What are you doing here in Dorchester, Lucy?'

'I am seeking my man, sir,' the woman whinged. 'I remember your name. It was Colm!'

McFeeley gently told her, 'You have to be strong, Lucy. They have put your man to death!'

Lucy Yates gave a sob and tears formed in her eyes. Yet to McFeeley it seemed that she was simply reacting to a sense of loss that wasn't really focused on her husband.

Pulling on McFeeley's hands, she pleaded, 'Come into the bushes with me please, Colm, I needs to be comforted.'

The prospect turned McFeeley's stomach. Yet he remembered what she once was, and could possibly become again, and he knew that, in her present delicate state of mind, he had a tremendous responsibility not to totally destroy her with a rejection.

'You *do* want me again, Colm?'

'I do,' he lied. 'It is time that worries me. I have to meet a gentleman at the manor.'

'Then go,' she urged with a pleased smile. 'I just wanted to know that you could still love me. Go, Colm, and I will wait for you on this very spot.'

'I will come back,' McFeeley promised.

After being treated to the luxury of tubs filled with hot water, McFeeley and Piper had been given civilian clothes that, though not a perfect fit, made them feel good. Lord Stawell had told them of how Lady Sarah had secured their reprieve and release, but when McFeeley had tried to thank her she had blushed prettily and reminded him that he had saved her life more than once. She had explained that neither she nor Lord Stawell could be seen to be taking sides, so he and Piper would have to make their own way to London on foot the next day. Rachel had puzzled McFeeley by keeping to the background.

Rachel did not put in an appearance when Piper and he were ready to leave the next morning. Sarah stood facing him on the lawn in front of the manor. He was sad as the time for them to part, most probably forever, came nearer.

'I trust, Lieutenant,' she said in her melodious voice, not able to bring herself to use his first name, 'that you will have no difficulty in rejoining your regiment when you reach London.'

'It shouldn't be too difficult. I'm hoping that I will be able to keep Jonathan Piper with me.'

Sarah smiled wistfully. 'He is a good man. So unlikely a theatre-goer. Rachel was—'

As if having broken some rule by mentioning the name of her companion, Lady Sarah didn't complete her sentence. As a diversion she did a little caress of the round stone head of a cherub that was testing the water of a carved birdbath with his toe.

Placing a hand on the cherub, McFeeley said, 'This little fellow is lucky, having no cares.'

'Don't envy him, Lieutenant. Being without cares means that he is also without the delights that feelings can bring,' she replied, blushing while providing him with enough of a lead to be bold.

'What of us and our feelings, Sarah?'

Looking away, out across the lawn to the dark-green perimeter hedges, she spoke reflectively. 'We would have to be made of stone where our feelings for each other are concerned, Colm. Our destinies were decided long before we met. Perhaps it would be different otherwise.'

'When everything has settled down, I could come to you,' he suggested.

Reaching out she patted his hand consolingly. This was the only physical skin against skin contact ever between them, and they were both unsettled by it. With a forlorn shake of her head, she told him, 'There would be too many invisible and insuperable barriers. The chains of birth, heritage, family and marriage bind me.'

'So what do we do?' he asked as Lord Stawell came out of the manor, beckoning to them.

Moving slowly away, she said, 'Each night take your first look at the moon and think of me, for I will be seeing the same moon and thinking of you. That way we shall always be together.'

At the last moment a bashful Rachel had emerged to bid them well in a barely audible voice. They were only a few hundred yards away from Stawell Manor when McFeeley's name was called from a group of trees set back from the bank of the river.

'Lieutenant McFeeley!' the male voice called again.

Cautious, due to the fact that they were unarmed, McFeeley called, 'Show yourself!'

'It is I, John Whiting, the Quaker.' An unkempt Whiting stepped from the trees.

McFeeley walked out to meet him and they shook hands. 'How did you know where to find me, John?'

'I was told where you were, Colm, by the lady who is waiting for you down by the bridge.'

What Whiting said brought Lucy Yates painfully back into McFeeley's mind. He was twisted by guilt at the realization that she had waited on the river-bank for him throughout a night in which he had lain in an unbelievably comfortable bed at the manor.

'Is she still there now?' he asked, hoping for an answer that he was aware he wouldn't get.

'She is,' Whiting nodded, his eyes revealing that he had assessed the situation regarding the woman. He changed the subject. 'Would you step into the trees with me, Colm?'

With Piper at his side McFeeley followed the Quaker. They were only a little way into the copse when they saw a woman, standing with her back against the wide girth of an ancient tree. An astonished McFeeley found himself looking at Lady Henrietta, who was smiling at him.

'Hello, Colm!' she said, as if he had left her just a few minutes ago in Taunton.

'You have heard of the fate of James Scott, Colm?' said Whiting.

McFeeley shook his head. 'I have heard nothing, John.'

'He was taken in the New Forest together with Lord Grey of Werke,' the Quaker said sadly.

'But now they are both in the Tower,' McFeeley was confident that he had it right.

'James is,' Henrietta said. 'In his wisdom, the king has released my husband. I want to go to London with you, Colm.'

'It is too long a trek for a woman, Henrietta. We have no horses,' McFeeley said emphatically. 'Surely you only have to wait, Henrietta, and Lord Grey will come to collect you.'

'It is not my husband that has me head for London,' Henrietta replied.

Looking at Whiting, McFeeley asked, 'How do you regard this, John?'

'I beg of you to take Lady Henrietta with you, Colm,' was Whiting's unexpected reply.

McFeeley was of a mind that John Whiting would see it all differently if he learned that Henrietta was pregnant. Yet this theory was destroyed when Henrietta said, 'As you know, Colm, I am carrying James Scott's child, which will prove favourable when I get to London.'

Whiting was nodding his head in agreement, staggering McFeeley further when he urged, 'You can see what a service you will be doing, Colm. Her plea to the king to spare His Grace will be made powerful by the fact that she is bearing the Duke of Monmouth's unborn child.'

Overruled and outnumbered, McFeeley warned Henrietta, 'It will be tough going.'

'I know,' she replied with a sweet and courageous smile.

'Will you be coming with us, John?' McFeeley asked.

'No, my friend. My fiancée awaits me back at Taunton, but my prayers will be with all three of you on every step of your pilgrimage,' Whiting told him.

'Then we will move out now so that we can cover many miles between now and twilight,' McFeeley said. Then, lowering his voice to speak to the Quaker, he said, 'Would you do something for me, John?'

'You don't need to ask, my friend. What is it?'

'When we have gone,' McFeeley said, 'will you go back down to the woman at the bridge? Her name is Lucy Yates, and I would ask you to take her back to her home at Axminster.'

John Whiting smiled. 'It will hardly put me out of my way, Colm. I will go to fetch her now.'

'There is no need. I am here!'

Lucy Yates stepped out from behind a tree and came forward. She had washed and tidied herself since McFeeley had left her, and was very much her old, attractive self.

'Lucy,' McFeeley said, recovering swiftly from his surprise, 'this is John Whiting, who will see that you get home safely.'

'It is most kind of you, sir.' Lucy Yates smiled at Whiting, but then became serious as she turned to McFeeley. 'I am not going home, but to London with you.'

'You are not thinking straight,' McFeeley pointed out. 'Your boy will be waiting at home.'

'My son ran off to sea the day you came to my place,' she told McFeeley, 'and as for a home, I no longer have one.'

'Then what will you do in London, madam?' Whiting inquired.

'I shall find work, sir. I am an able-bodied woman. But that is for the future. Today, tomorrow and the days that follow, sir, this lady,' Lucy Yates pointed at Henrietta, 'needs me to take care of her along the way.'

'I would welcome that. Thank you, Lucy,' a relieved Henrietta said.

Both McFeeley and Piper saw the situation more realistically, and trouble manifested itself insidiously that night as soon as they halted just outside of the town of Wimborne. McFeeley had chosen a small hollow with care. There were two grassy areas separated by a screen of bramble bushes that gave the women and himself and Piper some privacy. Before splitting up into this male/female arrangement for the night, they sat together eating the cold food that Piper had been carrying since leaving Stawell Manor, and drinking sparkling water from a stream.

Lucy kept very close to McFeeley, taking advantage of every move she made to press some part of her body against his. He was aware that Henrietta was observing this, a trace of amusement on her lovely face, and it embarrassed him.

'It would be charitable of you to take that woman tonight, Colm,' she said bluntly. 'I'd be lying if I said that I didn't want you myself, but Lucy's need is much greater than mine.'

'I will be lying over there,' McFeeley said, pointing to where Piper was bedding down. 'We must concentrate on reaching the city, Henrietta, and nothing will divert me from that aim.'

'Listen to me, Colm, listen to me!' Henrietta said animatedly. 'I am not crazy, but all of my life I have been subjected to things that I do not understand. I have learned that I ignore my feelings at my peril. At this very moment I am convinced that you must lie with that woman tonight! Promise me that you will.'

Making his nod a signal of reluctant acquiescence, McFeeley was about to leave when Henrietta's whisper reached him. 'Sometime, Colm, maybe within the next hour, perhaps far into the future, you will learn why I have asked you to do this. The answer always appears sooner or later. Take her to where I can't hear, Colm. I can be incredibly jealous!'

Lucy came straight to him as he walked away from Henrietta, pushing her body against his. Slipping an arm around a waist that had been thickened by having borne a child and hard physical work, he guided her towards a clump of bushes down by the stream.

As he always did, McFeeley had woken at daybreak. Lucy Yates was in his arms. Awaking her he disentangled himself; he wanted to get them moving off without delay. They had eaten breakfast on the move and within half an hour were entering the New Forest, a place that held many dangers, even in times of peace.

Thirteen

THEY HAD BEEN moving for about an hour between the trees, entranced by the colours of autumn, the undergrowth stroking them wetly as they passed through it, when the shout came in startling unexpectedness from somewhere among the trees.

'Halt there! Halt I say!'

The two women and Piper looked to McFeeley for an indication as to what they should do. He gestured for them to stop. Whoever had shouted the command could not be argued with, as McFeeley and Piper were unarmed. If this was a band of robbers they had unfortunately come across, then they had nothing worth taking. The voice shouted once more.

'Who do you say you are? Are you Monmouth rebels running?'

'We are not. We are but peaceful pilgrims,' McFeeley called back through the trees.

'I am Colonel Penruddock,' the disembodied voice shouted. 'Stand absolutely still until my men have checked you out.'

'The local militia,' McFeeley said to Piper in a low voice. 'Just stay calm and quiet. Once they've taken a look at us I reckon they will allow us to go on our way.'

Having reached up to the branch of a tree with her left hand, Lucy Yates relieved the tiredness of her body by letting her arm take her weight. She was giving McFeeley a smile to assure him that she wasn't worried by what was happening, when the branch she was swinging on gave way. It snapped with an alarmingly loud crack that brought a practically instantaneous bark of a musket from within the trees. With a gurgling noise, Lucy slumped to the leafy floor of the forest.

Beating away the undergrowth, McFeeley and Henrietta bent to take a look at the stricken Lucy. A bullet had passed through her throat to almost sever her head from her body. There was no doubt: Lucy Yates was dead!

'Here is the answer, Colm,' a shocked Henrietta said quietly.

For a moment he looked at the torn, bloody flesh and the lifeless body. Could this really be the same body that had writhed in his arms in the throes of a great passion just a few short hours ago? For a moment he resented the pressure Henrietta had placed upon him to make love to the woman, but then he was glad that she had. Henrietta had received some kind of message and it had been a reliable one. Lucy had died free of any strong desires tying her to the world of the living.

Coming to his senses, McFeeley yelled, 'Run!'

All three of them sprinted, crashing through the thick undergrowth, bashing and scratching themselves against the trees as they went. Shouts came from behind, but decreased in volume as they put distance between themselves and the pursuing militia. They made good time and had covered a lot of ground, so that when a breathless Henrietta was doubled over by a pain in her side, McFeeley called a brief halt.

'We have no reason to run,' Henrietta gasped as she regained her breath. 'It is them who are in the wrong for killing poor Lucy.'

'Which is why we are running,' Piper explained.

'I don't understand!' Henrietta plucked a wide-bladed leaf and wiped perspiration from her neck with it.

'Accidentally or otherwise,' McFeeley told her, 'the militia has killed a woman. They cannot leave us alive to testify against them.'

'We'd better get moving, sir,' Piper advised as the sounds of movement through the trees came to them.

Running once more, they kept going by McFeeley and Piper each linking an arm with one of Henrietta's and half carrying her along. It meant having to zigzag to find a wide passageway through the undergrowth, but it was the speediest way to get along.

They later came to a wooden fence with long, colourful flowers stretching up above it. 'There must be a house at the other side,' McFeeley whispered as they huddled against the fence.

'The first place the militia will look, sir,' Piper suggested as they slid along the fence and came to a high wooden gate.

'Maybe no; we've nothing to lose,' McFeeley replied, reasoning that the local colonel would not wish to antagonize the people he lived among.

Reaching up, he lifted a latch and the gate swung inwards. All three went through, finding themselves in a spacious garden and closing the gate behind them. Ahead of them was the rear of a house. It was a picturesque cottage with a coating of creeping ivy forming a dark green background for the flowers growing against the walls. There was a malt house on their left, and McFeeley hesitated over going to it because if the colonel and his men did come into the garden, they would head straight for it themselves.

'Look!'

It was Henrietta who had breathed the word, and McFeeley looked at her and then on to where an old lady had come to the door at the rear of the house. Shielding her eyes against a sun that was now low in the sky, she peered in their direction.

'She's seen us, sir,' Piper was saying, but then the old woman was waving an arm at them furiously, urging them to come to her.

They ran across the garden and up to her. The skin of her face was so lined that it appeared to have been pickled, and her grey hair was in two braids that were neatly fastened at the back of her head. Her slight body was bent with age, and the hands she was rubbing together were gnarled with just about every knuckle grotesquely enlarged by arthritis.

'Did you serve with His Grace the Duke of Monmouth?' she asked, and they all knew that it was wise to agree that this was so.

'And is it that bounder Colonel Penruddock that's after you?'

'It is, madam,' McFeeley replied. 'Do you know him?'

'Aye, I know him. He's a pig of a man who is a magistrate hereabouts. Now, come on the three of you – there is not time to waste!'

For all her frailty the old woman was extremely active. Leading them towards the malt house she opened the door and they saw that it was disused and full of rubbish. Tugging fiercely at the rubbish with her twisted old hands, she cleared a space and beckoned them inside.

'Go in and lie flat,' she told them, holding Henrietta back as she went to go into the building, 'Not you, dearie.'

When McFeeley and Piper had done as the old woman had told them, she piled the rubbish she had removed back on top of them, then closed the door and hurried off, taking Henrietta by the arm.

'You are with child, dearie!' the old lady said as she and Henrietta went into the house.

'How on earth can you tell?' an astonished Henrietta asked, looking down at her still flat stomach.

'You don't miss much when you've been in the world as long as I have, dearie,' the old lady chuckled. 'Is one of them with you your man?'

This time it was Henrietta's turn to smile, 'No.'

'But there is something between you and the older man,' the old lady insisted. 'As I said, dearie, I don't miss anything.'

'You're right, we do mean something to each other,' Henrietta confessed, 'but he is not the father. The child I carry is that of the Duke of Monmouth.'

Unprepared for the reaction in the old women, Henrietta took an involuntary step backwards as the old one fell to her knees, looking up adoringly at her.

'You are truly a blessed woman,' the old lady said as tears poured down her lined cheeks. Then she controlled herself and came up onto her feet. 'Come, dearie. Now there is all more the reason to hide you!'

Taking Henrietta to the side of a huge chimney, she pulled a dusty drape to one side to reveal a cavity in a thick wall. Henrietta squeezed in. It was tight, smelled strongly of damp stone and was very dark inside when the woman allowed the drape to fall back in place, but Henrietta felt secure.

The whole place was peaceful for some time then, with only the sound of the old woman moving around reaching the three concealed fugitives. Then there was the sound of the back gate opening, and the voice that had shouted at them called to the old woman.

'Are you at home, Mrs Olaf? This is Colonel Penruddock!'

There was the sound of the door of the house opening, and from their uncomfortable places of concealment, McFeeley, Henrietta and Piper heard the old lady reply caustically, 'I know who you are, Colonel. I'd recognize that mouth of yours in a gale of wind. You have not been invited on to my property!'

'We are here on military business; searching for three fleeing rebels. Have you seen anything of two men and a woman, Mrs Olaf?'

While Penruddock was conversing with the woman he was having his men make a search. The door to the malt house creaked open. McFeeley and Piper held their breath as hands pulled at the rubbish that lay on top of them. A sword was thrust down through the pile. Before the point of the weapon dug into the ground, it disturbed a rat. Giving a muted little squeal the creature scurried away, alerting the searching soldier so that he withdrew the sword and thrust it down through the rubbish once more.

This time the blade came so close to McFeeley that it sliced through the skin of his left forearm. Struggling against the instinctive reaction of pulling his arm away, which would have disturbed the rubbish and had them discovered, McFeeley gritted his teeth when the sword was withdrawn and warm blood began to trickle down his arm.

'Nothing in here, sir,' a voice close to them called.

'We'll take a look in the house, Mrs Olaf,' Penruddock's voice said.

'Will I achieve anything by objecting, Colonel?' the old woman asked.

'Not at all,' the colonel abruptly replied, and the sounds of the militia entering the house had McFeeley and Piper worrying over Henrietta.

But the search of the house went without incident. They heard boots scuffing their way out through the gate, which closed with a rattling bang. Then the old lady was tugging the rubbish off them. Back in the house she fussed over McFeeley's slashed arm. Washing and bandaging the arm, Mrs Olaf issued a warning, her eyes worriedly on Henrietta all the time.

'Don't think Penruddock was fooled. He knows that you are round here somewhere,' she said, wagging her neat grey head worriedly. 'He'll be waiting out there somewhere. We must take care of you, dearie. You have the future of our country in your womb.'

The old lady insisted on making them a hot meal. They had protested when she stated her intention, but the aroma of the food cooking had them realize just how ravenous they were. It was dark when they had finished eating, and Mrs Olaf had another surprise in store for them. Reaching into the wall cavity in which Henrietta had hidden away from the militia, the old lady pulled out two muskets, one at a time. As McFeeley and Piper grabbed the weapons, enjoying the sense of security the feel of the muskets gave them, their hostess went to the wall running alongside the heavy table at which they sat. First with her fingertips, then using both hands, she removed a loose stone from the wall. From the cavity inside she produced bullets, powder and ramrods.

'How did...?' Piper began, but Mrs Olaf stopped him with a raised hand.

'Ask not from whence they came, son,' she said with a sweet smile. 'Simply repay me by using those weapons well and wisely.'

'We respect your privacy, madam, but I daresay you have had a life filled with adventure,' McFeeley commented.

'My husband, John, was a member of Cromwell's House of Lords, my son,' the old lady said, eyes going a little vacant in reminiscence, 'and the Protector had no stauncher supporter than him.'

'Your husband has passed on, Mrs Olaf?' Henrietta asked with a womanly interest in the homelier side of things.

'These many years,' the old lady was saddened by recall of her loss. 'John played no small part in the trial of Charles I, and upon the Restoration he had to flee to Europe for his own safety. Not that it did poor John any good. He was murdered one morning on his way to church.'

'I am sorry,' Henrietta said feelingly.

Taking a look at the muskets, McFeeley suggested quietly and politely, 'And you are seeking revenge?'

'Against whom?' Mrs Olaf asked. 'This country of ours has been in turmoil for years. My faith was pinned on the Duke of Monmouth. Now we will just have to wait until the dust has settled!'

Anxious to be away, McFeeley stood up from the table. Concerned for the old woman, he asked, 'You do appreciate that if it is learned that you have harboured us you will be severely punished?'

'With that swine Penruddock involved, it is a certainty that I shall be.'

'Oh no ...' Henrietta groaned, giving voice to her and her two companions' concern over the old woman.

'Don't worry on my account,' Mrs Olaf told them perkily. 'I would much rather die for a good cause than from old age. Now, it is you three who we must think of. Take heed that Penruddock and his men will be waiting out there for you.'

This had been on McFeeley's mind. It shared his thoughts with others on the tragic death of Lucy Yates, and the fact that this gentle, caring old lady was likely to be sentenced to burning for high treason, which was the punishment for women, because she would be judged as having helped three Monmouth followers. It would be a miscarriage of justice in the extreme, as Henrietta was a lady, and Piper and himself soldiers of the king. But Colonel Penruddock's killing of Lucy ruled out any hope of putting the case of Mrs Olaf straight with him. McFeeley decided that he must concentrate on getting the three of them to London.

'With the hay in for the winter, Mrs Olaf,' McFeeley began, 'where is the nearest barn from here?'

'Less than half a mile away, over the back of that hill,' the old lady replied, pointing to a wall of the room, seeing the hill in her mind.

It was to the south, McFeeley recognized as he asked her a second question. 'Is the man who owns the barn any relative or friend of yours?'

'Nothing could be further from the truth,' Mrs Olaf replied with a little laugh. 'The barn is on Colonel Penruddock's farm. Ben Bendall runs the place, but Penruddock owns it.'

This was good news for McFeeley. Doing some rapid planning, he then told Henrietta and Piper, 'You two wait here for me, but be ready to leave once I get back. If I should not return within an hour, then you must move out and head for London. Take care, Piper, and take your musket and ammunition with you.'

As McFeeley divided the powder and bullets to take some with him, the wise old Mrs Olaf gave a smile as she said, 'I think that I know what you have in mind!'

Although he had neither seen nor heard anything definite, McFeeley was conscious of the colonel and his soldiers lurking somewhere in the night. But he moved stealthily, either slithering snake-like on his stomach or creeping on hands and knees until he was some distance from the house. He had covered the major part of the distance to the barn at a run then.

He found the barn packed to the roof with hay that had been tinder dry when cut and stored. It ignited that fast that flames were licking out angrily at him so that he was lucky to get out through the barn door without being burnt.

Dashing to a hedge he dropped to the ground underneath it, sliding himself into concealment, turning to keep observation on a barn that was now a blazing inferno with flames shooting up high into the night sky. He had only minutes to wait before there was much shouting and yelling as figures came charging out of the darkness into the orange glow of the raging fire. The figures wore uniforms and McFeeley, who had no idea what Penruddock looked like, heard his distinctive voice raised to shout panicky orders.

Satisfied that the fire, which was already sending up sparks that had ignited two smaller buildings and had set the thatched roof of a nearby cottage ablaze, would keep the militia occupied for some time, McFeeley headed back the way he had come at a fast sprint. With no need to keep under cover, he made good time, arriving back at the house to find Mrs Olaf, Henrietta and Piper standing out in the garden looking at what had the appearance of an exaggerated and fiery false sunrise.

'That's a really ambitious diversion, sir,' Piper complimented McFeeley.

Hearing the words, the old lady put a hand on his arm. 'I just knew that you were an officer!'

'It is you that concerns me now, Mrs Olaf,' he said, noticing how the poor light had aged her by accentuating the lines in her face. The fire was bright enough now, despite the distance, to tint her silvery hair pink in places. 'Once they have put out the fire they will come for you!'

'I shall be ready for them, my son,' she told him enigmatically. 'Now, take your charges off with you. I will be relying on you to get that lady and her unborn child safely to London.'

'You can depend on it,' McFeeley told her as they clasped hands for a moment.

Without a word, perhaps because none of them could trust themselves to speak, the trio went out through the gate at the foot of the garden. They had walked something like a hundred yards when McFeeley looked back, something he had been disciplining himself not to do, and saw the frail little figure standing watching them, framed by the gateway.

'Keep walking. I'll catch up with you,' he said gruffly to his two companions.

Eyes made weary by long years of living studied him curiously as he walked back to the old woman. She called to him urgently. 'You must go as quickly as possible. Off with you now! Don't fuss over an old lady. I have lived my life; the three of you still have yours in front of you.'

Coming right up to her, McFeeley leaned his musket against the fence and took both of her thin hands with their wrinkled, sagging skin in his. He held her gaze for a considerable time before he spoke. It seemed to him that if he continued looking into her eyes he would see both her past and his own future. Not wanting to view either, he lowered his gaze.

'I couldn't leave you with a lie,' McFeeley said softly and apologetically. 'I have met Monmouth and have admired him, but I am not of him. Forgive me for not telling you when we first met you, Mrs Olaf. You see, I am a lieutenant in the king's army.'

There was a stunned expression on her face for a moment that had McFeeley cringe inside at having induced her to sacrifice her life under a misapprehension. Then life flowed back into her eyes and tightened the skin of her face so that she was every bit as bright and intelligent as before.

'Thank you for coming back to tell me,' she said, giving one of her sweet smiles as her fingers tightened on his hands. 'What is in our heads, our choices, who we serve, are transient and not important. It is what we hold in our hearts that we must listen to attentively. You are a good man, my son, and if I have been of assistance to you that makes me both happy and very proud. Go with God.'

Before releasing her hands, McFeeley kissed her lightly on her corrugated brow. When he turned and walked away he was not in the slightest abashed to feel tears stinging his eyes.

They had walked all through the remainder of that night and the following day. Now, as the sun dipped to their left and the evening grew cold, they crossed Bagshot Heath and entered into the welcoming social warmth of the Greyhound Inn. McFeeley was confident that they had put enough distance between Colonel Penruddock and themselves to be able to relax. As head of the local militia, the colonel would have neither the resources nor, probably, the inclination for a long pursuit.

The only people they had encountered along the way had been a group of ragged gypsies at Old Basing, and some castaways a little further along. The latter had been desperate enough to be dangerous, but the sight of the muskets that McFeeley and Piper carried had discouraged them from making any aggressive move.

These muskets were now worrying the landlord of the tiny inn. A short man with a paunch that defied gravity, he shook his head doubtfully, bloodshot eyes on the weapons, when McFeeley requested a room for Henrietta and another for Piper and himself.

'Just for the one night,' McFeeley emphasized in the hope that it would help sway the owner of the inn.

'Can't help you, mister,' the landlord looked away, either shyly or slyly. 'As you can see, this is a small house and all the rooms are taken.'

Aware of how weary Henrietta was, McFeeley was disappointed. He looked towards where she had slumped onto a bench when they had come into the inn. The ground they had covered without rest had taken its toll on two hardened soldiers like Piper and himself, so he could only make a probably inaccurate and inadequate guess at how it had affected Henrietta. To her absolute credit she had uttered not one word of complaint, not even a solitary sigh.

'If it's the muskets bothering you,' McFeeley told the landlord, 'then forget it. We are soldiers.'

Whether the fat-gutted man believed him, or simply wanted to stop McFeeley from nagging at him, he said grudgingly, 'The three of you can lie in my barn for the night. I won't want nothing off you for it.'

This offer wasn't as good as having rooms, but it was probably better than they could have hoped for, and McFeeley accepted it. They had a refreshing drink and some bread and cheese, which eased but didn't satisfy their hunger, then went out to the barn.

There was enough straw when gathered up to make a bed for Henrietta at one end of the long barn, and for Piper and McFeeley to be able to bed down comfortably at the other end. A fairly sturdy breeze had sprung up to produce an orchestrated squeaking and creaking of the roof and sides of the barn. It was a disconcerting sound, and it was perhaps responsible for Henrietta calling McFeeley, as he was about to settle down for the night, eager to rest his tired body.

'Colm, I can't bear to be alone tonight!'

Gathering his straw up under one arm, McFeeley left Piper and went to the far end of the barn to lay the straw down, careful to place it several feet from where Henrietta lay.

'Are you still awake?' she called softly a few minutes later.

There hadn't been time to even get near sleep, and McFeeley stifled a minor irritation as he replied, 'Yes.'

'Do you think we'll reach London in time, Colm?'

'I'm sure we will,' he said, recognizing that she was speaking of pleading for the life of James Scott. 'As he is the King's nephew I can't imagine that he'll be executed!'

Henrietta wasn't convinced. 'That Quaker, John Whiting wasn't it? He was certain that James would be executed.'

'If that is so, then as I have said, he is the king's nephew so the execution is not likely to be carried out speedily. We'll reach there in time for you to see the king.'

'I pray that we are,' she said fervently. Then she fell quiet for some time.

The next time Henrietta spoke it was close to his ear. She had moved herself and her loose-straw mattress very near to him. 'I need to be held, Colm.'

One of her arms went around his neck, her breath was warm on his cheek, and her spare hand was fumbling with his clothing and her own. He knew that the inevitable was about to happen. It was something that he didn't want intellectually but couldn't resist physically. The knowledge that she was carrying Monmouth's child should have been enough to have him push Henrietta away, but he found that he was welcoming her.

'Sir!'

Piper's warning hiss had come through the darkness, immediately putting an end to what was developing into frantic play between male and female. Piper's call solved McFeeley's conscience problem, and brought him immediately alert.

'What is it, Piper?'

'I'm sure that I heard soldiers outside, sir.'

Sitting up, McFeeley was straining his ears when it became unnecessary. A stentorian voice came from outside. 'This is Colonel Penruddock, you men. Take heed. Open the barn door, very slowly, and throw out your arms. Then walk out slowly, holding your hands where we can see them and you won't be harmed. You have my word.'

Hurrying to pick up his musket, McFeeley went to stand beside Piper, who was already armed. The soldier asked, 'How many do you think we're up against, sir?'

'If there's only two of them, which I doubt, then it's one too many for us in this position, Piper,' McFeeley faced the facts.

'Then what...?' Piper began.

'Wait for a moment,' McFeeley said, going over to help Henrietta to her feet and taking her over to sit against the front wall of the barn before returning to Piper.

'She'll be safe there if they blast us when we open the door,' McFeeley said. 'We've got to take a chance on this being a squad of boys playing at being soldiers, Jonathan. I think that Penruddock is all that holds them together. If we get him, they'll run.'

'How will we get him without them getting us first, sir?' Piper inquired, not questioning McFeeley's ability, but with a soldier's need to know what tactics were to be employed.

'First we have to locate the pig,' McFeeley said, fondly using Mrs Olaf's epithet for the colonel. He raised his voice to shout. 'Can you hear me, Colonel?'

'I hear you!'

'This is Lieutenant McFeeley of the Kildare militia.'

'Don't waste my time,' Penruddock yelled back. 'Do exactly as I told you. Open the door, carefully, and throw your weapons out.'

Looking at Piper, McFeeley pointed to the right of the door in a two o'clock direction. 'That's where he is, Jonathan.'

'I hope that he stays there,' Piper said earnestly.

The possibility of the colonel changing positions was in McFeeley's mind, too. As he and Piper groped their way to the door in the poor light of the barn interior, and he gestured with his head for the soldier to quietly lift the latch, McFeeley called yet again.

'Colonel Penruddock!'

'What is it?' the colonel's voice came from his original position.

'Now!' McFeeley hissed at Piper.

Kicking the door open as Piper cleared the latch; they both took one rapid step outside of the door and opened fire, taking their aim from where they had heard Penruddock's voice. After the two closely sounding explosions of their muskets there came a disappointing silence. They were back inside, each standing on opposite sides of the still open door, backs against the wall, bent to the task of reloading their muskets, when they were rewarded with the thump of a heavy body falling outside.

'They've shot the colonel!' a male voice, raised an octave by panic, called.

'Is he hurted?'

'He's dead,' the first voice squealed back in what had become terror.

Piper hardly needed McFeeley's signal to act; both stepped outside and discharged their muskets in the direction from which the voices had come.

There was a cry of pain followed by a groan. Then came the pounding of running feet heading away from the barn. They had achieved what McFeeley had intended, much more easily than expected. He went back into the barn, reloaded his musket beside

Piper, who was doing the same, then put a hand under Henrietta's arm to help her to her feet.

'I'm sorry, Henrietta,' he told her, 'There can be no rest for us tonight.'

'If there's more militia close by, and they learn about the colonel, then they'll be down on us real quick, sir,' Piper said, unnecessarily but feeling better having heard the likelihood put into words.

'It will be tough going, but we can cover most of the ground before dawn,' McFeeley said as he helped Henrietta out of the barn. 'But we can't afford to make another stop before we get to London.'

Feeling Henrietta's momentary resistance, he peered at her through the darkness, concerned that she might be feeling too ill to walk. She was moving again, but her voice sounded strange as she told him, 'I have one of those feelings again, Colm. You know, the way I was before Lucy....'

'Who does it concern this time?'

'I wish that I knew,' she replied as they set off down the heath. It was afternoon when they reached London, which seemed to the three of them individually no different than when they had last seen it.

As they passed St Paul's Cathedral, which now had only a tenuous link with the sacred, it was busy with the tricksters and traders who operated in the middle aisle, while the smart and flashy folk promenaded. They paused, welcoming an excuse to ease their tired limbs, to watch a Punch and Judy show in the street, which was an innovation for all three of them.

'I doubt if anyone here really knows that the Monmouth rebellion took place,' Piper commented, causing them to compare this pointless, hedonistic way of life they were witnessing with the hardships and trauma they had endured in recent weeks.

They moved on through the chomping donkeys of tradesmen and the poignant cries for alms from the penniless. A swarthy man passed them with a dancing bear on a chain. The huge animal took short staggering steps on its hind legs, its forelegs held high above its chest, eyes rolling and big head swinging from side to side. This example of pseudo-entertainment seemed to mark a border between the frivolous and the sombre. Faces were sad as they went by them, and when they came upon a small group of weeping women, McFeeley stopped to make an inquiry.

'Has something happened?' he asked, prepared for any kind of answer. In these unsettled times it was possible that even the reign of King James II may have been cut short.

'Oh, it's terrible, sir, it's real terrible!' an old woman replied displaying a toothless top gum as she wailed.

'Our faith has been taken from us,' a younger woman said, dabbing at her running eyes with a kerchief.

The sorrow was evident but its cause remained a mystery as all of the women shrieked their grief in concert. Children stood and watched them curiously from what they believed to be a safe distance. Frustrated at receiving no real answer, McFeeley grabbed an arm, his fingers sinking through clothing to come to what was no more than bone.

'Tell me what has happened?' he demanded.

'Oh, sir!' The old woman with no upper teeth cried. 'That monster Jack Ketch has done for our dear Duke of Monmouth!'

'What are you saying, woman?' McFeeley asked, still gripping her arm.

'The dear man died a terrible death,' a younger woman moaned.

'At the Tower, sir,' the old hag said in her screeching voice. 'They executed His Grace, sir. We are doomed, sir. Our saviour has been put to death and the Protestant religion died with him!'

Anticipating that she would need support, McFeeley swiftly put an arm round Henrietta. His heart went out to her as she looked up at him, a courageous smile on her lovely mouth, tears sparkling in her expressive eyes.

She said very quietly, 'Another of my premonitions come true, Colm!'

'This James Scott business has been a lesson for me, my Lord Churchill,' King James said in what was, for him, a spirited manner. 'It does not gall me to say that I am grateful to my treacherous nephew, as the service he did me was unintentional. He taught me, my Lord Churchill, that I cannot put dependence in an army formed by disseminated units throughout the land. I plan a standing army, and will look to you for to provide at least the initiative.'

Claude Critchell cleared his throat to draw Brigadier Churchill's attention. Seeking the king, they had found him at Westminster Hall inspecting his law courts. They had thrashed between them what had to be said, but one had to be prudent when putting suggestions to his majesty. If James suspected that one of his subjects was waving a flag to promote someone, then he was apt to do the opposite of what had been hoped for.

'There will be promotion for you, of course, Brigadier,' James went on.

'On the subject of promotion ...' Churchill began.

'Do I detect the preliminaries of a request concerning this protégé of yours, John? Lieutenant McKinley, isn't it?' the king said rather sharply.

'McFeeley, Your Majesty,' Captain Critchell made the correction.

'McFeeley returned to London this very day, Your Majesty,' Lord Churchill said. 'He is a remarkable soldier, and both Lady Sarah, who also came back to the city today, and I have personal reasons to thank him.'

'Then I, too, shall show my gratitude for his service to me against James Scott. Whatever you recommend for the fellow, then I will give it my blessing,' King James assured Churchill.

'You are most gracious, Your Majesty,' Churchill said.

'Most gracious,' Captain Critchell added in support.

'Now, to other matters,' the king said. 'I am told that I must make haste to establish myself as a caring and merciful monarch down in the West Country, my Lord Churchill?'

'With the utmost respect to you and your administration, Your Majesty,' a careful Churchill replied, 'It would seem that there is much bad feeling in the aftermath of the Assizes presided over by Lord Chief Justice Jeffreys.'

'My Lord Jeffreys is thorough but does tend to be somewhat overzealous.' The king gave a smile that evinced his liking for Jeffreys. 'But he has done much to right the balance on his way back to London. In Hampshire he reduced the sentence on a woman found guilty of high treason. It would appear that this woman, a

Mrs Olaf, gave succour and shelter to some absconding members of James Scott's rebel rabble of an army. Because of her advanced age, Jeffreys would not allow the woman to be burned. He had her beheaded instead. That is the kind of leniency I believe the people are looking for, gentlemen.'

Neither Churchill nor Critchell could credit what the king had said, and they were still recovering from the shock of it when they were walking down the steps outside. There was greyness to the day that matched their mood. Across the street from them McFeeley and Piper, in their ill-fitting civilian clothes, the muskets that they carried looking out of place, waited as Captain Critchell had requested them to. An approaching carriage was well timed, bringing Lady Sarah and Rachel along with the horses held at a gait that would bring the carriage up beside the two officers when they reached the kerb.

Without looking across the road, Critchell said, 'I took the liberty of asking Lieutenant McFeeley to wait until our audience with the king had ended, Brigadier. Do you wish to discuss his military future with him now?'

'No, not now. Probably not for some time, Claude,' Lord Churchill said, wearing an unhappy expression. 'Everything is so unsettled! How could I possibly offer McFeeley anything, Claude, when I am not sure what my own position will be in a week, a month, six months from now?'

'It would be profoundly sad if he should be forgotten, Brigadier,' a worried Captain Critchell observed.

'I give you my oath, Captain Critchell, that Lieutenant McFeeley will not be overlooked. Whatever shape or form the army may take, he will have an important place in it,' Churchill said.

'My faith in you will remain inviolate into eternity, my lord,' Critchell said.

'That's a rather long term commitment, Claude,' Churchill smiled. 'Come, the carriage is here. The ladies will be impatient for dinner.'

Watching Captain Critchell come out of Westminster Hall with Lord Churchill, McFeeley straightened up from where he had been lounging against a stone balustrade. Piper came up to attention beside him. Critchell had already used his limited power to grant McFeeley's request that Private Jonathan Piper be permanently assigned to him, and had then asked McFeeley to wait because he, Captain Critchell, believed that Brigadier-General Churchill was to bring McFeeley's name to the King. But when the captain deliberately didn't look across at him, McFeeley accepted that he had waited for nothing. He clapped Piper on the back.

'Come along, Piper, it is time we returned to some proper soldiering,' McFeeley said as a carriage went slowly by.

First recognizing Rachel inside the carriage, and anticipating that she would avert her face when she saw him, McFeeley was right. But then he found himself looking into the beautiful face of Lady Sarah. Her eyes held his steady; messages passed rapidly between them. These were messages in some kind of mental code that their minds would decipher for them when the time was right.

Neither she nor he wanted the magically compelling exchange to end, but then the carriage rolled on rumblingly, taking her from him and to her waiting husband. The world that had been rent asunder by the Monmouth invasion was going back to rights. Lord and Lady Sarah were now reunited, and Lady Henrietta, whose grieving over the Duke of Monmouth had been short in duration but would linger in some form or other throughout her life, had gone back to Lord Grey.

As they walked away, Piper looked back over his shoulder at the carriage as it moved away, muttering a quotation. 'Against the ground we stand and knock our heels, Whilst all our profit runs away on wheels.'

'*Lady Flippanta*?' a sarcastic McFeeley asked.

'No, sir. That is by John Taylor, the Water Poet,' Piper replied. Then he put his usually well hidden sensitivity on show to say, 'This parting must leave an aching void inside of you, sir, as there is scant chance of you ever seeing the lady again!'

'One never knows, Jonathan,' McFeeley replied with a philosophy his head readily produced but his heart refused to support. 'There are no meetings without consequence.'

Epilogue

SUMMER HAD MANAGED to dry the mud of Slap Arse Lane, but a damp late autumn in Ireland had brought back bad conditions underfoot. To Colour Sergeant Gray the dampness had a second disadvantage in that it coaxed out the vile smell of the place. His dislike of making his way through a Sodom and Gomorrah that some dark force had transported from Biblical times to dump it in this cesspit area of Kildare, was as keen as ever. He was near enough now to see the smoke from the hovels. Soon he would be able to hear the trollops calling to one another; using language that he would die to shield from the ears of Mrs Gray. Gray's already flaring anger at this mission had been fanned by Private Jonathan Piper's slightly mocking attitude. Too clever by half, that one, Piper was a newcomer who didn't know the wiles of Colour Sergeant Gray, a patient man who knew how and when to pounce like a thief in the night to smash insubordination.

Gray was planning his vengeance on two assumptions. One was that Piper would not always have the protection of an officer, and two that Colm McFeeley would not remain an officer for much longer. Since coming back to Ireland, McFeeley had broken every rule in the book, and was now in the process of working his way through the pages a second time. Piper, an over-educated, sneering fellow, had used his flowery language just now when Gray had inquired as to the whereabouts of Lieutenant McFeeley.

Recognizing the expression of hate for McFeeley on the colour sergeant's face, Piper had answered with some stupid kind of quotation, saying, 'Deal with the faults of others as gently as you would with your own, Colour Sergeant!'

Gray had promised himself right then that once he had located McFeeley, he would return to camp and deal with Piper's faults: and he wouldn't do it gently.

'Would you want to spend a short time with me in the bushes, sergeant darlin'?' A young whore dressed in muddy rags stepped out of furze to accost him.

'Away with you, girl,' Gray roared angrily at the girl, sending her racing off until she slipped and fell into the mire on her face. He walked on, shouting back, 'If you ever come at me again I'll have you slapped in irons.'

Almost slipping over as he hurried on, the colour sergeant uttered a curse that Iris Gray had heard before, and objected strongly to. He saw two hazy figures standing close to each other up ahead. McFeeley's back was too him, but Gray knew every detail of the lieutenant's shape and found it easy to identify the man whom he disliked so intensely. As he had anticipated, the girl was unknown to him – they always were where McFeeley was concerned! With a delicately pretty face as yet untouched by the whoring profession she was entering into, she looked at Gray with large, slightly luminous eyes. McFeeley turned just his head.

'What is it, Colour Sergeant?'

'Compliments of Captain Critchell, sir,' Gray answered, almost choking on the title of 'sir' when applying it to McFeeley, particularly when the lieutenant was holding a whore in one of his arms. 'The captain requests your presence in the town, sir.'

'Very good, Colour Sergeant. I will find my own way there.'

'Captain Critchell asked that I emphasize that he wants you there immediately, sir!' Gray insisted.

'I would imagine that my idea of immediately and the captain's differ, Colour Sergeant,' McFeeley said as he walked away, an arm round the waist of the girl.

Filled with rage, the colour sergeant glared after McFeeley and the girl. Then he spun on his heel in the mud and went back up Slap Arse Lane, slipping and sliding as he went, irate enough to kill a whore with a single blow if one should be unfortunate enough to step out and offer him her wares.

Having got his amusement out of the colour sergeant, McFeeley left the girl with a kiss and a promise that he would return within the hour. As he hurried towards the town he thought how history was repeating itself. If Gray had been at his side now it would be identical to the time he had walked this route and had ended up involved with the Duke of Monmouth.

This notion of the past being run again persisted right up to when he entered the hotel, as untidy and ruffled as he had been previously. Meeting Claude Critchell, whose welcoming handshake was firm, McFeeley told himself that the feeling of familiarity had to end there; otherwise a resurrection of the Duke of Monmouth would be necessary.

But when he was taken in to Lord Churchill he was praying for at least one piece of history to recur so that he could be with Sarah again. He wished it were possible for him to inquire whether she was here in Ireland. Wisely, he remained silent.

'Well, Captain McFeeley…!' Churchill said from behind his desk. McFeeley missed the significance of the rank because he was thinking how the brigadier had aged in a short time.

McFeeley grasped that he had been promoted when he saw Critchell smiling happily at him. He knew that the captain was expecting to see a reaction in him, so he deliberately refrained from obliging him.

'We have another rather unusual duty for you, Captain,' Churchill said, apparently as disappointed as Critchell over McFeeley having shown no response to the indirect announcement of his promotion. Churchill suddenly let a smile ease the habitual sternness of his face. He stood and came round the desk, still smiling, although it had become more of a grin. 'Before we go into matters military, Captain, you'd probably like to know that you have become something of a celebrity in court circles back in London.'

'I don't understand, my lord,' McFeeley said uncertainly, perturbed to see how uncomfortable Claude Critchell had become.

'Of course you don't,' Churchill said patronizingly. 'You see, Lady Henrietta Grey has given birth, and His Majesty King James II is highly amused by her having produced a little McFeeley.'

A great elation surged through McFeeley. Never a man to accept authority or show any respect to the upper classes, he knew that he was about to enjoy himself immensely. This moment was well worth the trials and tribulations he had suffered in the campaign against Monmouth.

'Then you had better stop His Majesty from laughing as soon as possible, sir,' he advised Lord Churchill, 'for the heir to his throne is not a McFeeley. Henrietta has produced a little Monmouth!'